P9-DIA-114

The Look of Love

Center Point
Large Print

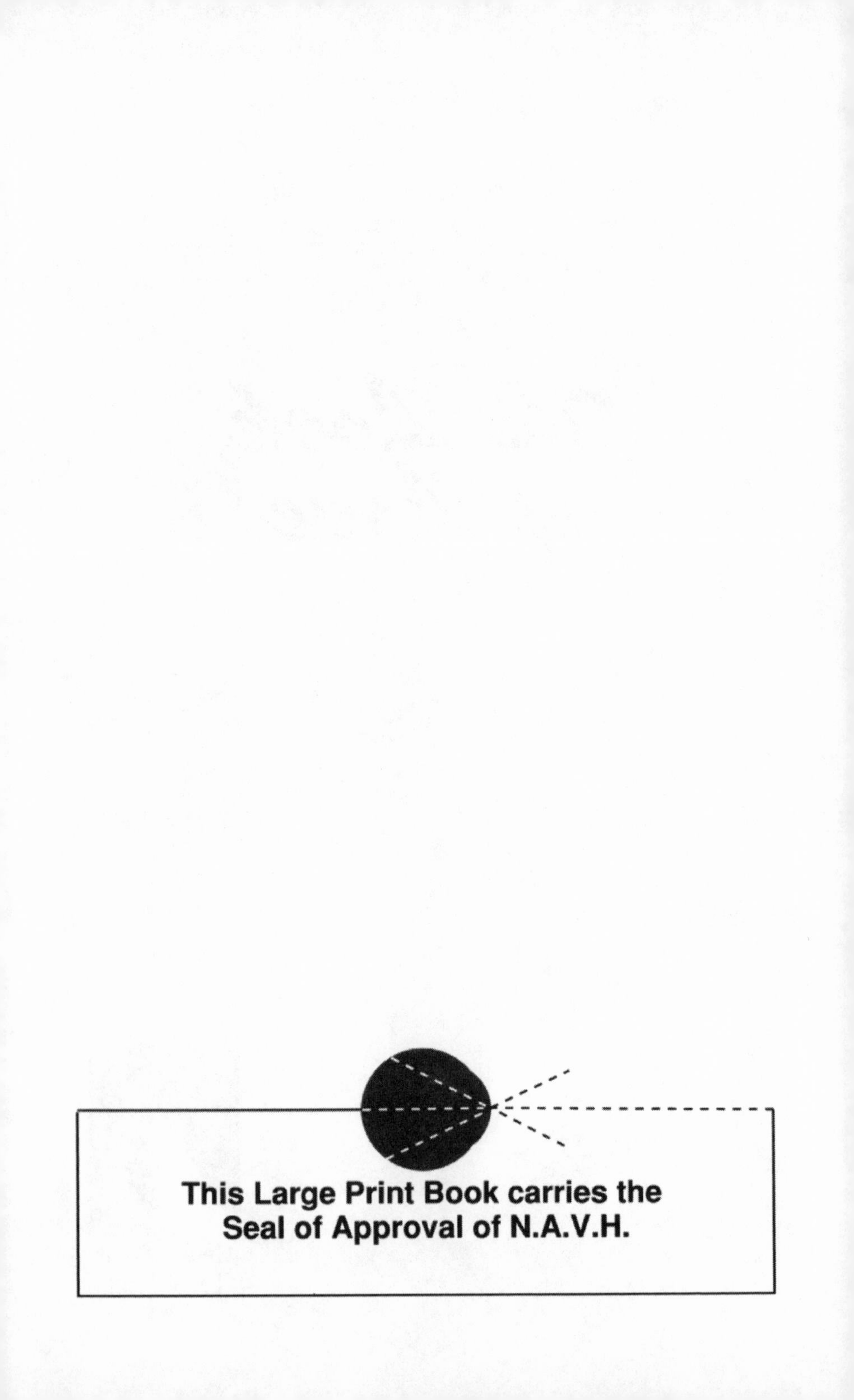
This Large Print Book carries the
Seal of Approval of N.A.V.H.

The Look of Love

Bella Andre

CENTER POINT LARGE PRINT
THORNDIKE, MAINE

This Center Point Large Print edition is published
in the year 2013 by arrangement with
Harlequin Books S.A.

This is a work of fiction. Names, characters, places and incidents are either the product of the author's imagination or are used fictitiously, and any resemblance to actual persons, living or dead, business establishments, events or locales is entirely coincidental.

The text of this Large Print edition is unabridged.
In other aspects, this book may vary
from the original edition.
Printed in the United States of America
on permanent paper.
Set in 16-point Times New Roman type.

ISBN: 978-1-61173-856-8

Library of Congress Cataloging-in-Publication Data

Andre, Bella.
The Look of Love / Bella Andre. — Center Point Large Print edition.
pages cm
ISBN 978-1-61173-856-8 (Library binding : alk. paper)
1. Large type books. I. Title.
PS3601.N5495L66 2013
813′.6—dc23

2013020262

Meet the Sullivans!

As a lifelong romance reader (who devours up to a book a day when my writing schedule permits!), my favorite romances have always been about families. I love following brothers and sisters and cousins from book to book, not only for the pleasure of watching them fall in love, but also to watch each of their love stories grow deeper and richer throughout the series.

I couldn't be more excited about introducing you to the six brothers, two sisters and fabulous mother who make up my Sullivans! From a winery owner to a movie star and even a librarian, while the Sullivan family runs the gamut of careers and personalities, they all have one big thing in common: they are there for each other, no matter what. Especially when the road to Happy Ever After isn't exactly smooth. . . .

In *The Look of Love*, when photographer Chase Sullivan finds Chloe and her totaled car in Napa Valley, she's so lovely, inside and out, he wants to love and protect her. Only, she has vowed never to trust a man again. But could Chase be the only exception?

I absolutely loved writing Chase & Chloe's sweet—and sinful—journey toward true love, and I hope you enjoy reading about my Sullivans as much as I've enjoyed writing about them!

Happy reading,

Bella Andre

One

Chase Sullivan was seven years old when he picked up his father's Polaroid camera for the first time and started taking pictures. For his eighth birthday, his father gave him his very own camera, both of them knowing by then that Chase was meant to be a photographer.

Chase took endless pictures of his seven brothers and sisters, his mother and his father—until he'd passed away when Chase was ten. His siblings hadn't always liked having a lens pointed at them, and more than once one of his brothers had threatened to knock the camera out of his hand if he didn't put it down.

And yet, even after over a decade of working as a professional photographer taking pictures of everything from desert landscapes to Olympic athletes, Chase still thought that his earliest subjects—his family—were some of the most interesting he'd ever captured.

Which was why he was happy to take on the role of official photographer at big family events. Especially one as important as his mother's seventieth birthday party.

His brother Ryan's house overlooking the San Francisco Bay was the perfect spot for the party.

Despite the vast size of Ryan's living room and kitchen, the place was packed with well-wishers who had come to celebrate the beloved head of the Sullivan clan.

Laughter and conversation were in high gear when Marcus, Chase's oldest brother and the owner of Sullivan Winery, put his arm around their mother's shoulders and brought her over to the big birthday cake. The noise level dropped as if on cue and Chase put down his beer and picked up his camera. He began by taking shots of Sophie, his younger sister, carefully lighting the birthday candles she had artfully arranged to spell out his mother's name as well as the number seventy.

As he looked through the viewfinder, Chase was struck, not for the first time, by just how much Sophie and his mother looked alike. Mary Sullivan had been a model when she'd met his father and, many decades later, she was nothing less than radiant as she stood surrounded by her children and friends.

His mother's hair was gray now and cut to curl at the base of her neck, rather than long and dark and glossy as it had been during her years on magazine covers, but in both of Mary's twin daughters, Sophie and Lori, Chase could clearly see the resemblance to his mother in her mid-twenties. Mary still had the same lightly tanned skin and long, elegant limbs, and he was often struck by the way her expression was a perfect combination of Sophie's innate calm and Lori's irrepressible energy.

He'd overheard more than one party guest remarking that it was hard to believe Mary was seventy years old when she looked at least ten years younger. Especially, many of them had added with a grin or a grimace—depending on which of her children they were looking at—when one considered that she had raised eight kids virtually by herself after her husband had passed away unexpectedly at forty-eight.

Chase's chest twisted, as it always did, whenever he thought of his father. He wished Jack Sullivan could be here with them all. Not only because he still missed his father every single day, but also because he knew how much his mother had loved her husband.

Forcefully shaking off the dark thoughts, Chase took a shot of the cake with all of the candles blazing, seventy plus one for luck. Marcus led them in a rousing chorus of "Happy Birthday," and soon, everyone in the room was joining in.

While his mother beamed at them as if they weren't butchering the simple song with their off-key singing, Chase moved to the outer edge of the crowd to capture as much of his family as he could through the viewfinder.

When the birthday song finally warbled its way to the end, Marcus squeezed Mary's hand, saying, "Time for you to make your wish, Mom."

She looked out at the crowd of people who loved her, her smile meant for each and every one of them. "So many of my wishes have already come true." Her grin grew wider. "And still, I want more. At least seventy more."

They laughed along with her, each of them knowing she had to be one of the least greedy people on the planet. Whatever wishes she'd made in her life had clearly been made for her children. She'd never remarried, never even dated as far as Chase knew. Instead, she'd focused on raising them, supporting them, guiding them. Now that they were all adults, she was still always there if they needed her . . . and even, sometimes, when they didn't realize that they did.

So as Mary Sullivan closed her eyes to make her wish, and then opened them again to bend down and blow out the candles, Chase hoped she was making at least one for herself.

Everyone applauded and he got a great shot of Marcus pressing a kiss to their mother's cheek, while Sophie wrapped her arms around Mary from behind. One by one, Chase captured the images he knew his mother would love of his brothers and sisters celebrating with her on her birthday.

Soon, Chase had all the shots he needed to put together a great photo book to commemorate his mother's seventieth birthday. He could have put his camera down, but he knew better. In a family of eight siblings, each of them had to carve out their unique place. The photos Chase had taken over the past twenty-plus years gave clear evidence as to the way their personalities had only grown more distinct with time.

Even before their father had passed away, Marcus had taken his role as oldest Sullivan seriously. At fourteen, all of his training paid off when he was able to immediately step in to try to fill their father's shoes. Chase knew they all owed Marcus for the childhood he'd given up for them, and was beyond glad that his brother had found his own calling in the vineyards and varietals of Sullivan Winery, which he'd founded ten years ago. Unfortunately, as Chase turned his camera to focus on his oldest brother, he found a frown on Marcus's face as he spoke to his girlfriend, Jill. She was evidently upset about something, her mouth pinched, her eyes narrowed as she gestured at the rest of them. Seeing frustration so clearly stamped on his brother's face, Chase lowered his camera. He didn't feel right about capturing this moment between Marcus and his girlfriend, not when he was certain Marcus wouldn't want any of them to know that all wasn't right.

Lori, his twenty-four-year-old sister and Sophie's twin, tugged on his elbow, and he gladly looked down into her grinning, mischievous face. "You look happy, Naughty. Have you and Nice made up yet?"

Long ago, he'd christened Lori *Naughty* and Sophie *Nice*. Were it not for the fact that they were physical carbon copies, Chase wouldn't believe for a second that they were related to each other. Unfortunately, for the past few months, the twins hadn't exactly been getting along. Not that either of them would tell their brothers a damn thing about why they were fighting, of course. Even when they were at odds, Chase mused, the twins always worked as a team.

Out of all of his siblings, Lori had always been his most willing subject. A fantastic choreographer, Lori had always loved to dance and from the age of two on she'd happily performed for him while he took frame after frame of her little body in motion as she twirled, leaped and shimmied. And yet, he believed his most striking shots of his little sister had always been taken after all the motion had stopped, and she had forgotten that she was being photographed. She channeled her love, her energy, her passion, into dancing, and when she was still, all of those emotions remained on her very pretty face.

In silent answer to his question about her twin, Lori looked in Sophie's direction and frowned. "Don't get me started on her," she said, before giving a quick shake of her head and turning back to Chase to confirm, "Oh, yes, I'm definitely happy." She directed his attention to where his brothers Zach and Gabe looked to be having a rather intense discussion, clenched fists and all. "Have you met Zach's date for the evening yet?"

"I have," Chase said as he shot the bottle-blonde in the sky-high heels a quick glance. The woman was pretty, just like all the rest of the women Zach went out with, but not particularly memorable. As he looked back and forth between his brothers, it didn't take long for Chase to guess what had Lori grinning from ear to ear.

"Gabe used to date her, didn't he?"

Lori laughed as she nodded. "He sure did."

Throw six brothers between the ages of twenty-seven and thirty-six together and things were bound to get messy. All eight siblings together under one roof meant lots of laughs, plenty of ribbing . . . and likely at least one major argument. But since it was obvious that neither of his brothers was serious about the girl, Chase figured there was a zero percent chance that they were going to come to blows over her other than as an excuse to blow off some steam with their fists.

Since high school, Chase had heard more than one woman exclaim over Zach's looks, and boy, did his brother work his genetic luck-of-the-draw. Given that Zach loved two things—fast cars and even faster women—Chase supposed it all had worked out just fine so far. Grinning as he took a few pictures of Zach working to lay claim to his own date, Chase decided he would torture a couple of friends who ran a successful modeling agency with these pictures of Zach next week. Because if Zach would ever agree to put down his wrenches and give up his race cars to pose in the latest designer clothes, even for one week, the modeling agent could charge pretty much anything he wanted for Zach's time.

Then again, Chase thought as he moved his lens to focus on Gabe, any agent worth his salt would try to get Gabe to sign onto his roster, as well. Even though Gabe was the youngest of his brothers, he also happened to be one of the biggest and strongest Sullivans. He had the most dangerous job of any of them, working as a fire-fighter in San Francisco. More than once, he'd had to leave parties like this one over the years when a call came in. And every time he did, every last one of the normally loud group of Sullivans took a quiet moment to pray for his safety. Tonight, Chase hoped the rain coming down outside meant Gabe would get to stay with them at least until the party ended.

He'd just lowered his camera when Lori said, "I don't know why Zach and Gabe are even bothering to argue over the girl, when she can't take her eyes off Smith." With a shrug over their movie-star brother's infinite allure to every female on the planet, Lori told him, "I'm going to get some cake before it's all gone. I'll be sure to get you a middle piece."

Chase lifted his camera back up as his sister flirted her way back into the center of the party. No question about it, his high-maintenance, stunning sister was going to make some poor guy crazy one day. And the guy would be lucky as hell to win Lori's big heart.

Of course, she knew the camera was on her, because she turned and winked at him and mouthed, "I told you so," as she gestured with her thumb to where Smith had just been cornered by Zach's date.

Chase almost felt bad turning his camera to his brother Smith. For the past fifteen years, Smith's love of acting—and his immense talent—had put him at the mercy of thousands of cameras and the worldwide media. Chase always laughed at the way people lost it around his movie-star brother. Smith was just as normal as the rest of them.

Although, he had to admit, chartering a one-hundred-and-fifty-foot yacht in Italy and filling it with stars wasn't exactly normal.

Even now, as the woman stood just a little too close while asking Smith for an autograph, Chase was struck by how well his older brother dealt with his fame. Still, while he never complained to them, Chase knew the pressure to always be “on” and play the role of “Smith Sullivan” for the entire world had to grate sometimes. It was why when they were together with just the family, Chase and his siblings made sure to treat Smith like he was no different than any of them.

Just to Smith’s right, their brother Ryan lifted a heavy chest out of the way so that people could have room to dance as the swing band started up. As a professional athlete, Ryan was tall and muscular and made the movement look effortless, but through the camera eye Chase caught the slight clench of his jaw as Ryan’s right shoulder gave just a little too far under the weight. As a kid, his brother’s number-one goal had been to pitch for the San Francisco Hawks. They’d had one heck of a celebration the day Ryan had been chosen as the Hawks’ top draft pick out of college. For the past ten years, Ryan had made those strikeouts look easy. But Chase knew just how focused his brother could be when he wanted something, just as focused as he’d always been on being the best damned pitcher in the National Baseball League.

As soon as Ryan cleared the dance floor, Lori put down her piece of cake, took his hand and pulled him onto it. Chase continued to photograph them as Ryan tried to draw Sophie in to dance with them, too, but Sophie simply shook her head and moved deeper into the shadows.

Sophie was Lori's direct opposite, *Nice* to Lori's *Naughty.* He couldn't imagine her being anything other than a librarian, and knew she absolutely loved her job at the main branch in San Francisco. Even when they were kids, whenever she saw him with his camera, she'd simply lift the book she was holding higher over her face until he gave up on her and went to find another victim. He knew she was steering a purposefully wide berth around him and his camera tonight. Chase had always thought that it was just as much of a gift to know how to blend in to the background as it was to know how to shine in front of a camera. From the time she was a little girl, Sophie had been mastering the art of observing. Watching. Taking it all in. He'd learned a lot from her over the years, and often thought of her as he stepped behind his camera.

A moment later, Chase felt a slender but strong arm move around his waist. He put down his camera to press a kiss to the top of his mother's head.

"Happy birthday, Mom. I hope you're having a good time."

She smiled up at him before saying the same thing she did every year when they all gathered together to celebrate her. "I'm having the best birthday ever, honey. Simply the best."

Together, with their arms around each other, and as they watched his brothers and sisters dance and laugh, talk and argue, Chase agreed. It really was the best birthday party ever.

A few minutes later, Sophie was more than happy to take some pictures of Chase with his mother. "Whatever you do, don't smile," Sophie told them both, a favorite family joke his father had come up with long ago when trying—and failing—to get eight unruly kids to all smile for the camera at once. He'd finally told them all not to smile, or else! Of course, being forbidden to smile for a picture had made them all giggle so hard that the family photo had come out perfectly.

Rain had started falling in earnest and he could see from the darkening sky outside the window that the weather was about to turn downright nasty. With an early-morning photo shoot scheduled at Marcus's winery in Napa Valley, Chase had already planned to leave his mother's party a little early. In the dark and the rain, the drive to Napa from the city would take even longer than he'd anticipated so it would be best to leave sooner rather than later.

With a promise to send his mother the photos as soon as he could, Chase slipped his camera back into his bag, gave Mary one last hug and then headed out.

Over an hour later, as Chase's BMW rounded a curve in the narrowing road that led to Sullivan Winery, his windshield wipers were barely making a dent in the rain and the view of the roads through Napa Valley was continually obscured.

For the next four days, Chase was doing a photo shoot at Marcus's winery for Jeanne & Annie, a growing fashion house that combined haute couture with homegrown style. The models and crew would be staying at a hotel in town, but Chase was going to be staying in his brother's guesthouse in the middle of the vineyard. The winery was the perfect location for the shoot, especially in the spring with the grape vines budding with bright green leaves and the mustard flowers blooming between every row.

A bolt of lightning suddenly lit up the sky, and if there had been enough of a shoulder on the narrow country road, Chase would have pulled over to take some shots of the storm. He loved the rain. Big weather changed the way things looked and could transform an ordinary field into a marsh full of a thousand birds making an impromptu pit stop. Conditions that sent most photographers into a tizzy—especially if they depended on the perfect sunset to nail their pictures—were exactly what got him going.

It was in those moments, when everyone was cold and nothing was going "right," that magic would happen. The models would finally drop their guard and let him see past their hair and makeup to who they really were. Chase believed there needed to be a true emotional connection with the camera for real human beauty—along with the beauty of the clothes or jewelry or shoes that they were wearing—to really shine through.

Of course, early on in his career, being around all that physical beauty had made Chase just as big a player as every other straight guy in the business. At first that had been one of the bonuses of his job, but when he hit his late twenties and realized that his flavor of the night hadn't lasted a full eight hours but his photographs were forever, he'd slowed down some.

Then again, between his recent trips in and out of Asia and the fact that there hadn't been anyone who got his motor going, he'd abstained from one-night stands for the past month. He was planning on breaking his dry spell tonight with Ellen, one of Marcus's head winery managers whom he'd met while planning the shoot. A few emails was all it had taken to set things up. A strings-free night of naked fun was just what the doctor ordered, even if Chase suspected Marcus wasn't going to be particularly happy about his brother having a fling with one of his employees. Well, he figured, they were all adults. . . .

The rain was heavy enough that Chase almost missed the flickering light off on the right side of the two-lane country road. In the past thirty minutes, he hadn't passed one car, because on a night like this, most sane Californians stayed home.

He slowed down and turned on his brights to get a better view through the pouring rain. Not only was there a car stuck in the ditch, but there was a person walking along the edge of the road about a hundred yards up ahead. Obviously hearing his car approach, she turned to face him and he could see her long, wet hair whipping around her shoulders in his headlights.

Wondering why she wasn't just sitting in her car, dry and warm, calling Triple-A and waiting for them to come save her, he pulled over to the edge of the road and got out of his car. The woman was shivering as she watched him approach.

"Are you hurt?"

She covered her cheek with one hand, but shook her head. "No."

He had to move closer to hear her over the sound of the rain hitting the pavement. The temperature had dropped and the rain was rapidly becoming hailstones. Even though he still had his headlights on, it was dark enough that it took his eyes a few minutes to adjust to the darkness. Finally, he was able to get a better look at her face.

That was when something inside of Chase's chest clenched tight.

Despite the long, dark hair plastered to her head and chest, regardless of the fact that "looking like a drowned rat" wasn't too far off the descriptive mark, her beauty stunned him.

In an instant, his photographer's eye cataloged her features. Her mouth was a little too big, her eyes a little too wide-set on her face. She wasn't even close to model thin, but given the way her T-shirt and jeans stuck to her skin, he could see that she wore her lush curves well. In the dark he couldn't judge the exact color of her hair, but it looked like silk, perfectly smooth and straight where it lay over her breasts.

It wasn't until Chase heard her say, "My car is definitely hurt, though," that he realized he had completely lost the thread of what he'd come out here to do.

Knowing he'd been drinking her in like he was dying of thirst, he worked to recover his balance. He could already see he'd been right about her car. It didn't take a mechanic like his brother Zach to see that her hatchback was borderline totaled. Even if the front bumper wasn't half-smashed to pieces by the white farm fence she'd slid into, her bald tires weren't going to get any traction on the mud. Not tonight, anyway.

If her car had been in a less precarious situation, he probably would have sent her to go back to sit inside her car while he took care of getting it unstuck. But he didn't like the look of the way one of her back tires was hanging precariously over the edge of the ditch.

Chase jerked his thumb over his shoulder. "Get in my car. We can wait there for a tow truck." He was vaguely aware of his words coming out like an order, but the hail was starting to sting, damn it. Both of them needed to get out of the rain before they froze.

But the woman didn't move. Instead, she gave him a look that said he was a complete and utter nut job.

"I'm not getting into your car."

Realizing just how frightening it must be for a woman to end up stuck and alone in the middle of a dark road, Chase took a step back from her before saying, "I'm not going to attack you. I swear I won't do anything to hurt you."

She all but flinched at the word *attack* and Chase's radar started buzzing. He'd never been a magnet for troubled women, and wasn't the kind of guy who thrived on fixing wounded birds. But living with two sisters for so long meant he could always tell when something was up.

And something was definitely up with this woman, beyond the fact that her car was half-stuck in a muddy ditch.

Wanting to make her feel safe, he held his hands up. "I swear on my father's grave, I'm not going to hurt you. It's okay to get into my car." When she didn't immediately say no again, he pressed his advantage with, "I just want to help you." And he did. Much more than it made sense to want to help a total stranger. "Please," he said. "Let me help you."

She stared at him for a long moment, hail hammering between them, around them, onto them. Chase found himself holding his breath, waiting for her decision. It shouldn't matter to him what she decided.

But, for some strange reason, it did.

Chloe Peterson had never felt so wet, so miserable . . . or so desperate. She'd been beating the speed limit for the past couple of hours, before the storm had kicked into overdrive. She'd slowed down considerably on the superslick pavement, but her tires were old and bald, and before she knew it her car was skidding off the road.

Straight into a muddy ditch.

It might have been easier—smarter, too—to sit in her car and wait out the storm. But she'd been too keyed up to stay still. She'd needed to keep moving; otherwise the thoughts knocking around in her head were going to catch up with her. So she'd slung her backpack over her shoulders and stepped out into the rain, just as it started to turn into out-and-out hail.

The hard little pellets hurt her skin, but she'd been glad for the cold, for the sting. Because it gave her something else to focus on, something besides what had happened just hours ago. She still could hardly believe that—

No. She couldn't let herself think too closely about what had happened. Tonight her focus had to be on getting out of the rain and finding somewhere safe and dry to rest until morning. Tomorrow would be soon enough to try to piece together how everything had gone so terribly wrong so quickly.

Chloe hadn't been exactly sure of her location, but she'd hoped she was walking in the direction of town.

All night long the roads through the wine country—roads she'd driven before in what felt like someone else's life now—had been strangely empty, but she'd barely starting walking away from her car when she'd realized headlights were coming up behind her.

Fear had knocked into her again as an expensive car pulled over to the side and she'd had to stop to brace herself to withstand it. She was all alone on a dark, wet, country road. She didn't have her cell phone, and even if she had, she doubted there was enough reception out here in the storm for it to get a signal. The fact that the car was expensive didn't settle her nerves. If anything, knowing that whoever was in the car had money only made her more nervous. Because if there was one thing she'd learned all too clearly over the past six months, it was that money meant power. Power over women like her.

And then the man—the very large man—had gotten out of his car and started walking toward her, telling her to get into his car.

No way.

He'd tried to convince her that she was safe with him. He'd said all the right things, but she'd had too much experience with people like that, who easily said one thing, then did another.

"I don't know you," she told him. He could be an ax murderer. She had feet. She'd walk and find a place to dry off later.

She could see the frustration on his face, knew he was about to try and reason with her again, when suddenly the sound of skidding tires came at them.

Before she knew what was happening, he was pulling her into his arms. She didn't have time to think of fighting him, didn't even consider it when she realized a fast-moving motorcycle was practically on top of them.

She closed her eyes, bracing for impact, when the man effortlessly lifted her and jumped into the ditch, holding her tightly against him.

She opened her eyes just in time to watch the motorcycle's back tires skid and then finally catch hold just in the place she'd been standing. Her heart, which had all but stopped, started racing again as she watched the motorcycle speed away.

She realized she was panting as oxygen raced back into her lungs. She was shaking, too, both from the cold and from the scare.

"Are you okay?"

Chloe looked up at the man who had shielded her from harm with his own body, and for the first time since he'd stepped out of his car, something other than fear ran through her as she was hit hard with the realization of just how attractive he was.

No, she silently admitted to herself. *Attractive* was a paltry word for a man like this. Even in the dark, she could see that he put other men to shame. Even in the cold rain with his hair and clothes plastered to his skin and several streaks of mud across his cheekbones, he was utterly gorgeous.

And her body was reacting to him with surprising heat.

Or maybe, she suddenly realized, that heat was coming from the fact that he was still cradling her in his strong arms.

That steady strength, along with the way he'd moved her out of the way of the too-close motorcycle without giving even one thought to his own safety, had her teetering on the edge of trusting him. And on any other night, perhaps it would have been enough. But was it?

Now that they were safe again, Chloe struggled to stand up in the slippery dirt as she tried to right her thoughts so that she could come to some sort of rational decision. She was also splattered with mud from where he'd landed in the ditch with her in his arms and her attempt to climb out of the ditch only made the mess worse.

"Wait a minute," the man said in a low but soothing voice. "Let me get us out of here."

A few moments later, after moving with surprising effortlessness through the mud and the rain, he put her down on the side of the road.

Her eyes had adjusted enough in the dark by then for her to clearly see into his eyes as he told her, "It really isn't safe to be out here. Not for either of us." He looked so sincere, and not at all like he planned on hurting her.

Common sense told her that this man, this stranger, was right, and yet, she was still wary. Incredibly so.

But at this very moment, out in the rain and the dark in a town where she knew absolutely no one, what other choice did she have?

In her mind she replayed the way he'd protected her from harm by not only pulling her from the path of the motorcycle, but also using his own body to brace their fall into the ditch.

"Okay. I'll go with you," Chloe finally said.

She sincerely hoped she didn't end up regretting her choice.

Two

Thank God, thought Chase, she had finally agreed to come with him. That motorcycle had scared the crap out of him. He hadn't had a moment to think—he'd just reacted and now he was incredibly relieved that he'd been able to save both of them.

Now, his instincts as a gentleman had him reaching for her backpack.

She immediately jumped back a foot. "Please, don't." She carefully banked that quick flash of fear before saying, "I can carry my own bag, thanks."

The way she'd leaped out of his reach as soon as they'd gotten back onto the pavement could hurt a guy's ego if he let it. At the same time, Chase knew it was just plain good sense for a woman to be on her guard with a strange guy in a situation like this.

Unfortunately, as she walked to his car, he found himself unable take his eyes off her sweetly rounded curves.

But any guy with sisters, especially two very pretty sisters like Lori and Sophie, who got into more scrapes than he was comfortable thinking about, gave an extra bit of consideration to his interactions with women. Chase and his brothers might like to play, but none of them would ever do anything dangerous or take a woman against her will. No, fact was they'd much rather have their women begging for it.

And this was no time to be thinking about sex. Not when he had a half-drowned woman on his hands—well, in his car, at least—since he'd promised her his hands weren't going to come anywhere near her.

Despite knowing the leather interior of his BMW was never going to be the same after the water and mud hit them, Chase didn't hesitate to open the passenger's side door for her and wait while she slid inside. Once she was seated safely with her bag clutched tight on her lap, he closed the door and ran around to the driver's side, jumping in behind the wheel.

Steam rose in thick waves from their clothes, and condensation quickly covered the inside of the windows, making the car feel even more intimate than it already was. So intimate, in fact, that Chase couldn't help but notice that his surprise passenger smelled good, like rain and freshly bloomed flowers. He turned on the heat to try to make her more comfortable and asked, "Do you want some dry clothes to change into?" He figured he could give her something from his own bags in the trunk.

Even as she shivered, she simply said, "No, thank you, I'm fine."

Clearly, she was anything but fine but at least the heat was now blowing out of the vents onto both of them. Hoping the heat would keep her from catching a cold, he decided to try and coax some important information out of her.

"Where were you headed?"

She was already so tense, and yet at his simple question she tensed even further on the seat beside him.

Instead of answering him, she said, "If you could just take me to the nearest motel, that'd be great." She paused for a moment before adding in a softer voice, "Someplace cheap would be best."

With his previous plans for a fun and relaxing evening falling apart one soaking-wet minute at a time—along with the fact that he was trying to repress the way the stranger's scent was driving his senses crazy—Chase's voice was gruffer than usual as he offered, "Look, I've got a free place for you to stay for the night. We can call road assistance from there."

It would be better to wait until she was dry and warm again to break it to her that even though road assistance would be able to pull her car out of the ditch, they probably wouldn't be able to make it run again. Heck, not even his brother Zach, who was a genius with cars, was likely to get too far with her hatchback.

"Thanks for the offer," she said, her words still wary, but firm, too. "Really, a motel is fine." She shrugged, an outline of moving shoulders in the dark interior of his car. "And don't bother calling road assistance," she said with clear resignation. "At this point I might as well leave my car in the ditch until I can arrange for it to be hauled off for scrap metal."

The exhaustion in her voice fought with an underlying strength for dominance. Chase couldn't help but be impressed with the fact that while she clearly didn't have the money to deal with any of this, she wasn't sitting in his car crying about it.

Chase knew he should just take her to a motel. Lord knew she'd told him to do that more than once already. But there was no way he could leave her in some dank motel in the middle of Napa Valley. Not if he wanted to be able to look at himself in the mirror in the morning without seeing the word *asshole* written across his forehead.

Besides, every instinct he possessed told him she needed more help than just a ride to a motel.

Of course, Chase had learned early on from his mother and sisters not to mess with what a woman wanted. He knew better, knew this woman would be pissed off with what he was about to do.

But none of that, none of the warning buzzers

that were going off in his head, were enough to stop him from deciding to help her, anyway.

He turned the key in the ignition and as he carefully pulled back onto the road, he realized he didn't know her name. Considering he was going to be taking her to the warmth and comfort of the large guesthouse at his brother's winery—whether she liked it or not—he figured a couple of formalities wouldn't be a bad thing.

"I'm Chase Sullivan."

No sound came from the passenger seat and, inexplicably, he found himself fighting a grin. Chase, along with his five brothers, had been magnets for women since adolescence. When, he tried to think, was the last time a woman hadn't thrown herself at him?

Then again, this one hadn't told him anything at all, had she? Not her name, or where she was headed.

Something was definitely up. It would be a much better idea if he could let it go, take her to a motel so that he could get on with his night of meaningless sex with Ellen at the winery, whom he'd called when he left his mother's party to let her know he was on the road and heading to Napa.

So then, why wasn't he doing just that?

And why did he feel strangely drawn to this complete stranger?

Chase let the silence ride out between them,

knowing she'd only answer if she felt comfortable enough with him to do so.

Finally, he heard her sigh a beat before she said, "My name is Chloe."

Chloe was a very pretty name, and she was a very pretty woman. He normally would have told her both of those things, but she was so touchy she'd probably take it the wrong way. He also noticed she didn't tell him her last name.

She craned her neck to look out the window at a dimly lit sign. "Where are you going?" she asked, panic clearly threaded through each vowel. "I'm pretty sure town is in the opposite direction."

Fortunately, right then he saw the Sullivan Winery sign, hit the remote to open the gates and started up the narrow road. His brother Marcus had built his winery on the most beautiful land in all of California's wine country. On a clear day, if you hiked to the top of the highest hill, you felt like you could see until forever.

If he could only convince her to stay the night in Marcus's guesthouse, Chase believed there was no way Chloe was going to be able to resist the beauty all around her come morning. And hopefully, the picturesque surroundings would help ease her worries enough that she would open up to him and let him help her with whatever trouble she was dealing with.

"This is my brother's winery. I know he'd want you to stay here, too."

"Chase."

Her voice held a strong note of warning, but it certainly didn't stop him from liking the way his name sounded on her lips.

"I told you to take me to a motel."

He thought about the different ways he could respond, if he should make excuses or be placating. But sensing she'd see through his bullshit in a way most women rarely did, he simply said, "Marcus's guesthouse is closer. Nicer, too."

She made a barely muffled sound of irritation. "Do you always ignore what people want and do what you want to do, anyway?"

Again, there were several possible responses. But only one honest one. "Pretty much."

"Your mother must be so proud," Chloe said sarcastically.

He liked the way the words rolled right off her tongue, as if she was getting a little more comfortable with the idea of being alone in his car with him, but a moment later, judging by the way she shifted uncomfortably in the seat, he guessed that she was worried about her off-the-cuff response.

Speaking as easily and gently as he could, he said, "Fortunately, I have five brothers and two hellcat sisters to distract her."

He hoped she'd give another unguarded response to that piece of information and was glad when she turned back to him and said, "You're kidding, right?"

"Nope. Eight of us in all." He took his eyes off the road long enough to take in her wide eyes and grin at her.

She shook her head and made another little sound that had his blood heating despite himself. "Your mother must be a saint."

Good. He'd managed to distract her for a few moments, long enough to pull up to the guesthouse. At least this time she hadn't seemed to be worried by what she'd said to him—or how he would react to it.

"Look," he said softly, "I know you'd rather not be here, but I can't see how it makes sense to pay for a room in some motel on the side of the freeway when there are five empty bedrooms right here."

"I don't know you," she said again.

Knowing he couldn't argue with that, he agreed, "I know you don't. And, trust me, if you were either of my sisters I wouldn't want you to trust some guy who picked you up on the side of the road in the middle of a rainstorm." As her body shifted yet again to face him in the car, he noted her obvious surprise at the way he'd agreed with her innate wariness of him. "That's why all I'm going to do is get you settled and then I'll leave and head over to my brother's main house on the other side of the property."

Chase waited for her to say no again. And the truth was, if she flat-out insisted on going to a motel, outside of throwing her over his shoulder and chaining her to one of the beds in his brother's guesthouse, he knew he was going to have to do what she wanted.

Jesus, he couldn't believe how hard he was having to work to push aside the flare of desire that tried to shoot through him at that whole tied-to-the-bedpost scenario he'd just come up with. Lord knew if Chloe saw her impact on him now, she was going to start clawing at the car door so that she could run screaming into town to get away from him. Thank God it was dark enough that she hopefully wouldn't notice his very obvious attraction to her.

"So," she said slowly, drawing the one word out, which had the unfortunate result of drawing his eyes to her full, expressive lips.

My God, she had to be one of the most beautiful women he'd met in months. Maybe ever. And beautiful women were his job. Chase was completely stunned by his reaction to her. Not only by how strong it was, but also by how quick it had happened. He barely knew her, had just met her on the side of the road. Not to mention the fact that she clearly wanted less than nothing to do with him. And yet, none of these things made him any less drawn to her . . . and to wanting the chance to get to know her better.

"You're not going to stay with me?"

Ah, finally. It was the first time she hadn't argued with him or told him she couldn't stay here. Seizing the moment, he said again, "I'll just get you settled and then I'll head over to Marcus's main house for the rest of the night."

Before she could change her mind, he reached across for her bag, but she shifted and opened the passenger's side door, moving out into the rain before he could help her with the damned thing. For some crazy reason, it had become a goal for him to carry it for her. He wanted to get her to trust him enough that she would accept his help.

She moved quickly to the covered porch of the guesthouse that Chase had stayed in many times over the years. It was so familiar to him, and yet as Chloe took in the facade of the beautifully designed stucco house with the tiled accents that had been flown in straight from Italy, the comfortable yet elegant outdoor furniture and the thick golden-toned wood front door, Chase felt like he was seeing it again for the first time.

His brother's winery truly was a wondrous place, and Chase found that he was very glad to be able to share it with Chloe, at least for one night when she clearly needed both beauty and warmth.

His brother's housekeeper had left the front light on for him and he was graced with his best view of Chloe yet. Her hair, which had started to dry just a little in the car, really was like silk, so glossy she could make a mint in shampoo ads. She also had a truly gorgeous figure. Not too thin, but with beautifully lush curves that made his fingers itch to touch her.

What the hell was wrong with him? He needed to stop thinking like that. Especially given that he'd taken her to his brother's place to help her out of a bad situation, not to help her out of her clothes.

As she waited for him on the porch, one hand clutching her bag tightly with the other placed over her right cheek again, Chase had to wonder why she was always hiding her face like that.

He had a bad feeling about it.

Knowing it wouldn't help her feel any more comfortable around him if he was scowling at her, he worked to focus instead on the way the porch light bathed her in a faint glow. Making a mental note to set up some shots with the models he'd be working with the following evening right where she was standing, he walked up the steps and headed for the front door.

"Let's go inside and warm up," he said, holding the door open for her.

"At least your mother taught you one thing," she murmured as she moved past him.

"Wow," she breathed as she stopped in the threshold to look around the beautifully decorated living room. "What a beautiful house."

Marcus definitely knew how to provide every luxury for his guests. Chase wasn't the only one who liked to come up to Napa to spend the weekend with Marcus, and he knew how much his brother loved having his family there with him.

"I know Marcus would want you to make yourself right at home," he told her, just as her scent wrapped itself around him again.

It was a hit of potent sensuality. Problem was, she was a gorgeous woman and he was a man who adored gorgeous women. But then her bag bumped against the door frame, pushing her hips into his groin, and he barely stifled his groan in time.

Jesus, if he didn't know better, if she were any other woman, he'd think she'd done that on purpose. But given the way she all but threw herself across the room and away from him, he knew there was nothing intentional about her effect on him.

It had only been a month since Chase had had sex, but his body was reacting to Chloe like it had been a year.

A gust of wind blew rain up onto the porch and Chase closed the door before it could blow inside. Chloe was standing awkwardly next to the kitchen island as he moved slowly into the room.

He worked to keep his eyes from devouring her as he asked, "Are you hungry?"

She shook her head, her hand back over her cheek.

"Thirsty?"

"No."

"Let me get you a towel and some dry clothes now," he said in his gentlest voice, hoping she'd at least let him do that for her.

"You said you had a place for me to sleep tonight," she reminded him. "That's all I need."

As she spoke, her hand slipped on her face. What he saw at the edge of her palm made him sick to his stomach.

"You're hurt." It wasn't a question. "You told me you weren't hurt, but you are. Let me take a look at your face."

She tried to take a step back but the granite kitchen counter held her where she was. "No," she insisted, "I'm fine."

He could see how hard she was trying to be tough and strong. But didn't she get it? He was right here offering to help her. And he wasn't going to let her keep suffering if there was something he could do to make things better for her.

Not moving slowly this time, not bothering to make sure he didn't spook her, he crossed to her and put his hand over hers.

The first touch had both of them sucking in a breath and he swore her pupils dilated a split second before she wrenched out of his grip with a strength that surprised him.

"I knew I shouldn't have come here with you," she said as she began to rush across the room.

But Chase was faster, pulling her into his arms before she could get away. He was just registering her soft heat, the press of her full breasts against his chest, the heated vee between her legs that so perfectly cradled his groin, when he saw what she'd been hiding from him.

"Jesus, Chloe, did that happen in the car? Why didn't you tell me how bad you'd been hurt? Did your face hit the steering wheel when your car landed in the ditch?" He narrowed his eyes as he studied the bruise close up. "Or did something else cause this?"

The huge mottled bruise was all the colors of the rainbow with a long scratch through the center. Tears sparkled in her eyes, but they seemed to be more from frustration than due to any pain she was feeling.

"It hasn't been my best night."

Yet again, she hadn't answered his question. But he figured it was pretty safe to assume the bruise hadn't been caused by her hitting the steering wheel when her car had crashed into the ditch. Any other woman would have been crying, but not this one, even though she'd clearly had a hell of a night so far.

"No kidding," he said softly.

The more he looked at her, the angrier he got about the bruise. He'd fought with his brothers enough times to know how bad it must hurt. And he'd also been on the receiving end of enough shiners from his brothers to know what it looked like when someone's fist collided with your face.

But even though he was filling up with absolute rage at the thought of anyone hurting Chloe like this, he knew better than to make a big deal out of it.

He wasn't going to bruise her pride . . . not when someone had already done a hell of a job on her face.

"Did you put any ice on the bruise?"

She shook her head. "No. I didn't have a chance."

When she clamped her lips shut as if she'd already said too much, he reluctantly let go of her and moved toward the kitchen.

Glad that he'd stayed in Marcus's guesthouse enough times to know where things were, Chase quickly found a box of plastic bags in a drawer by the sink. He went to the freezer to fill it with ice, then wrapped the whole thing up in one of the clean, soft, colorful kitchen towels he found in another nearby drawer.

Chloe hadn't moved from the spot where he'd stopped her from running. He could easily bring her the ice, but he knew it was important that she start to trust him—at least a little—if he was going to be able to help her. And every instinct he possessed had been screaming out from that first instant he'd spotted her that her damage was a hell of a lot bigger than just losing control of her car in the rain.

It sucked to be right sometimes.

"I don't bite. I promise," Chase said as he offered her the ice pack.

The very last thing he expected her to do was drop her gaze to his throbbing groin, raise an eyebrow and say in a rather sarcastic voice, "Really?"

Glad to see that any remnant of the tears that hadn't come were long gone, and surprised as hell at the way she'd just acknowledged his obvious attraction to her, he let loose his grin at her pointed comment.

"What I should have said is, I won't bite unless—"

She held up a hand to cut him off and finished his sentence. "Unless I want you to." She said it like she'd heard it a hundred times before. "Whatever. I don't want you to. Not now. Not ever." Her words were tired, hard, but thankfully, she chose to move toward him rather than farther away. "I'll take the ice, though."

He handed it to her and she was starting to thank him when she pressed it against her cheek a little too hard and gasped in pain.

"Here," he said, his chest clenching at the way her breath had hissed from her lips and her face had gone white. "Let me."

Moving closer again, he slid the fingers of his left hand beneath hers while cupping the back of her head with his right. He expected her to pull away from him, to tell him she could take care of herself, to insist that he keep his hands off her.

Instead, he was in for another surprise when she said, "You're good at this," in a soft voice that did nothing to stop the southerly flow of blood to his groin.

Chase was surprised to realize the ice had finally broken between them. All because of the attraction he couldn't control and her sarcastic comments about it.

Who would have thought that would do it? If anything, he'd been sure it would make her run.

What other surprises did she have in store for him?

And would she stick around long enough for him to discover them?

"Five brothers, remember?" he said with a small smile. "Although my sisters were the ones who usually left the worst bruises when we were messing around." He grinned. "Little brats."

She looked up at him then, and this time he didn't have any hope of controlling his reaction to the shot of desire that rocked him. Her eyes were extraordinary, a vibrant green along the rims of the pupils, but filled in everywhere else with blue. He'd already thought she was beautiful.

But now he realized that word didn't even come close to describing Chloe.

"You like your brothers and sisters a lot, don't you?" she asked in a soft voice.

He dropped his gaze to her mouth as she spoke, taking the chance to further appreciate the full curve of her lower lip, the sweet Cupid's bow of the upper.

No question about it, even though he'd only just met her thirty minutes ago, he was on his way to totally and completely losing his mind over this woman. One who obviously came with baggage.

He'd never been a man much interested in baggage. Looked like the universe was playing a fast one on him tonight.

Because he was definitely interested, despite all the reasons he shouldn't be.

"Do I have something on my mouth?"

Her irritation was, thankfully, fused now with a faint amusement at how clearly mesmerized he was. At this point, he'd rather have her laughing at him than running from him.

He refused to let himself think of later, trying like hell to keep his brain from heading toward the direction it was dying to go . . . the one where she was naked and he was tasting every inch of her beautiful skin.

First things first; he had to get her to agree to actually stay the night.

And not to run at first light.

"No," he told her in a low voice, "your mouth is perfect." A flush spread across the side of her face he wasn't covering with the towel and ice. "And yes, my siblings are great. I was a really lucky kid to have them around growing up." He thought about his mother's party and the pictures he'd taken of his brothers and sisters. "With eight of us in one small house together, we fought a lot, but we laughed even more."

Chloe's expression filled with longing before she turned her head away and lowered her lashes so he couldn't see into her stunning—and expressive—eyes anymore.

"My cheek feels better now, thanks. I'm pretty tired." He could see from the dark shadows beneath her eyes just how exhausted she really was. "Could you show me where the bedroom is now, please?"

He wanted to keep her there with him and keep asking her questions until she finally agreed to tell him who had hurt her. It didn't take a brain surgeon to guess that she was running from someone. Every cell in Chase's body wanted to protect her, but even though that initial icy barrier that she'd put up between them had thawed slightly, he knew she wasn't anywhere near ready to trust him yet.

"The bedrooms are just down the hall," he told her, but though it was long past time to let her go, he couldn't do it. Her warmth, her soft curves, felt too good, too right, for him to back away just yet.

Chloe, unfortunately, had no problem moving out of his arms.

Since the odds were pretty good that a guy had done the number on her face, he wondered, Was she married? Was this the work of an abusive husband?

Chase wasn't in the habit of scanning ring fingers for diamonds, but he didn't think before glancing at her left hand. He didn't even try to be subtle. Hell, she'd already seen that he wanted her. Felt it, too. He'd promised to keep his hands off for the night. But he'd said nothing about the future. And he needed to know if she was being beaten up by the guy she was married to.

She was holding her hand clenched into a fist, but he couldn't see a ring.

Good. That meant that once he found out what had happened to her, once she started to trust him, there wasn't one single reason he couldn't begin a slow and steady seduction.

When he finally looked up at her face, she was staring back at him with that same irritation he'd seen in her eyes earlier, only with none of the accompanying amusement this time.

Busted.

"The bedroom?" She lifted an eyebrow. Way up. "You were going to show me where it is."

He put his hands on her bag. "This way."

She reached for it, too, and they played a ridiculous game of tug-of-war over the army-green canvas bag for a few seconds. Chase knew he should just let her continue carrying it, but she couldn't have been more than five-foot-five to his six-three and he figured he outweighed her by about eighty or so pounds. He could carry the damn bag for her.

Still clutching it tightly in both her fists, she said, "You've really got a thing about carrying my bag, don't you?"

He was holding firm to his side as he replied, "I was going to say the same to you."

She dropped her hold on the bag so fast he stumbled back with it.

She shook her head and muttered, "I've never understood why men feel like they have to be so macho."

"Wanting to help you with this bag isn't macho."

She looked like she was on the verge of laughing—the first time he'd seen anything approaching a smile on her beautiful face—as she countered, "You sure about that?"

"Maybe it's just that my mother taught me right," he countered, throwing her earlier words back at her.

He didn't wait for her to argue some more . . . not when he was getting way too close to planting a kiss on that lovely smart mouth, whether she wanted him to or not. Either that, or find a way to actually make her smile. Or, better yet, to find out what her laugh sounded like.

He led the way down the hall to the master suite where he'd been planning to sleep. The other bedrooms were fully decked out with high-end mattresses, but he wanted Chloe to have the very best.

Chase opened the door and was about to reach for the light switch when he realized it was already on. It took his water-addled brain longer than it should have to realize that the bed wasn't empty.

And a naked woman was waiting for him on it.

Oh, crap. He'd forgotten all about Ellen, but Marcus's winery manager obviously hadn't forgotten about him. If things had gone differently tonight—way differently—he knew he would have been psyched to find her already stripped down and ready for him.

Only, after meeting Chloe, Chase was about as unpsyched by Ellen's naked presence in the house as he could be.

Ellen's eyes were wide as she looked between him and Chloe. Clearly, surprise had her frozen in place on the bed as it took her a minute to remove her iPod headphones. Obviously the music had masked the sound of Chase and Chloe's conversation in the living room and Ellen had had no idea that Chase wouldn't be walking through the bedroom door alone.

Before he could think fast and get Chloe the hell out of there, she stepped out from behind him. He waited for her to gasp in outrage, for her to do the inevitable—grab her bag from him and run back out into the rain.

But all that came was the low sound of her laughter. The very sound he'd been hoping to hear just seconds earlier . . . only he hadn't thought it would happen like this.

"Maybe," she said through her undisguised mirth, "there's another bedroom I could take?" She chuckled again. "Out of hearing distance, if at all possible, please."

He shot her a look that said she was crazy. Chloe couldn't seriously think he was going to have sex with Ellen while she was in the house, did she?

But then, he lost hold of the question entirely as her ongoing laughter wrapped itself around his senses.

God, he loved the sound of it. So easy. Straight from her soul. And her smile was absolutely beautiful.

Ellen was still stark naked on the bed, but he couldn't take his eyes off Chloe. He'd wanted to kiss her practically from the moment he'd met her. Now he wanted to kiss her senseless *and* make her smile, hear her sweet laughter again, just as much.

"Chase?" Ellen finally spoke, her voice a

little higher pitched than usual. “Who’s she?”

Ellen was only just moving to cover up now and as she did so he noticed she wasn’t really his type, after all. He much preferred Chloe’s curves to Ellen’s taut muscles. And dyed blond curls had nothing on brown hair that picked up the light as it shifted across her shoulders and back every time Chloe moved.

“I’m Chloe.”

Chase was more than a little surprised by how amused she was by the whole thing. Clearly, she was enjoying watching him deal with this predicament. Which was, he suddenly had to admit, pretty funny.

“Chase picked me up tonight.” She nodded in his direction and added, “You know the story—girl in trouble on the side of the road meets guy in a flashy car.”

Ellen looked more confused than angry as she wrapped a robe around herself, which he supposed made sense since it wasn’t like they’d been planning to do more than have a little no-strings fun with each other tonight. She looked at Chase and seemed to be trying to make up her mind about something before saying, “With you being a photographer and running with all those fast crowds, I should have figured you were into this sort of thing.”

Feeling as if he’d stepped into some kind of surreal scene being shot for one of his brother

Smith's movies, Chase had to ask, "What kind of stuff do you think I'm into?"

"You know, ménages and stuff," Ellen said, then bit her lip as she obviously thought over what she believed to be the new development in their evening. She turned her attention from Chase to Chloe. "Nice to meet you, Chloe, even if this is a teensy bit unexpected. I'm Ellen, by the way." She paused to take a deep breath before saying, "You're very pretty."

Chloe looked utterly bemused by the way Ellen was looking at her, clearly trying to size up her future performance in bed, since she now thought that was the kind of thing he was into.

"Thanks, I guess," she said to Ellen, "and you're pretty, too, but I don't think I'm up for any threesomes tonight."

The easy way she said it had Chase's brain spinning off in all sorts of crazy directions. Had she done a ménage before?

Just the thought of someone else touching her had him seeing red.

He'd never gone looking for serious, had been perfectly happy with one-night stands in the past. On the road as much as he was, keeping things clean and simple fit his life best, and Chase had never envied his colleagues who had a wife and kids at home waiting for them.

But from the first moment he'd seen Chloe, he'd wanted to protect her. Now, he had to wonder, could he already want more? Even though he'd only just met her, he knew attraction could come in an instant.

Could connection come that quickly, too?

"Oh, my God," Ellen said suddenly when she finally saw Chloe's nasty bruise. "What happened to your face?"

Chase hated to see every bit of humor leave Chloe's face.

"I'm fine," she told Ellen, before turning back to him to say, "I'll find another bedroom myself. Good night."

Chase wanted to go after her, but he knew he had to deal with Ellen first.

"Is she okay?" Ellen asked after Chloe had closed the door behind her. "That bruise looks really nasty." Before he could answer, she asked, "Has she seen a doctor? And did you really find her on the side of the road?"

He ran a hand through his wet hair, wishing he could answer Ellen's questions.

Instead, all he could tell her was, "She'll be okay." He'd make sure of it. "Look, tonight's not going to happen anymore."

Ellen smiled at him, their almost-fling instantly forgotten. "That's probably for the best, considering I work for your brother."

Chase was glad they both agreed that they'd just narrowly averted any potential problems.

"She really is very pretty." As she gathered up

her clothes in her arms and headed for the en suite bathroom, she winked at him and teased, "Pretty enough that I actually was considering that three-way for a moment there, even though it's not at all my usual style."

"No." His response was instinctive. "That never would have happened." He was never, ever going to share Chloe with anyone.

That was, if he ever managed to convince her not only to open up and tell him what had happened to her, but to stay long enough to see if the initial sparks between them could turn into something more.

Problem was, he thought as he walked out of the bedroom to let Ellen put on her clothes and headed down the hall to make sure Chloe had settled into one of the other bedrooms all right, he had a feeling convincing Chloe to trust him enough to give him a chance wasn't going to be an easy task in the least.

Three

Chloe wanted nothing more than to drop her bag on the bedroom floor, throw herself on the bed and curl up into a tight ball. But the wood floor looked really expensive and she'd already dripped on it enough. She knew how people with money lived, but even so, she was impressed with this gorgeous house in the wine country. And to think it was only the guesthouse. She couldn't imagine what the main house must look like.

She'd grown up in a lower-middle-class household with parents who always wanted more but never knew how to get it. So when she'd met her husband, and he'd told her he wanted to give her the world, she'd followed his promises straight to the altar.

Little did she know at the time just how little those promises would mean. He might have given her money to spend and pretty clothes to wear, but he'd also tried to take away everything that really mattered.

With a shake of her head, as if that would help clear the ugly memories from her mind, she headed for the bathroom. Putting her bag down on the tiled floor, she stripped off her wet, dirty clothes, put them in the sink and began to wash the mud out of them. She would have loved to throw them away, but she didn't have much with her and knew that she'd need them again in the near future. The best she could do for the time being was to get out the dirt with soap and water, wring as much of the water out by hand as she could and then hang them up to dry. Of course, she knew the house must have a washer and dryer, but spending the night in a stranger's house—not even the stranger who'd brought her here, but a brother she'd never met—was more than enough charity.

Finally finished dealing with her clothes, she moved to the shower and was reaching in to turn on the water when she changed her mind. The bathroom had a huge whirlpool tub. She almost moaned aloud at the thought of lying in the warm water with jets massaging her legs, spine and feet.

Chloe looked back almost guiltily at the bathroom door before realizing she was being silly. It was locked and she was finally alone. Since Chase was insisting she stay here tonight, what was wrong with availing herself of the facilities? At least those attached to her bedroom.

She hadn't been in a tub like this since she'd left—

No. She wouldn't let herself think of that tonight. Chloe knew she didn't have the luxury of pretending everything was okay—not by a long shot—but deep inside she felt safe in this beautiful house surrounded by grapevines.

She supposed, a few seconds later, that it was precisely that glorious sense of safety—and the memory of how nice it had been to feel so warm and protected in Chase's arms for the few moments that she'd let him hold her—that had her body acting so off-kilter when she stepped into the hot water.

Her skin felt extra sensitive as she slowly

submerged her legs and then hips and back into the large tub. Sighing with pleasure, she laid her head on the curved rim and looked up through a skylight that was pinging with the rain from outside. She hadn't felt feminine or sexy in a very long time. And yet, there had been no doubt that Chase had been attracted to her.

She should have been upset about it. After all, she'd just met him. And she was in no state of mind whatsoever to deal with anyone's attraction. Not his or hers. And yet a heavy, heated throbbing pulsed at the tips of her breasts, which felt even fuller than normal. Between her thighs . . . well, the truth was that she was burning up down there.

Heck, if she were being even the slightest bit honest with herself, she'd been on fire from the moment Chase had moved close, put one hand against her neck and held the ice pack against her cheek in his brother's kitchen.

Both she and the girl in his bed had the same taste, it seemed.

Thinking of the naked stranger—Ellen, she'd said her name was—and her crazy suggestion had Chloe unexpectedly grinning again as she scooted down in the tub and tilted her neck backward to get her hair wet in the hot water. *Mmm, that felt good.* She reached for the fancy bottle of shampoo by the side and began massaging the sweet-smelling liquid into her hair.

It hadn't been a great night by any means, but at least there'd been some unexpected humor in it. Especially the look on Chase's face when he opened the bedroom door and realized they weren't alone in his brother's guesthouse, after all.

Chase had clearly been surprised by the naked woman—and by the fact that she was only slightly fazed by the idea of more than one person in her bed.

Chloe's grin shifted into a semifrown. Not just because she hadn't thought people actually did that, but because she couldn't understand Ellen's thinking.

If Chase had been hers, she wouldn't share him with anyone.

The shocking train of thought stopped Chloe cold. Soap dripped into her eyelashes and she dunked herself under the water, hoping to wash her unwelcome thoughts away, too, while she was at it.

What was wrong with her? Was she really that blockheaded? That full of fantasies and foolish dreams?

She knew better, knew that the only person she should be trusting, for a very long time, was herself.

And yet, hadn't she been doing some verbal sparring with Chase out in the living room and kitchen? Borderline flirting, when she should have been wary. And then, when they'd found the woman waiting for him on the bed, maybe she should have been shocked, but instead Chloe hadn't been able to hold in her laughter.

Not when finally having a reason to laugh again had felt too good. She'd had to let it out.

Amazingly, for a few moments, she'd almost felt like her old self.

Once upon a time Chloe had been a sensual woman. She hadn't been one of those girls who was afraid of her own body. She'd loved being kissed. Caressed. She'd loved other things, too. Things her ex-husband had told her she was supposed to be ashamed of. But just because she'd done a crummy job of picking a husband didn't mean those urges, those desires, had ever really gone away.

They'd just gone into hiding.

And Chase was, quite obviously—and unfortunately—a master of hide-and-seek.

Chloe sighed as she ran a bar of soap over her arm. She couldn't believe her body had decided to leap to life now. Tonight of all nights, she should be focusing on getting sleep and food and figuring out what to do next.

Instead, she was lying in the bath thinking about Mr. Hotstuff with his green eyes and wicked grin. Not to mention the ridiculously great body—tall, broad-shouldered and muscular.

Frustration ate at her as she continued to soap her skin with more than a little vigor. She had a bad feeling that if she got up out of this glorious tub, instead of sinking into what was sure to be a fantastically luxurious bed and falling straight to sleep, she was going to be tossing and turning with unrequited lust all night.

No, damn it! When she'd left her now ex-husband, she'd vowed to take care of herself. At the time she'd believed that simply meant money and jobs and housing. Evidently, she thought with a slightly rueful shake of her head, it also seemed to mean that if she was feeling unaccountably aroused, she was going to have to take care of that, too.

She shifted in the tub at the somewhat shocking thought, and as the warm water floated over her curves, she tried to figure out how long it had been since she'd enjoyed sex. Since she'd been able to explore her body and give in to its needs.

How long had she been ashamed of her natural sensuality?

If only the answers weren't all so painful. If only the answers didn't make her feel so power-less.

No. She wouldn't go there tonight. Not after what she'd already been through.

Tomorrow would come soon enough. But tonight . . . well, maybe tonight was her chance to start taking some much-needed strides to reclaim a part of herself that she'd been forced to deny for too long. She couldn't rebuild her entire life from scratch tonight. That would take much longer than one evening in Napa Valley. But why shouldn't she give herself at least a small taste of the pleasure she'd denied herself for far too long?

Closing her eyes, she forced herself to unclench her jaw along with the muscles in her arms and legs. As she relaxed deeper into the warm tub, Chloe put her hands just above her breasts and held them there, feeling the quickening beat of her heart.

Her skin was warm from the water. Slowly, she ran her hands down her chest, over her full breasts, and she sucked in a breath at the surprisingly pleasurable sensations that shot through her. She used to love having a man's hands, his mouth, playing over her skin.

She hadn't conjured up sexy fantasies in a long time, but tonight it was only her and her hands and a tub full of steaming water. No one was here to tell her she was dirty or bad for liking what she liked.

Drawing on long-buried sensual memories, she let her mind drift to a scene where she was in a man's arms and his head was bent down over her breasts. And then he lifted his head and she gasped as a flush of arousal hit her right between her thighs.

Because the man looked just like Chase.

Chloe should have stopped touching herself

right then. She knew she should have had the self-control to get up out of the tub, to go get the sleep she so desperately needed.

But she'd gone without for so long. Far too long. She was thirty years old and heading straight toward her sexual prime, wasn't she?

It was one more reason to be angry about the way she'd let her life play out these past years.

And this, her innate sensuality, was one more part of her life to reclaim.

She looked around at the large tiled bathroom. The blinds were covering the window over the tub. Her knight in shining armor was busy with another woman in a bedroom down the hall.

Chloe knew she was safe here, safer than she'd been in a very long time. Tonight she had a chance to feel normal again. And she was going to take it . . . even if the gorgeous face of a man she'd just met—and was impossibly tempted by even though every last brain cell she had knew better—was the very man whose image was about to have her crying out with ecstasy in a few minutes.

Keeping one hand on her breasts, she let the other slide down over her rib cage, then her stomach, until she reached the thatch of soft curls between her thighs. It was instinct to let her legs fall open in the water.

Her breath quickened as she slid her fingers down lower. Even in the water she could feel how slick she was, how ready she'd been since practically the first moment Chase had touched her, his hand threading through the hair at the base of her neck as he held the ice to her cheek. She'd been all but seared by the heat of his body against hers, even as she knew he'd been careful not to press himself too closely to her.

She didn't have the first clue how she could have reacted like that to a complete stranger. Given what had just happened to her, the bruise still throbbing on her cheek, shouldn't she have been flinching and hating the feel of his hands on her?

But she hadn't been anywhere near hating Chase's touch. Far from it, considering the amazing truth that she'd been far more tempted to rub herself against him than shove him away.

As her fingers swirled between her legs, her mind flitted back to that moment when she'd looked down at his groin. Sex had been good once, good enough that she could still imagine the kind of pleasure a man like Chase could give a woman.

Sinking so deep into the water that her nose and mouth and eyes were barely above the surface, her feet slid out farther and she accidentally kicked something in the tub that sent the jets into overdrive.

Chloe's eyes flew open as the bubbling streams assaulted her sensitive skin. At first it was too much, too many sensations coming at her at once, but then, as she got more used to the water moving across her sore muscles, she found herself growing even more relaxed.

Lifting her hips into the jet streams felt decadent. Sinful.

And just plain good.

Moving her hand from between her legs back to her breasts, she cupped one in each hand as the water worked between her legs in the nicest possible way.

She rocked her hips up and down as she got closer and closer to the sweetest orgasm she'd had in a long, long time. Chase's face appeared again in her head and she didn't even bother to stop herself from fantasizing about what his kiss would taste like, about how it would feel to have his large hands on her instead of her own.

A strange sound tried to work its way into her subconscious, but she was too far gone to pay it any attention. And then Chase's name was on her lips as her entire body tightened down and then exploded in a thousand delicious pieces, her hips bucking closer to the wonderfully strong jets, her fingers tightening on her own breasts.

Oh, God, she loved this feeling, loved the wildness that coursed through her veins, and the calm that followed so closely after. Why had she gone so long without it?

Chloe felt so loose, so warm, that she was about to relax deeper into the tub when her brain rewound back to that moment when she'd been coming apart. To the sounds she'd heard, but dismissed as her body flew over the edge.

Her heart began to beat hard and fast again as she slowly opened her eyes. She was still disoriented enough from her orgasm for a few seconds that she was sure she couldn't be seeing what she was seeing: Chase, standing in the doorway of the bathroom, one hand on the door-knob.

Surprise—and dangerously strong lust—were written all over his face.

Four

Chloe closed her eyes again, held her breath and went completely under the water as the jets turned off on their own. She held her breath as long as she could, all the while praying that when she came back up the door would still be closed and locked . . . and that Chase seeing her not just naked, but touching herself in his brother's bathtub, would be nothing more than a bad dream.

Alas, when she came back up for air and opened her eyes, there he was, standing right where he'd been a minute ago.

Despite the fact that she was already in warm

water, she could feel an extra hot flush of mortification quickly covering her skin, head to toe.

At least, that's what she told herself it was.

With a snap of water and skin, she shoved her thighs together under the water in the tub, and lifted her knees to try and hide her naked lower body, while simultaneously crossing her arms over her chest to cover her breasts, which were exposed above the water line.

Forcing herself to meet his gaze—green eyes that blazed with enough heat to set off a fire-extinguisher—she said, "The door was locked!"

Good thing she already knew better than to expect an apology. Because Chase didn't look the least bit repentant.

"It must not have locked all the way."

Her lips shouldn't be on the verge of tilting up into a grin. None of this was funny. Rather, it would have been funny if it were happening to anyone else, like, say, in a movie she was watching.

But this wasn't a romantic comedy.

This was her screwed-up life.

"Do you always break into the bathroom when you have guests?"

At long last, he looked a teensy bit chagrined. "I didn't see your things in the bedroom. I thought you might have decided to leave again." He paused, his gaze softening behind the desire that still radiated from him. “I was worried about you.” He held out his hand. “And I brought Advil for your bruise. I know how much it must hurt.”

His sweetness hit her right in the solar plexus, right where she was still stupidly vulnerable, making her eyes close at the force of it.

She knew she should just keep her eyes closed. Because when she made the mistake of opening them again to be brave and look him in the eye, what she saw on his face made it impossible for her to tell the difference between his desire and his sweetness.

How could she when they were both wrapped up in one far-too-gorgeous package?

Oh, God.

She’d been so stunned by seeing him standing in the doorway that she’d completely forgotten the name that had passed her lips as she was coming.

His name.

Chloe gulped. Hard.

Knowing there was only one way to play it at this point, she said with far more bravado than she actually possessed, “I know a lot of Chases, by the way.”

He raised an eyebrow, the corner of his mouth twitching with an obvious urge to grin. “Really?”

He held her there in that half smile for longer than was fair. Especially when both of them knew she'd likely never met a Chase before in her life.

"People usually tell me it's a pretty uncommon name."

Well, what was she going to say to that? But now that the initial stab of mortification and surprise had passed, Chloe became even more aware of the position she was in.

Whatever Chase's mother had taught him, she'd clearly forgotten the lesson on leaving a naked girl alone to regain her composure. Because instead of letting her get out of the tub to get dressed in privacy, he let his appreciative gaze flicker up and down her bare skin.

Her hands itched to cover herself up more, but even though the naked girl on his bed had been a good thirty pounds thinner than Chloe, why did she have to be ashamed of her curves?

She'd been told one too many times by her ex that she needed to lose weight. She was never going to diet again. Not for anyone. She was keeping her muscles and curves, thank you very much.

Throwing on that cloak of bravado again, she said, "I'm still naked here, you know."

"You certainly are," he stated, his pleasure at her naked state obvious.

Why wasn't she more irritated with him?

More to the point, *why wasn't she scared?*

He was big. Way bigger than she was. His hands could do incredible damage to her. Not to mention other parts of his body that could hurt her.

And yet, even though she had every reason to be frightened of what Chase could do to her . . . she wasn't afraid of him.

At first, she'd been wary about getting into his car, but then, when he'd started talking about his big family, that wariness had disappeared. He clearly loved his brothers and sisters a great deal, and it was hard to picture a serial killer who had that kind of connection to his family.

She'd tried to force her wariness to reappear in the kitchen when he'd insisted on looking at her cheek, but the truth was, she hadn't been running because she was afraid he'd hurt her.

No, she'd wanted to run because of a different kind of fear entirely.

She'd been frightened of her response to him. Of how strong—and immediate—her attraction to him was.

And now, here she was, naked and wet in rapidly cooling water, still feeling that response. More than ever, in fact. Even after making a complete fool of herself by calling out his name in the midst of what should have been a totally private moment.

Irritated with herself for this strange weakness, and with Chase for being such an obstinate *guy,* she said with no small measure of sarcasm, "You don't take a hint very well, do you?"

He grinned, a beautiful smile that did funny things to her stomach. "I'm better with direct requests."

"Get out."

He grinned again, a good solid laugh coming alongside it. "Want a towel first?"

"So by *better* you meant *terrible?*" And yet, even as she said the words in the crispest voice she could manage, she was working like crazy to hold back the upward twist of her lips into a grin that matched his.

This time, she wasn't at all surprised when his response was to move farther into the room rather than out of it. He pulled a thick, plush towel off the heated rack.

"Here you go."

He held out the towel just far enough away that she'd have to stand up, step out of the tub and walk over to him to reach it.

Stalling, still trying to figure out just what it was about Chase that had her actually going along with this crazy game the two of them were playing with each other, she said, "So what happened to the other naked woman?"

"I sent her home," he said, as if it was the most obvious answer in the world.

Deciding there weren't a whole lot of reasons left to hold back her sassy mouth with him at this point—after all, she was naked in the bathtub and he was holding a towel out to her as a crystal clear challenge—Chloe made a little face and let loose with, "Poor thing. Was she disappointed by how fast you got off?"

A muffled laugh came from Chase. "I'm afraid this wasn't her lucky night. She put on her clothes and left right after you did."

Hmm. Well, that was surprising. She didn't know many men who could send home a beautiful naked woman without first taking what was offered.

Why wasn't he leaving her alone, too?

And why didn't she want him to?

Both of them knew that if she started screaming, that if she really wanted him to go, he'd go. Instead, they were playing this little game not just with the towel, but with the obvious attraction they each felt for the other.

It was a game she was having way too much fun with.

So much fun, in fact, that she knew if it went on much longer she was bound to do something really stupid.

Really, *really* stupid.

No.

She was done with stupid. Her marriage had been based entirely on stupid choices, after all. And look what that had gotten her. A big, ugly bruise on her face, her car in a ditch . . . while she hid out in a stranger's house and tried to use their attraction to ignore the fact that she still needed to figure out how to deal with her problems.

The frustrating thought had her forgetting all about the game she and Chase were playing, along with her own nakedness, just long enough that she stood up to grab the towel before she realized what she'd done.

Suddenly stunned, she stood before him, shockingly aware of each bead of water as it slid across her bare skin and back down into the tub.

Chase's green eyes dilated almost to black as he looked at her. "My God, you're lovely, Chloe."

She wasn't sure he was aware that he'd said the words aloud, but the reverence in them shook her.

No one had ever looked at her like that, like he'd never seen anyone or anything quite so pretty.

No. Not pretty.

Lovely.

Maybe it was the power of that one word, when up until now she'd only ever heard *hot* and *sexy,* that kept her standing there, still naked and dripping.

Waiting.

Anticipating.

Wanting.

She knew exactly what was going to come next, could practically choreograph what every single guy on earth would do in this situation. Chase was going to charm her into agreeing to have sex with him, and in the morning she'd hate him for taking advantage of her sensual weakness when her heart wasn't at all in it.

But, mostly, she'd end up hating herself for being weak and foolish, and for not guarding her heart and her body better.

Only, as the seconds ticked by in time with the overly loud beating of her heart, even though Chase clearly wanted nothing more than to rip off his jeans and join her in the tub, he didn't. And even though they both knew he was big enough and strong enough to be inside of her before she took her next breath, he didn't so much as move an inch closer.

Chloe couldn't believe it. She hadn't given him permission to touch her. And, amazingly, he wasn't taking it, anyway, wasn't taking whatever he could from her just because he was bigger and stronger than she was.

A sharp pang landed right behind her breastbone, right in the center of her heart, which had been so bruised and battered.

Was it possible that, for the first time in her life, she'd actually met a man who wouldn't touch her, who wouldn't try to make a move . . . unless she let him?

Was it actually possible that despite the intense desire in his eyes and the way the muscles in his jaw were jumping at the self-control he was using to remain right where he was, Chase would never lay a hand—or his lips—on her unless she out-right asked him to?

Could it be possible that he'd never press his lips against hers unless she begged him to kiss her, until she was ready and desperate for his touch, for his lovemaking?

Visions of that desperation shouldn't be so clear to her, shouldn't already be running through her mind like a sexy movie. But they were so ridiculously clear—and potent—that it took every ounce of self-control she had to force herself to shove them away.

"I'll take that towel now, thanks."

There'd never been a less sexy statement said between a man and woman.

So then, why did she suddenly feel so breathless?

Holy hell.

Chase had done his fair share of crazy things with women, but none of them had anything on seeing Chloe come in the bathtub.

And there wasn't a single model's body that he'd photographed over the years that had an ounce of the sensuality that infused every cell on Chloe's lovely naked body.

Looking down, he realized the towel was actually shaking in his hands.

Chase worked to calm down. He shouldn't

have stayed in the bathroom. He knew that.

But he hadn't been able to help himself. And he didn't think she had really wanted him to leave, either.

Still, some small voice of rational thought told him he should give her the towel before she dried all on her own, or caught a chill. He held the towel out to her and she tugged on it before lifting her eyes to his.

"Hotstuff?" Chloe asked.

He watched surprise register on her face when she realized what she'd just called him.

Hotstuff.

"You're talking about me, right?" he asked, glad to see her give him another one of those beautiful smiles that practically knocked him over. Her mouth was beautiful whether she was scowling or biting her lip. But when she smiled there was so much warmth he felt as if the sun had just risen to shine down over them both.

"It's a good nickname, don't you think?" Before he could answer, she reminded him, "You need to let go of the towel."

He knew that. But hell, he wasn't sure he could remember how to say his own name right now. So how was he supposed to get his brain to work enough to unwrap his fingers from the cotton?

"Sorry." And he really was sorry, especially when she quickly wrapped the large towel around herself.

"That bathtub is really great."

He was pretty sure he looked like an idiot standing there unable to respond. He'd accidentally watched her give herself what looked to be a really great orgasm and all she had to say was that the bathtub was great?

"I'm not sure the bathtub had anything to do with it," he finally said.

He loved the sound of her laughter, loved the fact that it sounded less and less rusty every time he heard it.

She shrugged as she walked past him, tucking the towel into place between her incredible breasts. "A guy should never underestimate the power of a well-placed jet," was her response as she walked up to the mirror and began finger-combing her hair.

When he just continued to stand there and watch her from behind, she raised an eyebrow in the mirror. "I'm sure you're tired."

Hell, no. He wasn't tired. Not when she was standing so close wearing only a towel.

"I don't need much sleep."

"Well, I do." With that, she walked out of the bathroom and to the door that led out to the hallway. "Good night."

He dutifully headed to the door, long after he should already have been on his way. "Good night."

Despite the fact that Chase wanted her more

than he'd ever wanted another woman, the kiss he wanted to give her wasn't one that would have her begging him for another climax.

No, what he really wanted to do was press a kiss to her forehead. He wanted to give her a gentle kiss that would let her know she was safe with him.

But he hadn't earned that kiss and instinctively knew better than to take anything from her that she hadn't offered.

He was halfway down the hall when he heard her say, "Hotstuff?"

Grinning again at the nickname she'd given him—that had to be good, right?—he turned around. "Yes?"

Despite the nickname, she looked serious again. Really, really serious. "Thank you. For everything you did tonight."

His chest squeezed at her heartfelt words. And at the *Thank you for everything you didn't do* that she wasn't saying, silent words that rang out just as clearly as the words she'd said aloud.

"You're welcome, Chloe." He smiled at her. "I'm glad you enjoyed the bath so much."

He could tell she wanted to laugh again as she told him, "You don't have to leave here and go to your brother's house. I think I'll be okay with you at the end of the hall rather than on the other side of the winery."

Hoping that meant she actually felt safer with

him in the house, rather than gone completely, he said, "Sleep well."

She cocked her head slightly to the side and said in a soft voice that tore at his chest, "You know what? I think I actually will."

And then her door closed and he stood staring at the place she'd been standing for a long while.

Chase Sullivan hadn't realized that tonight his life was going to change forever.

But it just had.

And, amazingly—shockingly—he wasn't the least bit interested in fighting that change. Instead, he was gearing up for a different fight altogether.

The fight for Chloe's heart.

Five

Chloe woke up warm and well rested. Oh, she'd missed beds like this—pillow-top mattresses with soft, silky sheets and thick duvets that were light and yet perfectly warm all at the same time. Still, becoming her own person again these past six months since filing for divorce, even if it meant she'd been sleeping on cheap, scratchy sheets and a rock-hard single bed, had been better than soft beds and fancy shoes.

That urgency to start running again tried to

steal through her, but for the moment she was just too darn comfortable to do more than stretch and snuggle down deeper beneath the covers. She closed her eyes and tried to go back to sleep, but despite how nice it was to lie in the middle of a big bed like a lump of lazy, rather than rush off to the diner she'd been working in these past months to serve greasy eggs, she just couldn't nod off. Not when thoughts of Chase kept sliding in, one after the other, insidiously sweet.

And hot.

She'd crawled naked between the sheets the previous night, so exhausted that she immediately fell asleep. But in the light of the morning that was now streaming in through the sheer curtains at the window, she remembered—in vivid, Technicolor detail—just what she'd done in the bathroom.

And just what he'd seen.

She instinctively covered her cheeks as they grew hot.

Chloe wouldn't beat up on herself for touching herself in the delicious tub. She wouldn't even call herself out for the way his name had fallen from her lips. And there really was no point in being angry with him for walking in on her "private time," not when the only reason he'd come looking for her was because he'd clearly been worried about her. He hadn't been hoping to catch her with her hand between her legs.

But what had come after—the fact that she hadn't flat-out insisted he leave the bathroom, the way they'd teased each other, the fact that she'd actually called him *Hotstuff* to his face—well, she could hardly believe any of it had happened.

And yet, despite the way her stomach clenched as she tried to force those memories away, the small spot of warmth that had settled in behind her breastbone before she fell asleep remained.

All because Chase hadn't come at her. He hadn't frightened her. Or tried to dominate her in any way.

Some women, she knew, liked that sort of thing. They found it exciting to have their power taken away. Once upon a time, she'd been tantalized by fantasies of being held down like that. Of being bound. Of being helpless in her passion. Of being able to let go completely with a man who loved her.

She couldn't imagine ever feeling that way now. No, she'd never let anyone take her power away ever again. And Chloe couldn't think of one possible reason that she might be tempted to let anyone control any part of her life like that. Not a single one.

She closed her eyes, knowing she was being a coward lying here in this soft bed. She should be on the phone, calling the police, filing a report against her ex-husband that explained exactly how she'd come by the nasty bruise on her face . . . and who was responsible for putting it there. She should have done it last night, but she'd been so spooked by the way her ex had come after her that she hadn't been thinking about anything but getting away. Far, far away from him.

But knowing what she should do and feeling strong enough to do it were quite clearly two completely different things.

Finally giving up on getting any more sleep, with her mind reeling in a dozen different directions, she pushed off the covers, slid out of bed and turned on the lights. A good night's sleep had helped clear her head enough that she finally noticed all the little things she hadn't seen the night before.

Everything from the furnishings in the bedroom to the plush carpeting beneath her bare feet and the curtains hanging in front of the windows spoke of wealth. Crisp white linens and the hardwood floors gave a light and airy feel to the room. But where her ex-husband and his family had made sure to scream their riches from the rooftops, Chloe got the sense that Chase's brother had purchased each chair, each pillow, even the linens, because he liked the way they looked and felt when you used them. Not because he was trying to impress anyone.

Pulling the sheets and comforter back up over the bed, she ran her hand over the soft bedcover one more time, telling it, “You were good last night,” like a fond lover before she headed for the bathroom.

She stood beneath the deliciously warm shower spray, feeling safe and warm, at least for a little while. She wasn’t going to hide here forever, of course. But for the rest of the day, if she could manage it without getting in anyone’s way, she’d hang out in the vineyards. Maybe even taste a little wine. Pretend her life was normal for a while.

Normal. That sounded really nice. Even if she wasn’t sure how “normal” it was possible to feel in a gorgeous wine-country house like this.

Forcing back the voice inside her head that told her avoiding the inevitable would only make it harder to take care of the ugliness later, she worked to convince herself that she deserved a tiny bit of enjoyment. Didn’t she?

After drying off and finding that her mud-stained jeans and T-shirt were thankfully dry and at least partially cleaner than they’d been last night, she put them on.

Okay, so maybe she’d taken longer than normal drying her long, straight hair, but that was only because it had gotten so tangled the night before and she wanted to make sure she had all the knots out. It wasn’t that she cared about looking good for Chase. And it wasn’t that she was nervous about seeing him again.

Oh, who was she kidding? No one, that's who.

The bruise on her face wasn't going to terrify small children or anything, but it wasn't particularly attractive, either. Add to that her well-worn jeans and T-shirt and she wasn't anywhere near looking her best.

Which was unfortunate, because if she was being completely honest with herself, she'd loved the way he'd looked at her last night when she'd stood up in the tub. Today, with her clothes back on, she really wished she could look her best for Chase . . . and that he would look at her that way again.

Just the thought of seeing Chase again had her heart pounding hard as she took a deep breath and threw her shoulders back before rounding the corner of the hallway to where it opened up to the kitchen.

It was empty.

Disappointment reared up in her before she could shove it down. Or pretend it hadn't been there at all.

There was a bowl of freshly cut fruit on the kitchen island, along with an array of pastries that had her empty stomach growling. She had already picked up a chocolate croissant—her favorite!—and bitten into it by the time she noticed the note tucked beside the pretty red-and-yellow fruit bowl.

Chloe,

Good morning. I hope you slept well. Sorry I couldn't stay to keep you company for breakfast. Please come join us out in the vineyards when you're done eating.

See you soon,

HOTSTUFF

P.S. Almost forgot. There's fresh squeezed OJ in the fridge. Gotta make sure you get your vitamin C.

Her surprised laughter rang out in the empty kitchen.

Chloe couldn't believe he'd signed his note with the nickname she'd given him. In her experience, men didn't have funny bones. Especially not when the joke was at their expense. But Chase had surprised her again and again, hadn't he? First, by appearing in the bathroom doorway while she was finishing up her bath, then again by not making a move on her, and now with the very sweet, very cute note.

Looking in the fridge, she found the juice and poured herself a tall glass. Settling on one of the bar stools, she picked up the note and read it again.

Us meant Chase and his brother, right? She fought back a prickle of unease that she might have to meet more people than that. Frankly, she didn't even want to meet his brother looking and feeling the way she did right now. But since she'd availed herself of his hospitality last night—right now, too—she wouldn't feel right if she didn't at least thank him for letting her crash in his guesthouse for a night. As soon as she was settled again, she'd get to work making him a new quilt as a proper thank-you gift. Quilting was her passion and maybe, once she cleaned up the mess that was currently her life and began it anew, she'd be able to turn the quilts she so loved to make into a business. She could make custom quilts or maybe even open a small quilting store in a cute cottage where she could teach classes to children and adults.

As she let herself enjoy the sun pouring into the kitchen along with a few of the dreams she'd set aside for so long, she pulled off flaky strips of the croissant and let them melt on her tongue. The croissant was down to little crumbles on the granite countertop and she was picking each one up with a wet fingertip before she admitted to herself that she was stalling again, hiding out in the guesthouse so she wouldn't have to face Chase.

It was a beautiful day outside. The storm from the previous night had cleared the air and she took a deep, cool breath of it into her lungs. If she was going to give herself one day away from her real life, she should go and enjoy Napa Valley while she was here.

Chloe stepped out onto the wide covered porch. Shading her eyes with one hand, before she even took in the beauty around her, she carefully scanned the area in front of her to make sure her surroundings were secure.

Because even though she felt safer than she had in a while, she also knew trouble could come from anywhere, just when she least expected it. Just as it had last night.

Every time she thought about what had happened the previous night, she felt so stupidly naive. How had she missed the signs that her ex had been on the edge? Thinking about it made her stomach feel like a tight fist was wrapped around it, clenching tighter and tighter.

Normal. She'd been planning to pretend everything was normal.

She took one deep breath and then another as she fought to repress her swirling emotions, her fears. Finally, when she felt steadier, she looked around her with a surprised gasp.

After the rain the previous night, the vineyard sparkled in the sunlight. The leaves on the vines were bright green, almost as if a child had painted the scene in primary colors with fresh crayons.

The vineyard was blissfully quiet, except, she noticed as she walked down between a tall row of vines, for the birds that were playfully calling back and forth to one another. As their cheerful songs filtered into her, she took a deep breath of the fresh air, the clean scent of dirt and growing plants and nature.

The beauty all around her was exquisite, the beautiful green of the vineyards and trees alongside bright yellow mustard flowers and purple sage. She felt like she could walk for hours, for weeks, and never get her fill of the views, the sunshine, the bright blue sky. The air smelled so good, perfumed by the vines and the flowers blooming all around them.

Unfortunately, a few moments later, her idyll was interrupted by the sound of quickly approaching footsteps and what sounded like a teenage girl sobbing. Chloe barely backed into one of the vines in time to avoid being trampled by a tall, thin girl who couldn't have been much older than eighteen or nineteen.

Chloe's heart thumped hard as she waited—and watched—for someone to come running after the girl. When the coast was clear a few moments later and she stepped back into the middle of the dirt path, she found the elaborate ties on the girl's dress had caught on a set of thick vines.

Chloe quickly made her way over to her. "Hold still for a few seconds and I'll get you unstuck."

The girl's eyes were wide and still full of tears as Chloe worked on untangling one of the silky threads.

Even though she was wondering what on earth the girl was doing wearing a dress like this—one

Chloe knew firsthand must have cost a fortune —in the middle of a vineyard on a weekday morning, she asked, "What's wrong?"

"He's so mean!"

Chloe's heartbeat, which had barely slowed, kicked back into overdrive. Feeling incredibly protective, she asked, "Who's mean? Your boyfriend?"

The girl shook her head, strikingly beautiful even with tear-streaked cheeks and tangled hair. "I wish. He's so gorgeous," she finally said, fresh tears falling down her cheeks, "and so, so mean!"

Why did they all do this to themselves? Chloe wondered. What was the allure of falling for guys who treated them like dirt? Was it some secret part of the kindergarten curriculum for girls? And, if so, why couldn't someone create a class on how to find men who were good, and kind and sweet?

Chloe absolutely refused to believe that a man had to use his strength against a woman to prove that he was strong. She suddenly found herself thinking of Chase again. Clearly, he was strong. But he hadn't tried to use his innate power to pressure her into anything. And it had only made her want him more.

As the thoughts raced through her head one after the other, Chloe finished untangling the silk threads from the vine. But even after she was done, the girl continued to cry—big, racking, dramatic sobs.

"Oh, good, you found her."

Chloe turned at the sound of a familiar voice. Chase? When had he come upon them? And how could his warm voice, the same one that had threaded through all of her dreams last night, have her body heating up this quickly?

The girl wrapped her long, slim fingers around Chloe's wrist and held on tight. Tight enough that any greeting Chloe might have uttered was swallowed up in a gasp of pain as long, perfectly manicured nails dug in between the veins in her wrist.

One look into his eyes was all it took for her to immediately forget the sting in her wrist. He looked so concerned. And so ridiculously beautiful that it actually stole her breath away. She'd seen him last night in the dark and rain, and then gotten a better look in his brother's guesthouse, but the way he looked in the sunlight? Honestly, it was a good thing the girl was holding on to her arm so tightly, if for no other reason than to make sure Chloe stayed on her feet.

She supposed he wasn't actually male-model handsome, but even if the bridge of his nose was just a little crooked from where one of his brother's fists had likely collided with it at some point, the way all of his features came together on his rugged face—along with the broad set of his shoulders, the narrow strength of his hips and the confidence in his stance—had her heart actually wobbling around inside her chest.

Chase's eyes were warm as he scanned Chloe's face. "How'd you sleep?"

Somehow, she managed a way too breathy, "Good."

He smiled, a big, heartfelt smile that immediately turned Chloe's insides to liquid goo. "I'm glad to hear it."

The girl dug her nails in harder to the thin skin on Chloe's wrist. "It's him," she hissed, frowning at the gentle interplay between the two adults who were completely ignoring her and her tantrum.

Chloe tried to shift her wrist from beneath the girl's talons. "What do you mean it's him?"

The girl pointed at Chase and exclaimed, "He's the one who made me cry!"

Chloe turned from the girl to Chase. Trying to get everything straight, Chloe said, "You made her cry?"

Rather than answer her question, he addressed the girl directly in a very patient voice. "Amanda, we're losing the proper light. I need you back in place on set. Now."

The girl's pout rivaled that of a three-year-old. "It's not fair."

Finally, Chase let a little annoyance creep into

his voice. “None of us have time for your tantrums today, Amanda.”

Chloe looked between the two of them in confusion. What in heck were they talking about? This pretty young girl couldn’t possibly be Chase’s girlfriend, could she? And what did he mean by “back in place on set”?

Still, she couldn’t forget the way the girl had been crying before he’d found them in the middle of the vineyard. Feeling protective, she moved to put herself between the two of them.

“Look, Chase,” Chloe began, “she’s really upset about something.”

The girl elbowed her out of the way and Chloe had a strange feeling that she’d just made the mistake of standing in Amanda’s limelight.

“I want to be in the front!” The girl’s big eyes were suddenly calculating. “Promise me I’ll be the lead for the rest of the day and I’ll go back.”

Chase’s expression didn’t change as he looked at Amanda. He wasn’t angry. He wasn’t laughing. He was simply focused. Determined. Chloe had the distinct sense that he rarely, if ever, didn’t get exactly what he wanted.

A slight shiver came over her as she remembered the way he’d looked at her with such intense desire the previous night. What would have happened if he’d thrown in this focus? This determination? Would she have ended the night alone in that big, delicious bed?

Or would she have had his big, strong body next to hers as company?

She barely managed to pull herself down to earth in time to hear him say, "Here's the deal, Amanda. Either you get back over there and do your job or I call a cab and let your agent know that this is the last time you and I will have the privilege of working together."

"But, Chase," the girl whined as she realized she wasn't going to get her way, "it's not fair!"

He shrugged, and pulled his cell phone out of his pocket. "Napa Valley. I need the phone number of a cab company."

The girl all but leaped across the path between the vines to grab the phone from his hand, her sharp nails raking even harder across Chloe's skin as she abruptly let go. Chase was faster than the girl, raising his hand high above his head and stepping to the side so that she had to catch a vine to keep from falling.

Chase put the phone back to his ear. "Yes, I need an airport pickup at Sullivan Winery."

"No!" The girl shrieked so loud Chloe's ears rang even as her wrist throbbed practically as bad as the bruise on her face had the night before. "I'll go back and do whatever you want."

Chase didn't shift the phone away from his ear as he simply told Amanda, "You won't question me again." It wasn't an inquiry. It was a statement.

The girl agreed, nodding her head. Hard. "It's just that I found out that my boyfriend is sleeping with my roommate and I hate them both and I'm so upset."

At that point, the girl had changed tactics, doing her best to blink her huge eyes at him and look equally pathetic and beautiful. Chloe knew if she ever tried to pull that off, she'd just look like she had a nasty cold.

"I'm really sorry I'm messing up the shoot," Amanda said in a voice that Chloe suspected was as contrite as she got.

Surprisingly, a hint of a smile played on Chase's lips. Was Amanda being forgiven that easily? In Chloe's experience, men weren't so forgiving. Then again, they weren't this good-looking, either. Clearly, Chase was breaking the rules left and right.

"Apology accepted. Now why don't you head on back and get your makeup cleaned up so that we can continue with the shoot while the light is good."

"Okay, Chase." The girl turned and trotted back on her mile-long legs, leaving Chloe and Chase alone.

"Teenage girls." He mock-shivered. "After dealing with my sisters for so long, I should have known better than to work in a field that depends on them."

"What's going on here?" Chloe realized, too

late, that she sounded like a bad fifties movie come to life, the matron walking in on a scene she couldn't comprehend.

"I'm a photographer. We're shooting a magazine spread here for the next few days."

Oh. Now things were starting to make sense. Especially all the talk of "shooting" and "good light."

"I meant to tell you last night, but—" he grinned at her "—I got a little distracted."

Just that quickly, the reminder of what had happened to "distract" him last night had her cheeks flushing and her entire body heating up. Her brain—and tongue—felt tied as she said, somewhat awkwardly, "I didn't mean to interrupt your work. I was just coming out for a walk." She gestured to the vines, the mountains, the trees, the blue sky. "It's so beautiful here. Absolutely lovely."

"Lovely," he murmured, and she was instantly reminded of the way he'd said, *"My God, you're lovely,"* the previous night.

Feeling her cheeks grow even hotter, she dropped her gaze to the dirt. "Thanks for setting out breakfast."

She watched his feet move closer, until he was standing close enough that she had no choice but to lift her head to face him.

"I'm glad you liked it," he said softly, and then he was brushing his fingertips across her cheek to the corner of her mouth. "You've just got a little bit of chocolate right here."

There was nothing for it but to stop breathing entirely while he was touching her. She couldn't remember a man ever being this gentle with her before.

Nor could she remember ever wanting a man as badly as she wanted him.

And then he moved his finger the slightest bit, so that it was in front of her lips, and some previously latent devil inside of her—the same one that had convinced her that touching herself in the tub last night would be a good thing—had her opening up her mouth and licking the chocolate off.

She heard a groan come from way down deep in his chest. "Chloe."

Oh, God, she was *this* close to kissing him, a man who was still a stranger despite the fact that he'd seen her naked and provided her a warm, safe place to spend the night.

What was she doing?

Six

Stumbling back, the branches from a tall grapevine lanced Chloe between the shoulders. "You should get back to work. They're probably waiting for you."

But Chase didn't move, didn't so much as shift his weight. Instead, he simply smiled at her, that intense heat still in his eyes. Along with something that truly had her shivering in her shoes.

Determination.

And focus.

"I'm sure they're still working on Amanda's makeup," he told her, but she heard what he was really saying loud and clear.

I'm not going anywhere. So why don't you stop trying to run and just give in to what we both want? It'll be good between us. So damned good. I promise.

Wanting desperately to negate the hot, pulsating desire between them, she said, "By the way, don't you think all caps is a bit much on the nickname?"

He frowned for a split second before he caught on and grinned again. "I figure if I'm going to have a nickname like Hotstuff, I might as well own it."

How could she do anything but grin back at him? He was just so darn likable. It wasn't his fault that he was sexier than sin. She shouldn't keep holding that against him.

"Come with me." He held his hand out. "I'll introduce you to the crew."

She looked down at his hand. She badly, so badly, wanted to take it. But she couldn't. Not if she wanted to actually keep her distance from him today, rather than end up in his arms begging him for the kisses and caresses he hadn't given her the night before.

Telling herself he'd understand if he knew her reasons—and that he probably already understood way more than she'd divulged to him due to the bruise on her cheek—she simply stepped beside him and started walking. She didn't have to look at him to sense his disappointment that she hadn't reached out to take his hand. But he didn't push her on it as he fell into step beside her.

"I absolutely love Napa Valley. This is such an incredible part of the country, full of such beauty and history," she said. "How long has your brother owned the winery?"

"Nearly a decade. We all thought he was crazy at first, taking those farming classes at UC Davis. Now we're all wishing we'd thought of it first."

She turned to him in surprise. "Don't you love what you do?"

The zing that shot through her body, head to toe, when his eyes connected with hers shocked her every single time. No doubt about it, Chase should be the one in front of the camera, knocking down female hearts like dominoes with that incredibly potent gaze, his green eyes holding more beauty, more heat, than she could believe.

"I do," he agreed. "But that doesn't mean I don't sometimes think about cutting down on the traveling and settling down with a pretty wife and a backyard full of cute kids."

"Are there cameras following us?" she joked, making a show of looking over her shoulder.

"No, why?"

"Because you just said pretty much what every single, thirty-year-old woman on the planet wants to hear. And you actually sounded like you meant it."

"What about you?" When she frowned at his question, he said, "Is that what you want to hear?"

Refusing to acknowledge the pang of longing, she shrugged. "I'm just thinking about making it through the next day, right about now," she said in as offhand a manner as she could manage.

She could see the models and crew waiting for him, but instead of hurrying over to them, he stopped walking and turned his back to everyone else. She had no choice but to stop, too, or walk right into the hard wall of his chest. His very broad chest.

"I took care of your car." He gave her a small smile. "It's been towed off to a better place."

Working to fight down the panic at being completely without a vehicle, she said, "It didn't have many miles left on it, anyway." She tried to smile back. "Thank you for dealing with it. I'll pay you b—"

He cut her off before she could finish her sentence. "Stay, Chloe." When she just didn't reply immediately, he said, "We'll be shooting here at the winery for the next few days. I was hoping you would stay."

She licked her lips, shook her head. "You're busy. And I need to . . ." She paused, knowing all she had ahead of her were problems, at least for a while.

"Stay," he said again, more softly this time, but with the determination, the focus, she was so afraid of threading through the one short word.

And, ultimately, that was the main reason she needed to leave. Because she had no intention of getting involved with another man. She was still learning how to be alone, how to rely on herself, how to trust again. It hadn't even been a year since she'd filed for divorce. She wasn't ready for another relationship.

And she definitely wasn't ready for Chase's determination. Or for his focus.

He was a man whom she could so easily—too easily—lose herself in completely.

She shook her head. "I'm sorry. I c—"

"Please."

He hadn't come any nearer, hadn't gotten in her face and demanded her agreement, but the gentle entreaty in his voice was like warm arms wrapping around her, pulling her close.

"Don't agree to the whole week. Just take it one day at a time."

And one night at a time, too.

She heard the words even though he hadn't said them. And that was when Chloe knew just how weak she really was, because even though she'd just recited to herself all the reasons she should go, she couldn't find a way to stop herself from saying, "Okay."

She could feel Chase studying her, knew he wasn't completely pleased with her answer even though she'd just given him exactly what he wanted. But whatever he was about to say was interrupted by a skinny young man with big, thick-framed purple glasses.

"Chase," the man said, "everyone's ready for you."

His gaze continued to hold hers for another long moment, before Chase slowly turned to the person she assumed was his assistant.

"Jeremy, this is Chloe. She helped me find Amanda and she's my very special guest. Be sure to show her a good time today, would you?"

Jeremy's eyes flashed over the bruise on her cheek before quickly flitting away. "Oooh, someone to share all the gossip with. Hooray!"

The young man reached for her hand and grasped it before she could pull away and then he was walking away with her and chattering in her ear about what a pain in the rear Amanda was, and how he'd had the misfortune of working with her too many times this year already, and how he hoped Chase had totally put her in her place, and could Chloe fill him in on absolutely every single word that had been said out in the vineyard.

Chloe threw a desperate glance at Chase over her shoulder, only to find him grinning at her. How did he always manage to be three steps ahead of her?

And—just as she'd asked herself last night—why the heck didn't she mind a whole lot more?

Fifteen minutes of nonstop chatter later, Jeremy had her settled into a comfortable chair where she could watch the action. Chase was photographing three young women in absolutely gorgeous ball gowns.

Amanda had been positively stunning. But all three of the models together? Chloe couldn't stop herself from turning to Jeremy and remarking, "That's a whole lot of beautiful up there, isn't it?"

Jeremy sighed and looked at Chase in clear admiration. "And can you believe he doesn't even know it?"

This time, there was no holding back her laughter, loud enough that everyone—including Chase—turned to look at her.

"I was talking about the models," she clarified.

Jeremy shrugged. "They're all right. But the Sullivan men are . . ." He sighed with deep longing and barely concealed lust as he kissed the tips of his fingers. "Perfection!"

Chloe would never have admitted it aloud, but the truth was she agreed with Jeremy's assessment: Chase was better looking than all of the models combined, and part of what made him so compelling was that he was utterly unaware of just how gorgeous a man he was.

Nonetheless, the young women were all shockingly attractive. Rather than being jealous, Chloe told herself she was glad they were there to remind her that she had nothing to worry about when it came to Chase. How could she have actually let herself get caught up in thinking, *Oh, no, he wants me so much,* and *What am I going to do if he's determined to have me?*

She chuckled again, realizing how ridiculous it seemed now that she'd seen the models he was practically close enough to kiss as he got into position for another shot. There might be a whole lot of beautiful out there in the vineyard, but there had definitely been a whole lot of delusional where she was sitting.

Silently continuing to laugh at herself, Chloe suddenly felt worlds better. Maybe she actually could take up Chase's invitation to hang out here in Napa Valley for a few days. Maybe she could extend "normal" for a little while, before she had to buckle down and face all that ugliness again.

Because, really, how could Chase possibly want anything from her when he had these other visions of gorgeousness around? Sure, Chloe knew she was cute. Pretty, even. But she certainly wasn't looking her best, with no makeup on and wearing crappy clothes.

What, she suddenly found herself wondering, would he think if he could see her in a pretty dress? With her hair up, something sparkling at her ears and pretty heels on her feet? Would he tell her she was lovely again? She worked to shake off the pointless questions as she watched him work for the next hour or so. She appreciated that he didn't play games with his models. Instead of flirting with them, or trying to pit them against one another in any way, he simply let them know when they were doing a great job, and as their confidence grew, so did their skill at posing for him.

Chloe was surprised to feel her creative juices flowing, even though she'd never paid much attention to either fashion or photography.

Her true passion was quilting, and as she watched him work, she realized that more than fashion was coming to life. The way Chase manipulated the canvas of models and clothes and the natural background of the vines and mountains and sky was so brilliant that simply watching him was helping her develop a new eye for composition. And new visions for the way she could block her next quilt.

Fortunately, now that she was firmly convinced she had nothing to worry about anymore when it came to Chase "wanting" her, she could allow herself to acknowledge just how fantastic he was. She even let her insides go a little gooey.

At least now she could chalk her feelings for him up to artistic genius . . . rather than how good-looking or how charming he was.

"Oh, my God, hot-boy alert!" Jeremy's voice sounded squeaky.

"What? Where?" Chloe asked, looking around and seeing that Chase was still busy shooting pictures a hundred yards away.

"To your right," Jeremy stage-whispered, and she followed his gaze across the field to the very good-looking man who was walking toward them.

"Who's that?" she whispered back, even though she didn't know why they were whispering.

"It's Marcus." Jeremy said the name reverently.

Oh, my. That was Chase's brother?

There were six of them?

Like Chase, Marcus was ridiculously good-looking. He looked to be a few years older than Chase, and even from a distance she could see he was a bit taller, with slightly more built-up muscles. His dark hair was just a little too long, and even in a suit, he was obviously very at home on the land. Clearly, Jeremy wouldn't be alone in falling all over Marcus.

And yet, while she recognized pure male beauty when she saw it, her heart wasn't pounding and she wasn't getting breathless, or anything. Chase was the only man who had ever made her want to call out his name while touching herself within an hour of meeting him.

Still, there was no denying the powerful allure of the Sullivan men.

"I really need to see a photo of the whole family," she muttered to herself, not intending for anyone to hear.

Of course, Jeremy heard and saw everything. "Their genes are insane," was his response. "Their mother used to be a model, back in the day. And their father was probably Cary Grant or something."

Chloe didn't say anything more—not now that she knew Jeremy was the worst, and most delicious, kind of gossip—but she was thinking that having six brothers and two sisters this good-looking all in one room together must be too much for the eye to behold. Hopefully, she found herself thinking, they were also all as kind as Chase had been to her from the moment he'd found her on the side of the road. Because if there was one thing she knew for sure, it was that good looks that didn't come with a conscience were never a good thing.

"Just watch. I can't even speak around him," Jeremy told her. "I'm going to go to pieces even though I know he'll never, ever play for my team and it doesn't make any sense for me to be so nervous. I hate how the best ones are all totally, completely hetero. If only one of Chase's gorgeous brothers was gay my life would be so, so much better," he said with a deep sigh.

As Chase's brother approached and she could see his face more clearly, Chloe was surprised to see that Marcus's expression was fairly serious, rather than playful like Chase always seemed to be. Then again, maybe it was because Marcus had a suit on, whereas her Sullivan was in jeans.

Her Sullivan?

What the heck was wrong with her? Chase wasn't hers. She was merely hanging out in this perfect world for a little while before heading back to her real life. She couldn't afford to get attached to anyone or anything here.

"Hey, Marcus." Jeremy stuttered out another, "Hi!" before he managed to get his trembling lips to shut.

Poor Jeremy. He was so nervous, Chloe actually forgot to be nervous herself. She even forgot to put her hand over her cheek to cover the nasty bruise.

She was about to reach out her hand to introduce herself when Jeremy's mouth opened again and he blurted, "This is Chloe. She's with Chase. He found her last night on the side of the road."

Chloe shot him a horrified glance. She knew she should have kept her mouth shut with Jeremy about how she and Chase had met, but he'd been so persistent with his questions that she'd finally shared the barest of details with him.

Clearly mortified by what he'd said the moment the words left his mouth, two bright pink spots appeared on Jeremy's cheeks. "Oh, God, that came out all wrong. What I mean is that Chloe met Chase last night and spent the night with him." His eyes grew even wider, as further horror filled them at what he'd just accidentally insinuated. "I—" he stuttered, as he looked down at a spot on the ground right between Marcus and Chloe. "I need to go check on some things." He turned and ran off.

Jeremy wasn't the only one who was mortified now. Willing her composure to come back after that extremely embarrassing introduction, she held out her hand.

"Hi, it's so nice to meet you, Marcus."

"It's nice to meet you, too, Chloe."

Marcus had a low, slightly rough voice that was undeniably attractive. Only for some reason, it didn't do anything for her. Well, hardly anything. Heck, she was human, wasn't she? It wasn't her fault that she wasn't completely blind to male beauty. And she had to admit that she was more than a little complimented by that quick flash in Marcus's eyes when he'd first looked at her that told her he thought she was an attractive woman.

"So, you met my brother last night?"

She swallowed, trying not to be defensive. "I did. On the side of a road, just like Jeremy mentioned. My car skidded into a ditch during the storm and I was lucky that he drove by."

"I'm glad he was able to help."

"And I'm glad to get the chance to meet you because I wanted to thank you for—" She felt terribly awkward as she said, "For letting me stay the night in your guesthouse."

The look on his face told her he had no idea she'd even been there. A beat later, he said, "Any friend of Chase's is a friend of mine."

He was very sweet, but she knew what he had to be thinking. It was what any person in his right mind would think upon hearing Chase had picked her up last night and taken her to the guesthouse. Just the two of them, all alone in the beautiful house, with all those beds . . . and bathtubs. What reason could there possibly have been for her and his brother not to get it on?

"Really, it's not what you—"

But she couldn't get the rest of the sentence out. Not without flashing back to that moment in the tub when she was coming and saying Chase's name and he was there.

So, yeah, maybe it was exactly what Marcus thought.

She felt a blush cover her cheeks as she realized there was, quite clearly, nothing she could say about the previous evening without sounding like a total freaking idiot.

Planting a smile on her face, she said instead, "Your winery is absolutely beautiful. Just stunning. It must be like living and working in a dream."

Marcus's grin told her that he was pleased with her compliments. "Thanks. How about I give you a tour?"

No question about it, their mother had raised her Sullivan boys well. The only problem, as far as Chloe could see, was that it had also turned them into lady killers, one and all.

How could a woman possibly resist those faces? Those bodies? Especially when they came with such great manners?

"That's very nice of you," she replied, "but I'm sure you have far more important things to take care of." And the truth was, while she'd love a tour of his property, she couldn't help but wish it was Chase offering to give her one, rather than Marcus.

"I love showing people around the winery and vineyards. That's part of the joy of this for me—watching other people take it in."

Just then, Chase stepped up. As the two men did their half handshake, half hug, Chloe barely held back a sigh of pure female delight at all that beautifully made testosterone in front of her.

"I see you've already met Chloe," Chase said to his brother as he fought back the urge to lay claim to Chloe in some obvious way. If she were anyone else, he would have put a hand on the small of her back, or even slipped his arm around her waist. But he knew better than to do either of those things. Not yet, anyway.

"Sure did," Marcus replied. "I was just offering to show her around."

It only took a millisecond—and one pointed look—for the brothers to have a very important silent conversation.

Chase: *I know you think she's pretty. Don't even think about it, not for a second. She's mine.*

Marcus: *I've got a girlfriend, remember? Besides, I wasn't going to lay claim to her. I can see that she's yours. You've got great taste, by the way.*

Chase turned to Chloe. "We're taking a break for lunch, and even though the models don't always eat, the rest of us do. How about you and I go for a short hike to the top of that hill and have a picnic?" He lifted the basket he'd had Jeremy put together that morning in anticipation of seeing her for lunch.

Fortunately, Marcus deftly let her off the hook from his previous offer by saying, "Looks like you're in good hands, Chloe. Hopefully I'll see you tonight for dinner with the rest of the group?"

Chase watched her expression shift to indecision. She'd agreed to stay the day, but now his brother was basically asking her if she was going to stay the night, too.

"I don't have anything other than this to wear," she said, gesturing to her clothes. "So, thanks, but it would probably be best if—"

Marcus smoothly cut her refusal off in a show of brotherly love at its finest. "My suit's coming off as soon as I'm done with my final meeting. Jeans are perfect."

With Marcus going out of his way to make Chloe comfortable, she finally agreed. "Okay, then. Thanks, I'd love to join you for dinner."

Chase owed his brother one.

The two of them hiked up the hillside and the view took her breath away.

Chase took a waterproof blanket out of the basket and laid it on grass that was still damp from the previous night's rain shower.

"Wow, you really come prepared."

"I've got a good crew."

She nodded. "You certainly do. They're all great." Jeremy had introduced her to Alice, the stylist, Kalen, the makeup artist, and Francis, who was in charge of lighting. The words, "I enjoyed watching you work," came out of her mouth before she could hold them inside.

His smile was like a warm caress over her skin. "I liked you being there." He laughed and admitted, "I was trying not to show off."

Amazed by how easily he could make her smile, she said, "Most guys don't admit stuff like that."

She half expected him to say something like, "I'm not most guys." Instead, he surprised her yet again by asking, "So, what do you do?"

He was being so careful with her. She felt it in every glance, every word. Even now, when he could so easily have asked her where she was from or why she was running, he was getting to know her another way instead. Just as he hadn't touched her without her permission last night. It was as if there was a silent agreement between them—he wouldn't push too far or get in too deep unless she allowed it.

The big question was, would she dare let him in?

Chloe didn't have an answer. How could she, when she was afraid to even acknowledge the question?

He handed her a gourmet sandwich full of goat cheese and grilled yellow and orange bell peppers, and as she took it from him, she said, "Well, most recently I've been waitressing."

He nodded. "But what do you like to do?"

Most people would have stopped at her day job. But not Chase. He was truly interested. And that honest interest went a long way toward shoving aside her reluctance to talk about herself.

She paused before answering, "I make quilts."

People never knew what to make of that. Most assumed it was a hobby. Others just thought it was plain weird or boring. Men, without exception, dismissed it as just another housewife craft. Chase, however, gave her a sincerely interested look.

"Tell me more."

Downplaying it like she usually did, she said, "I like seeing how fabrics come together in patterns."

"I don't know much about the quilting world," he said, "but I've photographed a few quilt shows and art quilts for various publications, and what I've learned about technique and the skill that's involved in making them has been really interesting. I'd love to know more. When did you start?"

Chloe rarely had a chance to wax on about her love for quilting. Not since she'd been a member of a quilting guild years and years ago. She missed those women—and their shared passion—terribly.

Which was probably why she actually found herself telling Chase, "I started quilting when I lost a close friend from college in a car accident. She had been so passionate about it. Her mom actually owned a store in town. It was the only way I could think of to keep up my connection to her. And it gave me something else to think about—the motion of my hands and the needle, the patterns of fabric and shape, the building of something that I could create. Sometimes I can almost feel her watching me from up above with a smile on her face."

"I'm sure she is."

Chloe started at Chase's words. Had she really just said all of that to him? Somehow he had gotten her to talk about her passion for quilting—a subject that would have put nearly every guy on the planet to sleep. But he wasn't snoring yet. And she found herself wanting to tell him more about herself, more than just her love for quilting.

She wasn't at all comfortable acknowledging that Chase had just become the exception. And that it had felt so good to share herself with someone who was really listening. Not when she knew that she was being stupid, letting herself think that this fantasy of sitting with a gorgeous guy on a hilltop in Napa Valley had anything to do with her real life.

It didn't.

She put down her sandwich and made herself face him, but before she could say anything, he said, "Uh-oh. That's not a good look."

She wasn't going to smile. There was no place for grinning when she needed to set him straight, when she was about to make her position on the two of them perfectly clear.

"Why are you being so nice to me?"

"I like you."

The glow his words caused was too bright. Too warm. Forcing herself to blot it out, she said, "You don't know me."

"I'm starting to."

No pause. No smooth words. No trying to charm her into agreeing with him. Didn't he realize just how much harder his honest responses were making this for her?

"Is this what you do?"

"What am I doing?"

"You keep helping me, making me breakfast, asking Jeremy to be nice to me all day."

He frowned and she could see that he was confused. "Is there something wrong with wanting to make you smile?"

Oh. Wow. Why did he have to say that?

She couldn't think of any other man who'd simply wanted to make her smile. Not even the man she'd married. Especially not the man she'd married.

Frustrated with herself for being so soft—so easy to turn to goo—she made herself come at him one more time with, "I get it if you're into saving people, but—"

"I'm not a saint, Chloe."

His low voice cut her accusation off in midstream, and she found herself unable to look away from his serious expression.

"I'll always take care of my family," he continued, "but I've never gone out looking for women who need to be saved. And even though I hope you'll soon trust me enough to tell me what happened to you, trying to boost my own ego by saving you is not why I asked you to stay."

Feeling like a big jerk for doing anything and everything she could think of to try and keep herself from doing something really, really stupid like falling for him, she said, "Look, Chase, you really have been nice." Despite having been slow to hand her a towel last night, she silently amended with a flush. "But, despite how great you've been—" she purposefully left off a reminder as to what she'd been doing in the bathtub the night before "—we're not going to . . . well . . . you know."

Ugh. She wasn't used to having conversations like this.

She half expected—half wanted—him to tell

her she was wrong. That they were, in fact, most definitely going to end up doing *well-you-know* if she stuck around much longer.

Instead, his expression grew even more serious. "Earlier, when we were out in the vineyard, when I asked you to stay, you didn't want to. But I didn't let up until you finally gave in." He ran a hand through his hair, clearly upset with himself. "I would never want to force you to do something you don't want to do, Chloe. I don't ever want to take something from you that you don't want to give me."

This was the perfect opening. It was her chance to tell him she'd never had any intention of staying, to make it clear that there was not going to be any further connection between them, and that it was time for her to be moving on.

So then, why did she find herself saying, "You didn't force me to stay. I wanted to stay."

The pure truth of that statement resonated within her solar plexus. Because it turned out the truth didn't care if she wanted it to be true or not.

"I want to stay," she said again in a firmer voice. She wanted to spend more time with Chase. She shouldn't. But she did. "But I don't want to be in the way."

"You could never be in the way," he said, and then with a grin that was softer this time, and somehow even more potent, he said, "You were saying something about how you and I aren't going to . . . ?" He paused, letting the unsaid words hang in the air between them.

She should have come back with a quick retort, something to put him in his place. But right at that moment, with the Napa Valley sun shining down on her and grapevines budding to life across rolling hills as far as the eye could see, there was nothing left but honesty.

"I haven't had a male friend in a very long time."

He was silent for a long moment, and even though the butterflies in her stomach had her keeping her eyes on the horizon, she could feel his gaze on her.

"I'd be honored to be your friend, Chloe."

Her breath caught in her throat then, and she liked him so much it was almost impossible not to grab him and kiss him.

Sure that he could hear her heart beating in her chest because it was so loud to her own ears, instead of kissing him she had to be content with whispering, "I like you, too."

Seven

Chloe wasn't used to sitting still. Especially not after the past year, when she'd had to keep working odd jobs just to pay the rent and eat and be able to buy some fabric to quilt together. She was happy to be back on set, but every time she asked Jeremy if there was something she could do to help, some task that would make their jobs easier, he held firm about her being Chase's special guest.

Worse still, all that staring at Chase was doing really funny things to her insides. To her outsides, too. Her skin felt sensitive all over beneath her clothes. Warmer than the weather warranted. Similar to the way she'd felt in the tub as the water had slid across her skin and she'd ended up flying apart with his name on her lips.

Chloe's uncomfortable musings were interrupted by a loud squeal that was followed by female cursing. Chloe craned her neck and saw that Amanda had tripped over a rock and her dress had a long, jagged rip across the front.

Chase called out, "Jeremy, we need a new dress. The same one."

Jeremy's face had gone even paler than it already was. "I don't think the designer sent more than one of that dress, but I'll look again to make absolutely sure." He scurried off to look through the huge containers of clothes.

Chloe spoke up without thinking. "I can fix it."

Chase turned his green-eyed gaze to her, and at the question in his eyes, she said, "I've worked with some pretty similar fabrics in my quilts. If Jeremy can't find a second dress, I can at least try."

"Amanda, take off the dress."

The model pulled it off without giving so much as a thought to the fact that she was wearing only very sheer panties beneath the gauzy fabric.

At first it had been a bit of a shock to see how comfortable these young girls were with their near-nudity, but then, Chloe figured if she'd had a figure like that when she was nineteen, she would have been smart to flaunt it, too.

More glad than she should have been that Chase didn't so much as glance at Amanda's perfect naked breasts, Chloe got up out of her seat and came to get the dress.

"Can you give me ten minutes?"

He looked down at the large tear and then back up at her in clear surprise. "You can have this fixed in ten minutes?"

She looked at it more closely, running her fingers along the tear. "I think so." Satins and silks were always harder to work with because every hole the needle made showed through, but she'd been eyeing the enormous sewing box all day. Now she finally had a reason to dig into it.

Chase called out for a break. She quickly threaded a needle with thin, transparent filament and began to work on the dress. She was so entranced by the soft fabric beneath her fingertips that it took her a few moments to realize Chase was sitting beside her.

"I'm so glad you decided to stay. What would I do without you?"

She almost stabbed herself with the needle. Thankfully, he clearly believed she was concentrating too hard to give him a reply.

Actually, she had to silently admit, she really wasn't concentrating all that hard. After the past year of doing side jobs for the local tailor for what amounted to little more than slave wages, she could sew up things like this in her sleep.

Only, it was more than a little unnerving to have Chase's full attention like this.

"Don't you have something else you need to be doing?" she asked him.

She could feel his grin without needing to see it. "Just keeping my friend company while she does me a favor."

Friends. He'd agreed to be her friend. And it had filled her with a delicious, forbidden warmth.

So then, why was she also just a teeny bit disappointed that he hadn't pushed her for more up on the hill? That he hadn't tried to charm her into believing that it was perfectly natural for friends to also touch and kiss and—

No. That was crazy thinking. And she knew exactly where that kind of crazy would lead.

Straight to a bed . . . with Chase in it.

"I'd like to help more," she told him as she worked to fight back the heat that coursed through her at nothing more than his nearness and the vision she'd just had of the two of them in bed together. "You've been so kind to me and I wish there was something more I could do to repay you."

"Chloe." The serious way he said her name had her looking up at him. "I wanted to help. You don't need to repay me for anything. Ever."

The intensity of his gaze—along with his utter dedication and focus on her—nearly had her stabbing herself again with the needle.

"I need to concentrate on this," she lied.

Because what she really needed was some breathing room from her budding feelings for him.

"Go check on something else," she told him in her best no-nonsense voice. "Please."

Before she looked back down at the dress, she caught a flash of his gorgeous grin. A grin that told her he knew exactly why she was sending him away, darn it.

Ten minutes later, she helped Amanda put the dress back on and found herself blushing as everyone on Chase's crew started clapping and telling her how great she was to have repaired it so quickly and so well.

"You are totally the bomb, girl," Jeremy said. He turned to Chase and asked, "Isn't she fabulous?"

Chase nodded, his eyes heated when he smiled at her. "She really is, Jeremy."

It wasn't long until the sun set and the models were beginning to fade fast with fatigue, their tall, slim frames slumping slightly beneath the weight of the magnificent dresses they were wearing.

"Let's call it a day," Chase said. "Great work, everyone." He made sure to include Chloe with his eyes, even though she knew she'd barely done anything to help. "Really, really great."

Chloe could see how much his praise meant to everyone. Including her.

"My brother Marcus is hosting all of us for dinner and drinks at his place tonight." He pointed to the big house across the vineyard. "Jeremy, why don't you take everyone over?"

Without being asked, Chloe helped the models out of their dresses, making sure to tell each one of them how impressed she was with the work they'd done before asking, "How do you hold those poses for so long?"

Amanda was already on her cell phone, but Jackie, a shy "older" girl (who was barely twenty-one, but Chloe had already learned that was borderline ancient in their business), explained, "I do a lot of yoga."

The girl's smile was beautiful and Chloe immediately grinned back at her.

"It was nice to have you on set," Jackie said. "Kind of like having my mom here to take care of us."

Chloe somehow managed to keep her grin in place.

She was only nine years older than Jackie. And yet, she supposed the model was right. If life experience was anything to go by, they were a century apart.

Jeremy loaded the huge van with trunks and racks of clothes and camera equipment, then called everyone together. "Are you coming, Chloe?"

She was tempted to go with the group, rather than stay behind with Chase. But she felt grimy. Even if she didn't have nicer clothes to wear to Marcus's house, the least she could do was smell better than this. A shower was definitely necessary.

"I'm going to freshen up a bit. I'll see you all there soon."

Freshen up a bit. Seriously, she even sounded like she was Jackie's mom.

After everyone left, she turned to look for Chase. Thinking of him made her insides go soft and warm.

At first she couldn't find him, and then she realized he was standing behind one of his big cameras . . . and it was pointed straight at her.

She instinctively put her hand over her cheek. Oh, God, what was he doing? And what would he see? Would he be able to look beyond the ugly bruise and see that she was a quivering mess of jelly on the inside? Would he see what a coward she felt like for not having called the police yet to report what her ex had done to her, for just hiding out here with him and the models and his crew?

And would he see the feelings that had grown for him inside of her all day, despite the fact that she knew better than to feel anything at all?

Angry at him—and at herself for even caring in the first place—she started toward him. He'd already lowered the camera by the time she said, "I thought you put all your equipment away."

"I always feel better if I've got at least one on me. Just in case there's something I need to take a picture of."

"You don't need to take pictures of me."

"I've never been able to resist photographing beauty," he said softly before tucking the camera inside his bag. "I'm sorry. I didn't mean to make you feel uncomfortable. I hope you'll forgive me."

The look he gave her—warm and soft, yet full of a desire he didn't bother to hide—had her realizing just how ridiculous she was being.

"It's just with this bruise . . ." she began, lifting her hand to cover it again.

"Are you ready to talk about what happened yet?" His words were gentle and clearly concerned.

She swallowed hard before shaking her head. "No." She took a shaky breath. "Not yet."

Before she could say anything more, he reached for her hand and moved it away from her face. "You're lovely, Chloe. You don't need to hide yourself from me. Or from anyone."

She was amazed that he didn't seem to think the bruise made her look ugly. And he didn't seem to think it made her look weak, either.

Their slow walk back to the guesthouse through the darkness with only the moonlight to light their way felt impossibly romantic. Far more romantic than she could allow it to be.

"So, when did you start taking pictures?"

He gave her a look in the near-dark, one that said he knew what she was after with her small talk. Or, rather, what she was avoiding.

"I used to steal my father's Polaroid camera and annoy everyone with it. When I was eight years old, he gave me a camera of my own. Not one for kids, but a real one that I had to work hard to figure out how to use. I still have that camera and use it on special occasions even though it's a classic now."

She grinned at the vision of a mini-Chase documenting the world around him, just as determined and focused then as he was now.

"Did you always concentrate on photographing people?"

"I've tried it all, landscapes and abstracts and

still lifes, but in the end I've always found people —and their emotions—to be more interesting than anything else."

All day she'd been trying to put her finger on Chase's magic. "*That's* what you were after today," Chloe said with a sudden hit of awareness. "Emotion." She met his gaze and knew that even though she wasn't one of his models, it was exactly what he was tapping into with her, too.

"You were a great help today, Chloe."

She flushed at his praise. "I'm glad I could help in some way." She gestured to the property. "Getting to be here today was wonderful. Like being inside a Napa Valley fantasy world where everyone wears couture," she said with a grin.

They stepped up onto the porch, and Chase opened the door for her. Always the gentleman.

She stopped short in the living room, causing him to bump into her. His heat seared her, and she jumped away.

"What's all this?"

A clothing rack, just like the ones the models' outfits had been hanging on at the shoot, was standing in the middle of the room. It was packed full of clothes that looked as if they would fit her, rather than size-zero, six-foot, nineteen- and twenty-one-year-old girls.

"I had a few things delivered for you."

She turned to him in surprise. "How did you

even do this? You were working the whole time, harder than anyone else."

She couldn't remember ever seeing him take a break, beyond having lunch with her. Even when the rest of the crew was relaxing between shots, he was busy setting things up or reviewing the day's work.

"You look great in your jeans," he told her, "really great, but I know you weren't crazy about heading over to Marcus's tonight wearing them. If there's one thing I can do, it's get nice clothes delivered fast."

My God, he was so sweet. And modest. But . . .

"I don't have the money to pay you back for these clothes, Chase," she told him in a voice she tried to hold steady. How she wished she could wear these clothes, even for one night, just to feel pretty again. But she couldn't. "It was a lovely thought, but I can't wear them tonight."

"Let me do this for you," he said softly.

"I can't."

But, oh, how she wanted to. Even in her previous life with her ex-husband when she'd had money, she'd never worn clothes this gorgeous.

"You can." Chase didn't move closer, but the warmth of his words moved over her skin like a caress as he said, "I'm not going to come back later and demand anything from you. But I would very much like to see you in one of these dresses tonight."

Instinctively, she knew he was telling her the truth. He would never hold anything over her. So then why did that almost scare her more?

Chase was great. Beyond great. She should stop acting like a nervous cat already, claws popping out at the slightest noise.

Feeling like an ungrateful jerk over the clothes, she asked, "Can we start over and pretend we just walked in?"

"Sure."

He was so cute about it that he actually walked to the door and held it open for her. Clearly, his sisters had trained him well on how to respond to women's careering emotional states.

Following his lead, she walked outside on the porch and let him open the door for her again. "Wow, Chase," she said as she smiled at him. "These are such pretty clothes. Thanks so much."

He smiled right back. "You're welcome."

It took every bit of control Chloe had to force herself to step away from him, rather than move closer. Yet again, she wanted to put her arms around him and kiss him. She'd never been like this before, vacillating from one extreme to the other . . . from wanting to run away one second, then wanting to run straight into his arms the next.

Chase walked over to the rack of clothes. "This one."

He was holding up an amazing dress with a

long flowing skirt and a fitted bodice. It was midnight-blue—her favorite color—and she already knew it would fit like a glove. She doubted he would mind if she picked a different dress to wear tonight, but she wanted to please him . . . just as he'd pleased her by surprising her with such generosity and thoughtfulness.

"I just need a few minutes to shower and get dressed," she told him, then took the dress from him as she walked past. She felt his eyes on her back all the way down the hall until she closed the bedroom door behind her.

The shower felt like heaven, but she knew Chase was waiting for her so she didn't linger. The tub had beckoned, of course, but she wasn't sure she could face Chase again if she accidentally set off the jets and he heard them go on. Instead of making her blush, the thought actually made her smile even as her body heated up another couple degrees at the memory of being naked in this bathroom with Chase just twenty-four hours ago.

She dried off, then opened the toiletry and makeup bag she was amazed that he'd had set out for her, as well. She was most grateful for the makeup, because it meant she could cover up her bruise a little better. True, everyone had already seen it, but that didn't mean she liked looking at it every time she looked in the mirror.

Chase had thought of everything. How on earth was a girl supposed to *not* fall for a guy like this?

Forget his looks. He was amazing on the inside, too.

Then again, hadn't she thought her ex was great at first, too? Wasn't that why she'd married him . . . only to end up living a nightmare instead of a fairy tale?

Forcing the icky thought away, she finished blowing her hair dry, then slipped into the beautiful dress and picked a pair of heels out of the half dozen pairs of amazing shoes that had been placed in her bedroom while she showered.

A shiver ran through her at the knowledge that Chase had been just beyond the bathroom door while she was naked. Had he been tempted to break in again like he had last night?

And what would she have done this time? Would she have acted like she didn't want him in there?

Or would she have opened up the shower door and invited him in?

She tried as hard as she could to put herself back in her mindset from earlier in the day, when she'd first seen the models and had been able to convince herself that there was no way Chase would be interested in her with them around.

But after a full day with them, she knew without even the slightest doubt that there was nothing going on between Chase and any of those young women. Nor would there ever be. They looked at him with stars in their eyes, while he looked at them like they were his younger sisters.

Chloe could no longer deny that he didn't look at her like that.

He looked at her the way a man looked at a woman he desired.

Only, she found herself thinking before she could stop herself from going there, *there was more behind his gaze than just desire.*

Her heart fluttering wildly, she stepped out of the bedroom into the sitting room. Chase was silent for a long moment, which only made her heart beat faster.

Finally, he said, "You're lovely."

Lovely.

Did he know the effect that one word had on her? Did he know how special he made her feel, again and again?

Desperate to cut the sensual—and emotional—tension between them, she said, "Whoever picked out this dress has a great eye."

But he didn't let her break their connection, as he replied, "It's not the dress. It's you."

She worked not to deflect his compliment again. Once upon a time she'd known how to say thank you.

"Thank you," she said, taking in his dark jeans and the white button-down shirt that he'd rolled up a couple of times at the sleeves. "You look nice, too."

"I thought we'd walk over to Marcus's house." He looked down at her shoes. "Will that work?"

"Are you kidding? I used to practically live in heels like this."

He gave her a questioning look and she silently cursed herself. Fortunately, though, just as he'd been so nice about not pushing her about her bruise earlier, he didn't push her on this statement or ask her any questions about her past.

But she knew that if she stayed much longer, he would ask again . . . and she'd find it harder and harder not to tell him everything.

Chloe felt surprisingly comfortable at the small party at Marcus's house. Although, she thought as she glanced around her to take it all in, his property was really more of a Tuscan-style estate. Surrounded by hundreds of acres of his vineyards, the land directly around his home had been landscaped into a botanical paradise full of ancient oak trees, mature olive trees, fruit trees and a classically designed vegetable garden on the side of the house.

And yet, even though she'd never seen a house more beautiful, and knew it had to be worth an absolute fortune, she was so much more at ease in Marcus Sullivan's home than she had ever been at her ex's expensive childhood home, or the homes of the "friends" they'd spent time with. Even in her own home while married to him, she had to admit to herself, she'd felt out of place, almost afraid to move too quickly for fear she'd break something "priceless" on a table or shelf.

Marcus was the consummate host, making sure everyone's glasses were full and that the underage models stuck to juice and sparkling water even when they pouted and blinked their big, pretty eyes at him to try to get him to change his mind.

After she'd had her fill of the incredible spread and Jeremy had officially exhausted her gossip quota for one lifetime, Chase reappeared from the shadows.

"Are you having fun?"

She smiled at him as she said, "I am. Thank you so much for including me tonight."

It should have been a relief when he'd moved away from her not long after arriving at the party, especially after their silent walk from the guesthouse. But even though she truly had been having a great time tonight, she'd missed being with him. Her gaze had strayed to him from across the room one too many times. And he'd almost always caught her looking . . . because he'd been looking for her, too.

"Can I get you anything else to eat or drink?"

She shook her head, putting her hand over her stomach. “I’m stuffed, thanks.” Feeling a little loose from the wine, she said, “There is something I’d love, though. I’ve been dying to see a family photo.”

“I can already tell you I’m the best-looking Sullivan,” he joked.

She laughed out loud, since Chase was one of the least egotistical men she’d ever met. Confident, but not cocky.

“Why don’t you let me be the judge of that?”

He held out a hand, and she took it without remembering that it wasn’t a good idea to touch him. But, oh, it felt so nice to hold his hand—big and strong and warm—if only for a few short moments.

It occurred to her that she might be just a teensy bit tipsy as they walked into a room that she assumed was Marcus’s study, but it was so nice to feel relaxed again. She’d been so tense for so long. As long she could remember, actually.

Chase picked up a framed eight-by-ten photo from the bookshelf and handed it to her.

Chloe worked to keep the awe from her expression at what an incredible sight the Sullivans made together. Still, she couldn’t take her eyes off Chase. Even in a photo he commanded her attention.

He was standing next to his mother, nearly a foot taller, with his arm around her as she leaned her head on his shoulder. She looked happy and content, surrounded by her children.

Longing to be part of a family this close hit Chloe so hard, she almost dropped the glossy photo.

And then, she saw something that had her mouth falling open.

"Oh, my God. You're Smith Sullivan's brother?"

Jealousy wasn't something that Chase knew a lot about. So the sudden hard hit of it, right in the pit of his gut, stung pretty damn bad.

"I am." He waited for her to ask if she could meet Smith, or to start peppering him with questions about his movie-star brother.

Instead, she simply turned and stared at him for a long moment. "I guess I should have seen the resemblance." And then she said, "Tell me about everyone else."

Seriously? She didn't want to know more about Smith, who happened to be one of the biggest movie stars in the world?

This time he was the one giving her a funny look and she shifted uncomfortably under his gaze, her free hand automatically coming up to cover her cheek. "Is something wrong?"

He quickly shook his head. "No. Not a thing."

He wanted to move her hand from her cheek, wanted to tell her again that she didn't need to hide any part of herself from him. But he'd made himself a promise to let her lead their dance.

He wasn't a saint. Not even close. But he knew keeping that promise was the only way she'd ever really trust him.

Chase knew how to persuade a woman with kisses, with the touch of his fingertips across her skin. But he didn't want to be the only one wanting.

He wanted Chloe to want, too, just as badly as he did.

Enough that she'd have to act on that want.

Enough that she'd have to push past fear and trust him.

Up on the hill at lunchtime, she'd asked him to be her friend. Chase couldn't remember the last time he'd remained just friends with a woman that he wanted. And yet, when he'd told her he'd be honored to be her friend, it hadn't just been a line. He'd meant it. There was something about Chloe that brought out his protective instincts and made him want to know her secrets. He was curious, of course—anyone would be with the bruise she wore on her cheek and the way he'd found her on the side of the road. But he knew he had to be careful not to push her or she'd run. He had to tread delicately. And he hoped talking about his family would help ease her into becoming even more comfortable with him.

"Ryan is a year younger than me." At her questioning sidelong glance, he added, "I'm thirty-two." He turned back to the picture. "He plays pro baseball for the San Francisco Hawks."

She murmured something about being impressed, but it was clear from her reaction that she wasn't a baseball fan. He grinned, thinking about Chloe meeting Ryan and not fawning over him. His brother would be crushed. Smith would likely feel the same way. He couldn't wait to introduce her to his two famous brothers.

"Gabe is my youngest brother. He's a firefighter."

"Wow, a firefighter. That's a really dangerous job." She looked at Gabe's picture again and then back at Chase. "Doesn't your mother worry?"

"At this point, between the eight of us, I think she's pretty much thrown in the towel on worrying."

Chloe shook her head. "No," she said softly, "she's your mother. She still worries. About all of you. Because she loves you."

In an instant, he was caught up in a perfectly clear vision of Chloe as a mother, how sweet and loving she'd be. His voice felt raw as he agreed. "That's why we've tried to give her a little peace, now and again, as we get older. At least I have, anyway."

Chloe smiled at him, and his chest clenched tight at her beauty, and the way just one small smile absolutely transformed her entire expression from pretty to radiant.

"Who's this?" She pointed at one of his sisters.

"Nice." When she gave him a confused look, he realized he'd used his sister's nickname and corrected himself. "I mean Sophie." He pointed to her twin. "That's Lori, aka Naughty. They're the youngest of all of us."

She chuckled. "Why do I have a feeling your sisters don't much care for those nicknames?"

"Sure they do," he insisted, before admitting, "even though they're always telling me they don't."

Chloe shook her head and muttered, "I can't imagine dealing with one big brother like you, let alone six." She arched a brow at him. "I'll bet you know exactly what's best for them, don't you?"

He grinned at her unrepentantly. "Of course I do."

She snorted, then looked at the picture again. "They're both very pretty. I sure hope they got some good ones in on you and the rest of your brothers for being know-it-alls."

Chase winced in memory. "More than once, you'll be glad to hear."

She laughed again, and if there was a sweeter sound in the world, Chase hadn't heard it yet.

"What do they do? Lori looks really athletic."

"She's a dancer and choreographer. She started out working with cheerleaders and now she does a lot of the stuff you see on TV." Damn, he loved those girls, and would always want to protect them. “Sophie is a librarian in San Francisco. She’s smart as a freaking whip, and always had her head in a book. Still does.”

“Wow, very impressive. A movie star. A winery owner. A pro baseball player. A firefighter. An auto-shop tycoon. A choreographer. And a librarian. No wonder you’re so proud of your brothers and sisters.”

Chase and his siblings didn’t always see eye to eye; fists were sometimes raised and thrown in the heat of anger. But he’d give up his left arm—hell, both of his arms—for any one of them.

“I already know about Smith. He’s a little older than you, right?”

“Thirty-four.”

“Your parents were certainly busy,” she said, before pointing at another of his brothers. “And who’s this?”

“Zach. He’s twenty-nine. He owns half of the auto shops in California,” he said, just barely exaggerating considering his brother was a bona fide mogul with a wrench in his hand, “and he races cars in his spare time.”

Recognition lit in her eyes. “Are those Sullivan Auto ads I hear all the time on the radio his?”

Chase nodded. “He’s a business mastermind who’d rather spend his life under the hood of a vintage car.” Or in a woman’s bed. But Chloe didn’t need to know that. Especially given that Zach was a good-looking bastard. Quite possibly the best-looking of them all. Including Smith, whose looks were integral to his profession.

"Marcus is the old man of the group at thirty-six."

Laughing at just how off base it was for him to call Marcus an old man, she said, "So, there are eight of you between the ages of twenty-four and thirty-six." She raised an eyebrow. "And none of you are married yet?" Her surprise was evident.

He shrugged. "Nope. We're all expecting Marcus and his girlfriend to do the deed soon." Although after what Chase saw at his mother's birthday party, he wasn't so sure anymore. Neither Marcus nor Jill had looked particularly happy. "Bets were placed a long time ago on who would be shackled with the ball and chain first."

She laughed out loud at that. "See, now you're talking like a normal guy. Using the words *shackled* and *ball and chain* in reference to getting married."

Funny, he thought as he enjoyed her laughter, up until yesterday he'd been right there with the rest of his siblings on thinking marriage was a long way off. Hell, when he'd originally planned to come up to the winery, he'd even scheduled a one-night stand. But now, after meeting Chloe, he wasn't so sure.

He knew it was crazy. Knew how hard it would

be for anyone else to believe that it was possible to fall this fast, or this hard, this quickly.

He couldn't explain it.

But he suddenly found that he didn't need to.

Chloe had unexpectedly come into his life, and now that she had, he didn't want her to leave it. Or to leave him.

So even though it was crazy, and even though the rest of the world might not understand him or his choices, Chase realized that he didn't mind being led straight to the edge of the cliff. Not as long as Chloe was standing there, too.

And they were falling together.

Turning back to the picture, she said, "Your mother is beautiful."

"She is. She's great."

"She looks so happy to be with all of you." Chloe's eyes were big and full of concern as she asked, "What happened to your father?"

When he hesitated before answering, she bit her lower lip. "That was really rude. I'm sorry, you don't have to answer."

"No, don't be sorry, Chloe. You can ask me anything."

Her gaze flew to his again. "But we just met last night. We don't know each other that well," she protested, and it was as if she'd just been privy to his thoughts about how crazy this all was between them. How sudden. How powerful.

Crazy, sudden, unexpected: none of those

things bothered Chase. Hopefully, soon, they wouldn't matter to Chloe, either.

"I was ten when my father died," he told her, the pang right behind his breastbone reminding him how much he still missed his father . . . and how much he wished he'd at least been able to say goodbye. "He went to work that morning and he had an aneurysm. One of his employees found him in his office on the floor."

"Oh, Chase, I'm sorry."

She put her hand on his arm, and even though he thought he hadn't truly needed to grieve for his father in nearly two decades, her touch gave him comfort.

She looked back at the picture, and he could see her studying his mother's face with fresh emotion. "Did she remarry?"

He shook his head. "No. She never dated, either."

"No doubt she must have been too busy to have a social life for herself," Chloe murmured. "I can't imagine how she managed with eight kids all by herself."

Beyond glad that she hadn't shied away from what she wanted to know, he said, "It wasn't easy. Especially not at first. We all helped out. At least, the big kids did." He gave her a small smile. "I make a mean mac and cheese."

"Yum," she said in a soft, not altogether convincing voice.

"Want to hear my secret?"

"Uh . . . okay."

He leaned in a little closer, close enough that he could breathe in her sweet scent, along with the heady aroma of red wine on her lips. "You've got to watch the pot carefully and know just when to stir."

Attraction flared between them again at his teasing words, both of them knowing that what he was really doing was gauging her reaction to him.

Because he wanted her.

And he knew she wanted him, too.

Marcus found them in his study and glanced down at the family photo in her hands. "Whatever he's saying about us, Chloe," he teased, "it's all lies."

Chase watched her grin up at his brother, glad to see that she was so comfortable with his family. "So I guess that means you're not a superhero, after all?"

Marcus laughed, clearly pleased with her comeback. "Everyone left to go dancing in town. To be nineteen again," he said with a shake of his head. "How about I open up a bottle of the good stuff for the three of us?"

"The wine you've served so far tonight has been amazing. You have better stuff?" Chloe asked, incredulous.

"Prepare to have your mind blown," Marcus replied.

Despite the fact that his brother was clearly enjoying being around Chloe, Chase couldn't shake the sense that something wasn't right with Marcus. As the oldest Sullivan, he'd always carried more of the burden of making sure everyone in the family was okay. But tonight he seemed edgier than normal. Wound just a little too tight, even after changing out of his suit and tie.

Before meeting his girlfriend, Jill, Marcus had been just as much a dog as the rest of the Sullivan boys, a veritable connoisseur of beautiful women. But in the past two years, he'd straightened up to the point where Chase almost didn't recognize him. Where was the brother who knew how to have fun? How to laugh at stupid jokes? How to kick up his feet and enjoy the present instead of always preparing for the future?

Chase missed getting up to no good with the oldest of the Sullivan clan, but since he'd assumed his brother was preparing to marry Jill and settle down to have a bunch of kids, he'd figured it wasn't his place to pry. Only, after what he'd seen between them at his mother's birthday party, he suddenly wondered if he'd figured wrong.

"Is Jill going to be coming up to Napa this weekend?"

Marcus tensed. "She's got a lot of work to catch up on with some high-profile projects."

"It isn't work she can take care of from here?" Chase asked, knowing Jill spent most of her time online and on the phone versus having to be on-site in meeting rooms all day.

Chloe looked between Chase and Marcus, clearly sensing the tension in their conversation.

"It's easier for her to get it done in the city," Marcus explained as he led them into the living room, which looked out over the moonlit vines and pool patio. And as he uncorked a dusty cabernet bottle that still smelled of the caves, Chase understood that their conversation about Jill was over. At least for the time being.

Because if Jill didn't like coming up to Napa to stay with Marcus at least part of the time, it seemed that his brother and his brother's girlfriend were going to have some pretty major problems going forward. After all, the wine country was at the heart of not only Marcus's business, but this land was where his heart was. As far as Chase was concerned, any woman Marcus married needed to love it, too. And who in their right mind wouldn't?

As Marcus handed Chloe the glass of wine, Chloe said, "I really shouldn't have any more, but how can I resist?"

The three of them sat down, and Chase loved how easy she was with his brother. Just knowing

Chloe was near, just being able to see her smile, to hear her laugh, made everything so much better. And his life had been pretty damn good before she came into it, so that was really saying something.

"Everyone was saying what a great help you were at the magazine shoot today," Marcus told her.

Chase could see how pleased she was at his compliment. "I had fun."

"She completely saved the day, actually," Chase put in.

Chloe rolled her eyes. "That is so not true. I simply sewed up one dress that had a small tear in it."

It was a tear that could have cost them a very important shot, but before he could tell them that, Chloe took a sip from her glass and said, "Oh. My. God. This wine is so good it should be illegal."

Marcus smiled. "I'm glad you like it. This is the cabernet that put Sullivan Winery on the map."

She inhaled from the rim of her glass before taking another sip. On a near-moan, she said, "No wonder everyone started talking about your winery after tasting this. What I'm feeling isn't even close to *like*. It's *love* all the way."

In an instant, Chase's desire for her skyrocketed. All it took was hearing her moan . . . and say one little four-letter word.

A word that he hadn't even been searching for. Because he hadn't realized it was missing from his life.

Until now.

Until Chloe.

"So," Marcus said, "where are you from, Chloe?"

She instantly snapped to attention, sitting up so fast in her seat that the wine sloshed almost to the rim of her glass and over. Her face was flushed as she said, "I'm in the process of moving, actually."

She took a big, nervous gulp of wine and Chase tried to use Sullivan telepathy to tell his brother to shut up.

It didn't work.

"Where to?" Marcus asked.

Chloe took another gulp and swallowed hard before replying. "I'm still looking at my options."

After Marcus leaned over to refill her empty glass, she shot up out of her seat. "I've got to go visit the powder room. Excuse me."

Chase waited until she'd left the room to tell his brother, "You upset her with your questions."

Marcus frowned. "Sorry about that. I didn't realize it until it was too late." He shot Chase a serious look. "What the hell is going on? She's got that bruise pretty well covered up tonight, but how'd she get it in the first place? Did that happen when she drove off the side of the road? Or is there another story behind what happened to her?"

Every time Chase thought about how she'd gotten the bruise—it wasn't more than an educated guess at this point, but he was pretty sure some guy had hit her—he wanted to hammer his fist into something.

No, not *something.* Straight into the face of the guy who had hurt her.

"I don't know for sure. She hasn't trusted me enough yet to say." He gave his brother a warning look. "Don't push her anymore. On anything. I'm getting closer, but I don't want her to run from me like she just ran from you."

Marcus raised an eyebrow. "You like her."

"It's way beyond like," he said, echoing Chloe's comment. Only he was talking about something a hell of a lot more important than an expensive drink. Talking more to himself than his brother at this point, he said, "I just need her to stay a few more days. And then maybe she'll give me a chance to see where she and I could take this."

His brother was silent for several long moments before finally commenting, "I've never seen you like this before."

Chase had known other people would find his instant connection with Chloe to be crazy, even his own siblings. And the truth was that even though he'd already decided he wanted it—and her—it was crazy enough for him to shake his head and admit, "And here I thought I was coming here for nothing more than a photo shoot and a few days of meaningless sex with—"

Marcus cut him off, assuming, "With one of your models?"

Chase snorted. "No. No way. I stopped sleeping with models years ago." He knew his brother was going to be pissed off when he told him about Ellen, but it was probably better if they talked about it now over an expensive bottle of wine, rather than somewhere fists could be raised. "I was planning to hook up with Ellen."

Marcus narrowed his eyes. "My employee, Ellen?"

Now that it hadn't happened, Chase could see the foolishness of his earlier plan. "That's the one."

"Goddamn it, Chase," Marcus said in a heated voice, "you can't screw around with someone who works for me. All I need is for her to get a broken heart on account of you or Zach or Gabe and then having her take it out on my winery."

Chase held up his hands. "Look, the hookup didn't happen, okay? So don't get all bent out of shape about it. I met Chloe before Ellen and I could get into any trouble. And you'll be glad to hear that Ellen not only seemed fine with being let down, but also clearly agreed it was a bad idea." Ignoring his brother's glare, he gave in to the need to confide his feelings to someone, and admitted, "I've never been like this before, never felt like this with anyone but Chloe. And I haven't even touched her yet."

Damn it, he was saying too much. Marcus didn't need to know what he and Chloe had—or hadn't—done. No one needed to know that but the two of them.

Chase refilled their glasses before turning the tables on his brother and asking, "Are you sure everything is all right with you and Jill?"

"She's fine." The muscle that had started jumping in Marcus's jaw when Chase mentioned his employee was now pulsing fast and furious as he stood. "I'm going to head to bed for the night. Got a busy day tomorrow."

Chase stood up, too. This time around the Sullivan telepathy was working perfectly. Something was up with Jill and Marcus—and his brother had no intention of talking about it with him.

Chase wished like hell he knew how to bring the old Marcus back. As the eldest of the Sullivan siblings, after their father died, Marcus had immediately stepped into his place. Chase had memories of his brother changing diapers and wiping noses. Making sure everyone got to school on time with their homework in their backpacks. Fortunately, in their twenties, as everyone grew up and needed him less, he'd been able to break out of that responsible shell and cut loose for a while.

Once upon a time, Marcus had been the biggest player of them all—almost as if he was making up for lost time. Women would throw themselves at him, and he'd catch each and every one of them.

But now, ever since he'd been with ice princess Jill, he'd changed again. Receded back into that too-responsible, too-mature shell.

Funny, Chase realized with a start, that while he was thinking his brother needed to shake off the chains and get back out there into the playing field, here he was looking at doing the exact opposite.

But the truth was, Chase had burned through more than enough women.

People could call him crazy for falling so fast, but he wouldn't care. Because he was ready for that special one . . . and something deep down in his gut was telling him that he'd found her.

"I should check on Chloe," Chase told his brother. "I've got to make sure she didn't get lost in your palace on the hill." But before he left, he put his hand on his brother's shoulder. "Thanks for the party tonight, and for letting us use the winery for our shoot. This place is going to look great in pictures."

For a moment he thought his brother might have heard what he didn't say: *I'm here if you need to talk. Anytime. About anything.* But then, Marcus was saying, "It's my pleasure," before heading out of the living room and up the stairs to his bedroom.

A couple of minutes of searching later, Chase found Chloe standing out on the back deck, her glass empty again. For a long moment, Chase stopped and just stared.

She was stunning.

Not because of the moonlight. Not because of the dress.

It was all Chloe.

No other woman had ever taken his breath away like this. And he doubted any other ever would.

“There you are.”

She turned her face to his and it was full of so much emotion—and longing—that it was all he could do not to reach for her.

They were completely alone out on the back porch. His brother was in bed, everyone else was gone. And he could tell just from looking at her that the wine had blurred some of her edges.

Unable to keep away, he moved behind her, putting his hands on either side of the rail. “Some moon tonight, isn’t it?”

He expected her to push away from him, but strangely, she did the exact opposite by turning slowly in the circle of his arms so that she was looking straight at him with those big, beautiful eyes that mucked up his insides.

"Chase."

Jesus, he was teetering on a thin edge, so close to her and yet so damn far.

Honor. Why had he decided that honor mattered? Everything would be so much easier if he simply took what he wanted . . . and worried about the consequences later.

But even though she wasn't drunk, he knew she wasn't sober, either. And that he needed to take her back to the guesthouse and put her to bed.

Alone.

Only, he obviously wasn't strong enough to do any of that. All he could do was say her name. And want her more than he'd ever wanted anyone or anything in his whole life.

"Chloe."

Her full lips parted slightly at the sound of her name. For the first time, she wasn't trying to hide her desire from him.

"It's inevitable, isn't it?" she asked him in a soft voice that reverberated all the way through him.

Hell, yes, it was. But he couldn't put words in her mouth. Not now when every word, every look, every touch, was so damned important.

"What's inevitable?" His words were raw. Full of the need he couldn't hide.

Her eyes dropped to his mouth.

"This kiss."

Nine

As Chloe threaded her fingers through his hair and pulled his face down to hers, it took every ounce of control Chase possessed to keep his hands on the rail.

But when her lips touched his, just a whisper of a kiss . . . his control was lost.

He wanted to touch her everywhere at once, but it was a straight shot for his hands from the rail to her lower back and the incredibly sexy curve of her hips.

Her mouth was so soft, so damn sweet, as she pressed one kiss after another against his lips. If he could, he would have prolonged the gentle exploration. But he'd been waiting too damn long for this kiss. Running one hand up her spine, he cupped the back of her neck, threaded his hand into her silky hair and held her captive beneath him while he tasted her.

She gasped against his mouth, and somewhere in the back of his head he started to wonder if he was hurting her. He was about to force himself to lift his mouth from hers when he felt it: her tongue coming out to stroke against his.

Jesus, he'd thought about this moment a

hundred times in the past twenty-four hours, but nothing he'd come up with, nothing he'd envisioned in his fantasies, came anywhere close to the reality of how soft, how sweet, how sensual, kissing Chloe really was.

Chase had always loved kissing. To his surprise, most women liked to rush past that part of their sensual dance, even though sometimes a kiss could be just as good as full-blown sex.

Better, even.

Especially when he was kissing Chloe.

He could have spent hours on her mouth, learning her taste, her pleasure. Judging by the way she was kissing him back, with a passion that echoed his, he had a feeling she would be up for exactly that.

Slowly stroking his tongue against hers, he reveled in the taste of her, the feel of her, the little moans of pleasure she was making as they connected so intimately. Drawing back slightly, he gently sucked her lower lip in between his teeth for a soft nip at the sensitive flesh there, being sure to give her upper lip the same treatment. And then their tongues were back at it until she did the same to his mouth, tasting, taking, nipping, biting his flesh so perfectly.

"Chloe." He groaned her name against her lips, and she licked across his once more before looking at him, flushed and lovely and awash with desire.

She was panting when she admitted, "I've never been kissed like that before."

The innocence of her words, the look on her face—like she'd just experienced heaven—had him taking her lips again. Devouring them.

Chase didn't have any idea how long they kissed like a man and a woman who were starving for each other, but all the while he was intensely aware of the soft press of her breasts against his chest, along with the sexy curve of her hips where he was holding her against him. He was torn between continuing to kiss her lips and tasting his way down her incredible body.

Just then she shifted slightly in his arms, pressing her breasts and hips even closer into him, and the decision was taken away from him.

He'd been blessed enough to see her beautiful naked skin when he'd walked in on her in the bathtub the previous evening. But he hadn't been able to touch her. He hadn't been able to run his tongue over her. He hadn't been able to kiss every dip and curve.

Now, nothing could have stopped him from having all that. From having *her*.

Chase began to run kisses over her face, across her cheekbones, over her chin, down to her neck. He licked into the hollow of her collarbones and felt her weight come more firmly against him, as if she could barely hold herself up.

Chase had learned early on how to elicit a sensual response from women and he'd always enjoyed their pleasure as much as his own. But Chloe's response—and his need for her—was different from that of any other woman he'd been with. Their connection was not only more immediate, it was also stronger, ran deeper . . . and was so much hotter.

When he ran his tongue over her skin again, the softly desperate sound she made had him moving his hand from where he'd been cupping her neck down to a thin strap on her shoulder. She was soft, so damn soft that he almost lost the thread of what he was doing, but then she took a deep, shaking breath, her breasts moving against his chest, swelling up beneath the top of her dress.

And he remembered exactly why he needed to slide the strap off her lovely skin.

A picture of her breasts—water from the bathtub beading and sliding over her soft flesh—would be forever imprinted on his brain. But now that he was just seconds away from actually being able to touch, to taste them, Chase could barely get his hands to work right.

He needed to get the straps off.

And then, silk was sliding down over her shoulders and he didn't even need to give her dress a yank, because Chloe was two steps ahead of him, lifting her arms from the confines of her dress and shimmying her upper body so that the bodice slipped one inch, and then another, and then one more still, until her breasts popped out from beneath the thin fabric.

Desire momentarily immobilized Chase as he drank her in. Her breasts were perfect, full and round, beautifully natural in the way they lay against her chest, tipped up to him with desire.

Finally coming unstuck, but still utterly mesmerized, his hands warred with his mouth for the pleasure of being the first to touch her.

His hands won by a hair as he reached out to cup her, his fingertips stroking across the hard peaks of her breasts before cupping the softest flesh he'd ever felt in his entire life.

"Oh, God. Chase."

He tore his gaze away from her breasts, from the contrast of her pale skin against his tanned fingers, to see that she was staring in wonder at exactly the same thing. Her eyes lifted to his a moment later and the heat, the pleasure, in them had him pressing his mouth to hers again, her breasts still in his hands.

Their kiss took on a different sheen this time, the desperation for each other kicking up another notch. Chloe was rubbing and pressing her breasts against his hands, almost as if she was begging for something. As if she was begging for more.

"Watch, Chloe." Drawing back from her mouth, he trained his gaze back on her breasts as he ran his thumbs over the taut peaks. "Look how responsive you are to my touch."

She whimpered as he caressed the taut flesh again, harder this time, and then again. Her nipples puckered beneath his thumbs.

"Please, Chase."

He barely heard her request, her words more breath than anything else, but he understood exactly what she was saying. Because he needed the exact same thing she did.

Chase bent his head down and she arched her back to make herself more available to him. In one smooth motion, he laved his tongue over her incredibly soft skin. A part of him wanted to spend all night there, with his tongue on her breasts, running it across every inch of her. But his lips, his teeth, had other ideas, and it was barely a moment later that he was closing his mouth down over her nipple, swirling his tongue over her even as his teeth lightly scraped the rigid, aroused flesh.

She made a soft moan then that had him throbbing dangerously in his jeans.

There was nothing feigned about her response. Chloe was pure sensuality, just as he'd known she would be. He'd watched her come apart in the bathtub, and yet, being a part of that pleasure tonight, being the reason she was drowning in desire, put what he'd been feeling for her in another stratosphere entirely.

They'd talked about being friends—she'd told him how much she needed that—but after spending the past twenty-four hours in a nearly constant state of arousal for her, he couldn't stop himself from bunching her skirt up his hands and running one hand up her bare thigh.

Turning his attention to her other breast, his mouth closed down over it just as his fingers found her panties, damp with arousal.

"Yes," she gasped as he tugged on her breast with his lips, moving his hand up between her thighs so that he could slide his fingers in beneath the thin fabric of her panties.

Worries, concerns, reservations—they all flew out the window as he found her slick, and so damned hot, with his hand. She was practically bucking in his arms, arching into his mouth, opening her legs to give him better access to every part of her. Moments later, Chloe was crying out her pleasure and her inner muscles were clamping down on him in a beautiful, out-of-control rhythm. She was a living, breathing orgasm beneath his mouth and hands.

Her release seemed to go on forever, from one peak to the next, and Chase felt like the luckiest guy on the planet. He wanted to do nothing from here on out but make her come. Watch her come. Listen to her come.

He wanted to give up everything for her, if he had to. And it would all be worth it, just to be witness to such overarching, all-consuming pleasure.

Amazingly, when she finally settled back down in his arms, instead of being satisfied, she looked up at him and said, “Please, Chase. More. I need more.”

He knew just what she was asking for—she wanted him to take her, right then and there on his brother’s porch in the middle of the vines.

Chase had never wanted anything so bad. *Never.*

Only, when she’d been asking for more, her words had slurred together. Just the slightest bit.

But he heard it.

Worse, he could see now that her eyes were a little unfocused. Maybe even blurry. And not just because of her orgasm.

Chase didn’t want to have to ask himself if she was drunk, if she wasn’t totally in control of what she was doing with him out on his brother’s porch. He wanted to believe that the slurring had everything to do with how good he was making her feel and not the number of times her wine-glass had been refilled. He knew he could do anything he wanted to her right now, turn her around on the balcony so that her hips were pressed up against his groin while he lifted her skirt. He could fill his hands with the perfect, heavy weight of her breasts while he slid into her from behind. And both of them could get what they desperately needed.

But, damn it, he just couldn't do it.

Not when he knew he'd never—ever—be able to live with himself if this went even further and Chloe woke up in the morning not knowing what she'd done. Not if she had one single regret about him.

Chase couldn't be one more man to take something away from her.

Which meant that he needed to stop this.

Now.

Not wanting to startle her, he slowly moved his hand from between her legs, letting the dress fall back down. A moment later he was gently pulling up the bodice, covering up breasts that he would kill to taste again.

"What are you doing?" Her words were heavy with both desire and confusion. "Why are you stopping?"

"I think it's time to get you home to bed."

Her mouth moved into a sensual pout. "I'm not tired, Chase. Not yet."

Sweet Lord, it was hard not to take another kiss from that mouth. Even harder not to rip off her dress and take her right there on the wood-plank decking.

"You're lovely, Chloe, so damned lovely," he ground out through his unquenched desire, "but I can't take advantage of you like this."

The pout turned stubborn and, if it was possible, even prettier. "You're not taking advantage of me," she insisted. "I'm the one who kissed you, remember?"

This was even harder than he'd thought it would be. Because the last thing he wanted to do was hurt her feelings. He didn't want her to think he didn't desire her like crazy.

"I want this more than you can imagine, but I need you to be completely with me when we finally make love."

"I was with you." She lifted her mouth back to his, whispering, "I'm still with you," against his lips as she kissed him softly, then licked out against his lower lip.

He couldn't hold back his frustrated groan as he made himself drag his mouth away from hers. "I don't want you to look back at this tomorrow morning and hate me because I took advantage of you when you were drunk."

"I'm not drunk!"

"You're not completely sober, either," he made himself say in a gentle voice.

Suddenly, the fight went out of her. And she looked crushed. Completely crushed.

Hating to see that look on her face, hating the fact that doing the right thing had hurt her, anyway, Chase said, "You don't know how hard this is for me to do."

Her steps were mostly steady as she turned and

began to walk away from him, but every now and then she seemed to catch and right herself on her heels.

Chase knew he was right to have done what he did. But it didn't make him feel any better. Not when he could feel Chloe's hurt and embarrassment radiating from her during the silent walk back to the guesthouse.

She didn't so much as look at him as she waited for him to unlock the front door. Even though he was desperate to reach for her, to pull her against him, he let her walk past.

"We'll talk in the morning."

She stopped then, looking at him over her shoulder for a moment. Her bright eyes were dulled now. Without saying a word, she walked into her bedroom and closed the door with a soft click.

He got into an ice-cold shower and the mental picture of her breasts in his hands, the taste of her on his tongue, the feel of her aroused, slick flesh pushing and squeezing against his fingers, had him needing to take himself into his own hands despite the freezing water. Chase couldn't stop wondering—what was wrong with him?

He'd had a warm, wet and willing woman in his arms just minutes ago.

And he'd walked away from her.

Ten

Chloe packed her bag first thing the next morning and put her jeans and T-shirt back on.

Last night had been too close. She'd wanted Chase too much.

Which was why she couldn't stay here any longer.

A new basket of pastries and fruit was on the counter for her again, and pride should have dictated that she walk right by it, but that would have been plain stupid. She didn't have the money for a taxi. Which meant she was going to be walking out of here, down long country roads until she could find a bus stop.

Pride was fine and dandy. But not when she was going to desperately need the fuel to keep going.

Only, what had tasted so delicious the previous morning was sawdust in her mouth now, and she had to force herself to eat the croissant she'd picked up.

Of course, the folded note with "Chloe" written on it in Chase's handwriting didn't help, either. As she chewed and swallowed, she stared at the paper.

She swore Chase's note stared back at her.

It would be better not to read it. It would be

smarter just to walk out of here, say her thank-yous and goodbyes and forget she'd ever met a beautiful man whose kisses tasted like heaven.

But Chase had been nothing but kind to her. So kind, in fact, that instead of taking her the way she had so desperately wanted the previous evening, he'd not only put a halt to their kisses, but also actually pulled his hand from between her legs after she came for him and walked her home without another touch.

Oh, God, that first kiss had been intense. Wicked. Perfect. She could have kissed him all night. Chloe had dreamed of that kiss all night long, could still feel the way they'd almost been taking breath from each other's lungs. She'd woken up aching for another kiss . . . and for the chance to cuddle up with Chase under a blanket somewhere and just kiss and kiss and kiss all night long.

If she'd just been angling for another orgasm, she might have been able to deal with the ache. After all, she'd proved in the bathtub a couple of nights ago that she could give that to herself.

No, it was that urge to cuddle with him, that desperate desire to feel warm and safe, which frightened her. She had to leave.

But the truth was, she'd wonder what had been in his note every second of every day if she didn't look at it. As she grabbed it off the countertop the edges crumpled with her rough nervous handling.

Chloe,
I hope you slept well. One day soon, I'm hoping to be able to enjoy breakfast with you. I'm looking forward to that. A lot.
Please join us again today. Everyone thinks you're great.
See you soon,
~~Hotstuff~~
HOTSTUFF
P.S. It does need all capital letters, don't you think?

Somewhere between the *A lot* and the crossed-out *Hotstuff,* all the tingly, mushy feelings that Chloe had been trying to squash inside of herself popped back to life. Bigger and stronger than they'd been before, even.

Last night she'd been riding a light buzz and enjoying herself until Marcus began asking innocent questions. She'd gotten nervous and worried about all the problems she hadn't dealt with yet and started guzzling his wine.

Any other guy but Chase would have taken advantage of her slight tipsiness, especially with the way she'd been begging for him. But, yet again, just as he had in the bathroom that first night, he'd walked away from temptation. Not because he didn't want her, but because he'd known she wasn't all there, that the wine had dulled her senses and reactions just enough for her to give up control without a thought of protecting herself.

They'd been so close to what she'd wanted and a not-so-secret part of her wished that he hadn't stopped them from making love, that he had just taken advantage of the fact that she was a little drunk.

What was wrong with her? If that's what she was wishing for, then she had some serious problems. And Lord knew if she couldn't control her mind—or body—around Chase any better than that, staying was definitely out of the question.

It didn't matter that she still had nowhere to go. It didn't matter that her situation with her ex hadn't changed and that she still needed to deal with the police and see what they could do—if anything—to help her. He was doing an amazing job of making her feel like a princess, but her life wasn't a fairy tale; it was in shambles. Enough of this fantasy winery land, with the beautiful clothes, pretending that this great guy was hers.

None of that was reality, and there was no such thing as Prince Charming. Staying here, pretending, was just prolonging the inevitable for another three days: dealing with her ex, making sure he never hurt her again and then rebuilding her life from the ground up and making sure it was the life *she* wanted this time.

She took a breath and tried to prepare herself for the difficulty of saying goodbye to Chase.

Because something told her it was going to be harder than getting hit in the face by her ex. More painful than driving into a ditch. And worse than standing in the middle of a hailstorm.

Chase hadn't just been nice. He hadn't just been sweet. He'd also been incredibly honorable from the first moment he found her on the side of the road in the pouring rain.

She owed him the same respect. She wasn't just going to sneak away. She wasn't going to just leave him a note like a coward.

She needed to head out to the vineyards where he was photographing the models with his crew, pull up her big-girl panties and say a proper goodbye to his face. Sneaking out was for wimps. Even though the wimp inside her longed to prevail, it was time for her to learn how to be strong.

And it was time to tell Chase goodbye.

"Chloe, thank God you're here!"

Jeremy looked frazzled. And not just because he'd been enjoying the fruits of Marcus's cellar along with her the previous night.

"Chase was just about to send me to the guest-house to see if you were up yet." His glasses were on crooked as he explained, "Alice has the stomach flu."

"I'll go check on her," Chloe immediately offered.

Jeremy grabbed her arm. "No! I mean, a doctor has been in to see her, but we can't risk anyone else getting sick if they don't have the flu already."

Chloe shook her head. "But I'm not part of the crew. I can stay with her and then you all can—"

She felt Chase's presence a split second before he moved into her line of vision. His smile made her stomach do flip-flops. "Good morning, Chloe," he said, and then without pause, "We need you to take over for Alice."

Chloe blinked once. Twice. "Me?" She frowned. "What makes you think I can take over for her?"

"You were a lifesaver yesterday," Chase replied, as if it were the most obvious thing in the world.

"A lifesaver?" she echoed with disbelief. "I sewed up one dress with one tiny tear."

"You did more than that," he insisted. "I saw you talking with Alice, helping her put outfits together. She changed course a couple of times yesterday, and it was because of your suggestions."

Chloe shook her head. "They were offhand comments. I wasn't trying to take over her job."

"I know that. She knows that. But the fact is, you've got a great eye for color and pattern. You instinctively know what works. And the models trust you. They like you. That matters more than you know. If they feel great, they look great."

She opened her mouth to protest again, but before she could, he moved a little closer, close enough that her already racing heart all but jumped out of her chest.

"We all need your help. *I* need your help."

How could she say no to him? He'd saved her that night on the road. Instead of being picked up by a rapist ax murderer, Chase had been a full-on knight in shining armor. And now he needed her help.

But just then, just as she was about to tell him she'd stay to help, his gaze moved to the bag over her shoulder, then to her jeans and T-shirt, before returning to her face. When his gaze met hers again, she could see that he knew exactly what she'd been coming here to do: to say goodbye.

He didn't hide his disappointment from her. And, oh, she couldn't believe how much she hated seeing it. She wanted the man back who looked at her like she was beautiful, like he wanted her so bad that he was barely a breath away from taking her.

That was when she realized that even though she'd come to say goodbye to his face, it didn't change the fact that she was running again.

"I'd love to help." She looked between Chase and Jeremy. "Just tell me what you need me to do and I'll do it."

Jeremy dragged her off almost before the

words were out of her mouth. But not before she caught Chase's smile. And the fact that whatever disappointment had been there was now erased . . . desire and appreciation taking its place without even missing a beat.

The day flew by. Chase didn't really need much direction with the clothes, and Chloe felt that he was only asking her opinions to make her feel involved. At first she was reluctant to say much. She didn't want to screw up his photo shoot, after all. But, just as it had been the day before, it was hard not to get swept up in the magic of it all.

They were creating beautiful fairy tales out in the vines and, without overthinking it, she began to cinch in the waists on dresses and sew up hems. Not only that, but when she actually disagreed with the way the accessories he'd put together were clashing, and he took the shots both ways, she was amazed to realize that her choices were the better ones.

And through it all, even though they were surrounded by the crew, attraction pulsed between them.

A part of her wanted to run again. After all, she had so much practice with running that it seemed the easier choice. But with every hour that she spent working with Chase and his crew, she realized she simply couldn't leave them in the lurch. Plus, in those moments when she forgot to worry, she realized she was enjoying herself. A great deal.

At the end of the night, Amanda said, “We heard there’s an awesome Mexican restaurant downtown.”

Chase raised an eyebrow. “Everyone had more than enough to drink last night, courtesy of Marcus’s cellar.” When everyone looked crest-fallen, he said, “Okay, maybe one margarita per person. Max two.”

As everyone grinned, Chloe could guess how he was with his sisters. Loving. Protective. Careful with them. But not overwhelming them with rules and regulations.

He was obviously a great brother.

And he’d make a great father.

Father? What was she doing thinking about things like that? she wondered as the thought stopped her in her tracks. But she didn’t have time to dissect it because Jeremy had just asked, “Should we save you guys seats?”

Chloe felt Chase’s eyes on her, knew he wanted her to make the decision to either go with the group and hide out in the crowd like a coward . . . or face him alone.

Planting a smile on her face that she was sure no one bought, she said, “I think I’m going to hang out here at the winery again tonight.”

“I’m going to stay on-site tonight, as well. Have

a good time without us," Chase told his crew and models. "But since I don't want Kalen to have to work any harder than she already is on makeup, make sure you get some sleep tonight, ladies."

When everyone had left, Chloe said, "I'd like to go check on Alice. I hate that she's been all alone today."

Chase nodded. "That's exactly where I was headed."

As they drove over to the hotel where the crew was staying, the silence between them was fraught with all the things Chloe knew couldn't remain unsaid for too much longer. Soon, his patience was going to run out with her. And then she'd have to talk about what had happened. Her throat closed up even thinking about it, and she was glad when they got to Alice's hotel, even if she felt kind of horrible about the fact that Alice's illness was saving her from having to figure out how to be alone with Chase . . . and keep resisting him.

Only, when they knocked on Alice's door and the young woman croaked out, "Who is it?" in a very sleepy voice, Chloe belatedly realized it might have been a better choice to leave Alice alone for the night to sleep off her flu.

"I think we woke her up," she said to Chase right before Alice opened the door.

She looked horribly pale and weak as she said, "Hi, guys." She held up a hand. "Don't come too close, I don't want you to get this." She turned a little green as she put one hand over her stomach and said, "No one should have to feel like this."

"Alice, is there anything we can get you?" Chase asked.

"No," she said, "the nurse you sent over this morning has come back to check on me a couple of times. All I want to do is sleep now."

After saying a quick farewell so that Alice could collapse back on her bed, they headed back to Chase's car.

"Poor thing," Chloe said, and then, "That was really sweet of you to send a nurse out to make sure she was doing all right."

"She got sick on my shoot. It was the very least I could do."

Chase waited until they'd pulled back up in front of the guesthouse before turning to her. "We need to talk."

"I know."

She could feel his eyes on her. Intense. Heated. And a little bit hurt.

"You were going to leave." It wasn't a question.

"Yes," she admitted softly, "I was."

He was silent for a long moment, long enough that her gut twisted tighter and tighter with every moment that ticked by before he asked, "Why?"

She shook her head, hating how difficult it was

to be honest. But knowing she had to be. “I obviously can’t control myself around you.”

Finally, thank God, Chase’s mouth moved up into one of those beautiful smiles of his. “I’m glad.”

“No,” she insisted, “it isn’t a good thing.”

“Why not?” He wanted to know, and she could hear the heat now in his words. Could feel it radiating off him, as a matter of fact. “Why do you think you need to control yourself around me?”

She opened her mouth to tell him all the reasons why, but suddenly, all she could remember was how good it had felt when he was kissing her, how shockingly good his hands had felt as they moved across her skin.

Oh, God, everything had been good. So, so good.

“I—” She stopped, tried to straighten out her head before continuing, but it was difficult when her attraction to Chase was this strong. “We—”

Darn it, instead of her thoughts straightening out, they were spinning off in a crazy direction.

A really crazy direction.

She was changing a lot of things in her life, right? She was going to stop running. She wasn’t going to back down from a threat anymore. And she was going to stand up and take what she wanted when she wanted it.

Lord, did she ever want Chase.

She couldn't be thinking this, knew better than to even go there, but—

"Oh, hell," she muttered.

Chase lifted an eyebrow at her soft curse and she made herself face him squarely.

"I can't believe I'm about to say this." She swallowed, then grasped her hands in front of her in a nervous gesture she couldn't contain. "I honestly don't even know *how* to say it."

"You sure know how to keep a guy on the edge."

Chloe took a deep breath and forced herself to just spit it out. "Maybe we should have a fling."

Just as she'd been able to feel the heat of his desire, now she felt how strong his surprise was at what she'd suggested.

"A fling?"

She could feel a flush moving across her skin. "Sure. Like you said, why not?" Beyond nervous, she started babbling. "Last night was really great and you're right—I was a little drunk, and I probably would have woken up in the morning and felt weird about it all." She forced herself to slow down and to look him straight in the eyes as she said, "But I'm not drunk now."

"No," he said, his intense gaze never once leaving her face, "you're not."

"I've decided I'm going to stay to help. For the rest of the shoot. I'm not going to pack my bag up again and come find you to say goodbye.

No matter what happens, you can count on me."

Somehow, she'd assumed that if she suggested a fling, if she swore to him that she was going to stick around his brother's vineyard until the photo shoot wrapped up, he'd jump all over it. When he didn't, she suddenly felt terribly awkward.

But even as she wondered why he wasn't just grabbing her and taking what she was trying so pathetically to offer, she couldn't stop herself from saying, "You and I obviously have something between us. We're both consenting adults. It just seems to make sense while I'm here and you're here that we could maybe just, well, enjoy that."

Slowly, carefully, he asked her, "Are you saying you want to have sex with me?"

Oh, God. She could almost climax just from the husky sound of his voice . . . and from the thought of actually—finally!—getting to have sex with him.

"Yes." The word came out shaky with need. "A lot."

At that, his mouth quirked up at the two words she'd stolen from his breakfast note.

She could feel, could see, how much he wanted her. And yet, he still wasn't pulling her into his arms, wasn't just taking her right there between the rows of vines under the rising moon.

"Of all the things I thought you were going to

say to me tonight, Chloe," he said slowly, carefully, "this wasn't on the list."

Seriously? She'd just killed herself laying it all out on the line and he was going to be honorable again, wasn't he? That was what all of this was about. That was why he hadn't just taken her already, hadn't dragged her up against him and ripped off her clothes.

She loved that he was trying so hard to think of her own welfare. But not sleep with him now that she'd made the decision to have a fling with him?

No, no, no!

"Kiss me again."

She could see how much he wanted to kiss her, and yet instead of pressing his lips against hers, he used them to say, "I promised myself I wouldn't take anything from you that you didn't want to give."

"I want to kiss you, Chase," she told him in a voice that shook with that wanting. "And I want you to kiss me. All day long I've wanted you to kiss me."

Chase took her hand, hurried up the front steps and kicked open the front door, not stopping in the living room even though it meant waiting another few seconds for the pleasure he'd been craving. He wanted her in a bed, the way he'd been picturing her for forty-eight straight hours, naked and flushed with desire—and pleasure—for him.

In the end it felt like hiking halfway across the county just to get to the bedroom, but then, finally, they were inside the room. Chase closed the door and locked it before forcing himself to drop her hand and step back a few inches. All he wanted was to *take,* but he knew he couldn't. Not until he made sure, one more time, that Chloe would be okay if they did this.

"Are you sure you want to do this?"

"Yes."

She hadn't hesitated, but still he had to ask, "Absolutely certain?"

"Yes."

Again, there was no hesitation, only a growing irritation in her eyes that he was stalling. But he cared about her too much to do anything to hurt her.

"Once we start, I'm not going to be able to stop. I want you too badly."

At that, the faint irritation in her eyes was pushed aside by need, her eyes dilating from the force of her arousal.

He didn't want to scare her—didn't ever want her to be scared again—but she needed to know. "This is your last chance to change your mind."

Before he could take his next breath, her fingers threaded into his hair and her mouth was on his, her tongue pushing against his. He lifted her into his arms and moved to the bed, his mouth never leaving hers for a second. There was no finesse, no gentleness, in their kisses.

How could there be when they were both pure need?

Just that quickly, all thoughts of honor were forgotten.

All that mattered was Chloe. Worshiping her body.

And loving her.

Eleven

Chloe could hardly believe she was lying on the bed looking up at such a sinfully gorgeous man as Chase pulled his T-shirt off and threw it on the floor. Seeing all those muscles, his incredible washboard abs, all but paralyzed her.

She'd never seen anyone like him, live and in person, before.

"You're so beautiful." The words were out of her mouth before she even realized they were coming.

He responded by moving over her on the bed, placing his hands on either side of her face and kissing the rest of the breath from her lungs. One of his legs came between hers and she couldn't stop herself from closing her thighs around him and thrusting her hips up against his taut leg muscles.

She was already so close, knew she could probably come with nothing more than another one of his mind-blowing kisses and the friction of his thigh against her. Heck, she'd almost come just from the sound of his voice a few minutes earlier. That was how strongly he affected her.

"Chloe."

Her name was a whisper of need from his lips to hers, and before she knew it he had her T-shirt and jeans off. When she was wearing nothing but her bra and panties—thank God she'd at least kept her nice lingerie from her earlier life—he shifted away to stare at her.

She knew she wasn't nearly as thin as the models he worked with, knew that her body wasn't perfect, not by any means . . . but, amazingly, she could tell that Chase didn't care.

He liked her just the way she was.

"Jesus, Chloe. You're killing me here." He reached out and ran one slow finger from her chin down her neck, making her arch into his hands as he trailed his gentle, heated touch down to the valley between her breasts. "You're so damned lovely."

"You've already seen my body," she reminded him.

"Not like this. I couldn't touch you then." His eyes lifted from her curves to her face. "And I couldn't kiss you the way I wanted to kiss you."

How did he manage to keep stealing her breath when she was beyond certain that he'd already stolen it completely away just moments before?

"Show me," she pleaded. "Show me how you wanted to kiss me."

She could have sworn a growl rumbled in his chest as he slid one hand into her hair, the other beneath her hips to press her more firmly against him.

His mouth was hot, yet gentle, over hers—that first, desperate rush to have each other turning into such sweetness, such joy, as he tasted every inch of her lips with his, pressing soft kisses into the corners, the flesh at the center, the Cupid's bow of her upper lip. And then his tongue licked along the curve of her lips, a slow, sensuous journey that awakened every last cell in Chloe's body. Until, finally, he dipped his tongue in between her teeth and she met him halfway, taking everything he was giving her and returning it multiplied.

Her entire body had turned soft, pliant against him, and she could feel herself throbbing between her legs.

"Please," she whispered when he lifted his head so that they could draw some oxygen into both their lungs, "I need—"

She hadn't put words to her desire for so long that she found the words drying up on her tongue.

Fortunately, it seemed that he already understood, because instead of pushing her to tell him what she needed, he asked her, "Will you trust me?"

Only, it turned out that wasn't any easier. She wished she didn't have to think about it. But she did. Trust wasn't just something she could give out easily anymore, not even when the beautiful man she was in bed with had proved himself again and again to be kind and gentle.

"I want to."

His smile warmed her from head to toe before he pressed a kiss just below her earlobe. "Wanting to is a perfect place to start."

Loving the fact that he wasn't pressuring her to try and give him something she wasn't capable of giving, as he shifted again on the bed and began to run his tongue across the swell of one breast, she let loose a low moan of pleasure.

From one breast to the other, he didn't rush, didn't hurry despite the desperate sounds she was making. The look he gave her was more than a little wicked when he lifted his head from her chest.

She opened her mouth to try to tell him what she needed, opened her mouth to speak, but again, the words wouldn't come.

"Never be scared to tell me what you need," he told her in a low voice that rumbled over her skin like a sensual caress. "Never be afraid to tell me what you want."

"More." The one word was all she could get out.

His response to her request was to brush the pad of his thumb over one of her breasts, and she actually gasped at the sensation.

She'd never known a smile could be so full of desire until she looked into his eyes. He stroked her nipple again and this time she instinctively arched into his hand. It was so much easier now, with his hands on her, touching her just the right way, to say, "Yes. Please. More of that."

His hands moved behind her back, and then he was pulling her bra off and the air felt cool on the aroused skin of her breasts.

"I'll never, ever get tired of looking at you." Even though his hands were large, her breasts overflowed them. "I'll never stop wanting to touch you."

Somewhere in the back of her brain, an alarm sounded, telling her *never* wasn't the kind of word someone used when they were simply having a fling. But she was too busy holding her breath, waiting for what was coming next, to pay attention to that faint warning.

"I'll never stop wanting to taste you." He lowered his head until the soft hair on the top of his head was brushing against her skin, and then his tongue was flicking out to tease her.

They'd been here last night, with his mouth on her while she melted into a puddle of need, but he hadn't been telling her how much he desired her as he kissed and touched her.

Out on his brother's porch, they'd been stealing a moment. Tonight, there were no limits. And she knew he wouldn't stop after making her come this time.

The only question that remained was, would she get scared and decide to run again? Or would she be brave enough to take all of the pleasure that Chase could give her?

The gentle pull of his lips on her breast, the perfect scratch of his teeth against her sensitive, taut flesh, had the questions scattering away as her entire focus narrowed down to those few square inches that he was torturing so beautifully.

And then he was kissing his way down her stomach, making her squirm as his tongue dipped into the hollow of her belly button. She was lost in sensation when she felt the bed dip again and realized he was kneeling between her legs. A gentle press of his large hands on the inside of her thighs had her opening up for him.

She should have been shy, should have wondered how she could lie there and let him just look at her like that, almost naked except for a pair of fairly indecent panties, but she wanted him so much that she didn't care how long they'd known each other.

Only, a moment later when he pressed his palm against her core and she felt just how wet she was, something in her brain clicked over to memories, bad ones, where she'd been vulnerable like this with another man.

A man who had hurt her.

Chase had been wonderful so far, but what if he turned on her? She didn't really know him. How could she in only forty-eight hours?

Oh, God, what was she doing, lying here spread-eagled for a man who was, for all intents and purposes, a stranger?

"Chase, I—" She tried to close her thighs and covered her breasts with her hands.

He stilled the moment she stiffened and immediately said, "One word and I stop."

She knew what she should do. She should get up off this bed, put her clothes on and try to pretend none of this had ever happened.

But, oh, how she wanted this. How she wanted Chase.

He'd told her just before they'd ripped off each other's clothes that if they started down this road, he wouldn't be able to stop. And yet, here he was, offering to do just that if she needed him to.

It was more than she expected a man to do, but even as she was amazed that he'd done it, she had to wonder why she'd always expected so little.

Finally feeling trust begin to root a little deeper within her heart, she whispered, "What word should I use if I want to stop?"

She was surprised to see his mouth move up into a small smile that also held a great deal of relief in it.

"How about *bananas?*" he suggested.

Amazed to find herself almost smiling back at him, she confirmed, "So if I need to say that word, we'll stop."

He nodded. "Instantly."

She couldn't believe how quickly talking that out—and knowing he'd be true to his word—made the fear recede.

And the heat resurface.

Suddenly, instead of embarrassment, instead of hesitation, there was only need. So much need that as his hand moved between her legs again and found her so slick and hot and ready for him even through the lace fabric of her underwear, she had to press herself even harder against the heel of his hand, had to say his name again as a plea for even more.

"It's even better than I thought it would be," he murmured against her skin.

Somehow, she managed to get her brain to click into gear, to take in what he'd just said. "What's better?"

"You. This." His eyes roved over her body, to the place where his hands were covering her panties, then up over her breasts, to her face. "I've been picturing you like this for so long."

She had to smile then, despite the throbbing

ache between her legs, as she reminded him, "We've only known each other two days."

"It's been a rough forty-eight hours." He moved his palm away from her damp core and slipped his fingers into the side of her lace panties. "Every single second of them, I've wanted to be here with you. Like this."

The way he slid the lace from her hips was pure sensual torture.

And then, she was completely bare before him.

"So damn lovely." The awe in his murmured words made it easy for her not to shut her legs as he stared at her. "And so wet. For *me.*" His hand was back a moment later, sliding over her sex. "All for me."

His touch, his fingers on her, was more than she thought she could bear and her begging shifted gears. "I can't." She panted, feeling wild and out of control. "It's too much." But even as she said it, she knew wild horses couldn't drag the word *bananas* from her.

And when he didn't hear the seven-letter word, he urged her, "Come for me, Chloe."

Her eyes locked onto his in the exact instant that his fingers slid into her and her body obeyed his request. Her back arched, her head fell back against the pillow, her eyes closed tight and she cried out his name. Her orgasm seemed to go on forever until she felt limp. Utterly wrung out. Not sure when she'd be able to even move again.

Until she felt that soft brush of hair against her skin. Not on her chest this time, however.

On the inside of her thighs.

She tried to sit up on her elbows, but her muscles were all still too rubbery. "Chase?"

Her only answer was the slow swipe of his tongue against her most intimate flesh. He cupped her bottom in his hands and dragged her closer to his mouth.

Chloe knew she couldn't possibly come again. Not after the orgasm he'd just given her. She would be good to go for a while now. She opened her mouth to tell him so, but before she could get even one single word out, she realized just how good he was making her feel.

She was still sensitive, but unlike most guys, Chase seemed to understand that without being told. Instead, he focused his attention on drawing perfectly light circles around the flesh that was growing tighter and tighter with every passing second.

She supposed she should have known this was coming, that he wasn't going to stop without tasting her *everywhere.* She'd felt wild when he'd made her come with his fingers, but that wildness had nothing on what came over her when his tongue and fingers started playing her with the genius of a maestro.

"Oh, God. Oh, God. Oh, God."

The second time around she wasn't even sure

when her orgasm started, couldn't spare a thought for how Chase could have possibly gotten her there again so quickly. Lost in a world of sensation, of pure ecstasy, the beauty wasn't just from the way Chase was touching her, licking her.

What she was feeling was all wrapped up in the man himself, in every kind thing he'd said and done for her since that moment by the car.

Sex wasn't just sex anymore. Instead, it was something so much bigger, something utterly interconnected to a part of her heart that had been dead for so long she'd thought it would stay forever buried.

It was that realization that had her falling down from the peak. Way too fast.

She would have tried to hide her reaction from Chase if she could have, but he was too good at reading her.

And she wasn't nearly in the frame of mind to play games.

"Talk to me," he said.

In an instant, he was beside her on the bed, cradling her in his arms. She could feel his erection—still trapped in his jeans, huge and throbbing against her hips—but even though she'd had two orgasms and he'd had none, he clearly wasn't in any hurry to finish what they'd started.

Didn't he realize that only made things worse? That he only scared her more when he acted so sweet, when he put her first? Because he made her want things, long for things she'd tried to convince herself she didn't need anymore.

She shook her head and made herself say, "Just take me." Her breath hitched in her chest, and not just because she was still recovering from two back-to-back climaxes. "I want you to just take me."

But instead of doing what any other guy would have done, he simply raised an eyebrow. And looked even more concerned.

"I will," he promised, "but first I want you to talk to me."

She swallowed. "You already know how much I want you." She gestured to her body. "You would have known that if I hadn't said a single word."

He kissed her then, once on the lips, softly, before saying, "Tell me how you're feeling, lovely girl."

The endearment had her tensed muscles turning to mush again. "Stop doing that."

He frowned. "What am I doing? Did I hurt you?"

"No." Frustration with herself—and with him for being way too awesome—made the word staccato and sharp. "You know you didn't hurt me."

"Then what's wrong?"

"You're too great!"

The three words came out at almost a wail,

and he shifted her in his arms, as if he might understand what she was getting at if they only changed position. A moment later, she found herself flat on her back with Chase levered over her, his weight trapping her against the bed.

"You don't like great?" He was running one hand down her arm as he asked the question.

"I do, but—"

Wrapping his fingers around her wrist, he gently lifted her arm above her head and leaned in to run kisses and love bites up the sensitive skin on the undersides of her arms.

"But what?" he asked between kisses.

"It's just that—" Her words fell away as he repeated the gentle caress and kisses with her other arm, lifting it above her head, too.

"Right there," he murmured, looking down at the way her ribs were arching slightly, lifting her breasts up to his chest. "So pretty." He circled the tip of one breast and it begged for more, tightening beneath the sweet caress of his fingertip.

Oh, God, it was hard to form rational thought when he was doing that, but she had to at least try.

"This is supposed to be sex." His eyes met hers and she clarified, "Just sex."

She watched him go still above her, and when his hand tightened on her wrist at what she'd said, the clarification she'd just made about the fling they were having, for the first time since she'd been in his bed, she couldn't stop herself from thinking how big, how powerful, he was. If he wanted to hurt her, it wouldn't matter if she yelled, "Bananas!" as loud as she could.

"I'm sorry," he whispered when she stiffened. "I won't do that again."

Before she even realized what had happened, he let go of her wrists and had them switch places so that he was lying on his back and she was sitting up, naked and straddling him.

"No fear, Chloe." He brought her hands to his lips and kissed them. "I can't stand to see that frightened look in your eyes when we're together. I won't hold you down again like that. I promised you I'd never hurt you and I meant it."

"I know." The two whispered words floated between them as they stared at each other like that for a long moment.

Emotion pulsed and flowed, rose without ebbing. This was what she was really afraid of, she knew.

Not that Chase would physically overpower her.

But that the strength of his emotions might actually slip in beneath her armor. The armor she needed firmly in place so that she could deal with her problems without completely falling apart.

And yet, at the same time that her heart was

grappling with fear and love and pain and trust, her body was crying out for more.

For Chase.

The way she was sitting on his hips perfectly positioned her over his erection. Even the slightest movement, as small as a breath, had the zipper of his jeans rubbing against her groin. Looking down at Chase, his beautiful, bare chest laid out beneath her for the taking, pure female instinct sent her hands off to explore his muscles, to play in the light dusting of hair on his chest and below his belly button.

"You should be a model," she told him, hardly able to believe that he was really here with her now as she took in his incredible male beauty.

She watched him try to grin, but it never quite replaced the need on his face.

"I'd much rather stay behind the camera," he replied, "but I'm glad you like what you see."

It sounded like he was gritting out each word and she knew why. In this position, his erection had, shockingly, grown even bigger beneath her.

"I want to see more of you," she said softly.

Sliding a little lower down his body, she was barely aware of the fact that her bare breasts were directly over his face as she concentrated on undoing the zipper of his jeans.

He tried to distract her by cupping her breasts and tasting both at once. She moaned and nearly gave in to him, to the delicious persuasion of his lips and tongue and teeth. But God, she wanted him naked, too, wanted to see all of him just as badly as he'd seemed to want to see her bared and spread before him.

With increased focus, she slid his zipper down the rest of the way, and even behind the fabric of his boxers his erection jumped toward her. She tried to take his jeans off, but her hands were suddenly shaking.

"I'm right there with you," he said in a husky voice before he took matters into his own hands and took care of his clothes.

Chloe knew better than to stare. She wasn't a virgin. But no naked male she'd ever seen in person—or even in a photo—had looked like Chase. His stomach rippled with muscles; his biceps and triceps flexed as he pulled off the final pieces of his clothes to reveal long, strong muscles running down his thighs.

She couldn't stop the thought that he was built like a knight.

Her knight.

And then he was kissing her, both of their naked bodies pressed against each other, and just that skin-to-skin contact, the feel of him, hot and hard, the hair on his legs scratching against her, the muscles of his stomach and chest and arms pressing into her, was the most erotic thing she'd ever experienced. Even more than her orgasms.

Her words "You feel so good" were out and

between them before she could hold them back.

"So damn good," was his response, and this time she was the one kissing him, wanting to climb inside of him and never come out into the real world again.

Complete. She felt complete with him. Except, as her body reminded her, for one thing.

She needed him inside of her.

Now.

Her hips moved into place over his and she was so close—oh, God, just one more inch and he'd be pressing against her, into her—when his hands moved to her hips and held her still. "Wait a second."

Misunderstanding him, thinking the whole honorable thing was popping back up at just the worst possible time, she said, "I want it, Chase. I want you inside of me. So, so bad." Her desire was so big, so overpowering, that she momentarily lost her fear of speaking what she wanted aloud.

She belatedly realized he was tearing something open. A condom wrapper. Another time she would ask him where it came from, but right now, all she cared about was getting it on him.

And getting him in her.

Together, they worked to slide the latex protection over his hard shaft, and then he was lifting her again, over him. The first press of his thick, broad head into her made her breath come out in a gasp.

"We'll go slow," he told her, but she didn't want to go slow.

She wanted all of him. She wanted fast. She wanted hard. She wanted to be so full of Chase that there was no room for anything else, no room for fear or worry or thoughts of what the future might hold.

She looked straight at him, let herself fall into his beautiful eyes, so intense, so full of desire and arousal . . . yet so gentle all at the same time.

"I want you." Her words rang out like a vow in the bedroom.

"Then take me."

He was making it her choice. Despite how hard he was, despite the fact that he could be inside her before she even blinked, he was still making sure he didn't take anything she wasn't ready to give.

She sank down onto his shaft with a moan of deep, deep pleasure. When they were groin to groin, she stilled over him to appreciate how good he was making her feel. Beneath her, she could feel how tense every muscle was, but he let her settle deeper onto him at her own pace.

She began to lift off him—wanting to feel that delicious slide of heat and power, wanting him to make her entirely his—and her inner muscles clenched tight around him.

"Chloe, sweetheart."

She put her hands on his chest and felt how fast, how hard, his heart was beating beneath her palms.

And then she was riding him until her thigh muscles were screaming out, and he was driving into her, farther, deeper, than she thought he could go. Nothing had ever felt like this.

She had never felt like she could fly before.

Oh, how she flew, higher and higher until she was crying out Chase's name and he was rolling them over, his heavy weight crushing her into the mattress as he moved with her, up to the peak and then over.

Chase had done more than show her how to fly.

He'd flown with her.

Chloe woke up the next morning just as Chase was about to leave the bedroom.

She waited for regret to move through her at waking up in a man's bed, expected fear to pulse through her veins at the way she'd naively trusted him.

Her belly did feel a little tight. But apart from that, she was surprised to realize that she felt pretty good.

Verging on great, actually.

Pushing her hair out of her face, she sat up. Shocked by the way her muscles were protesting the sudden movement, she felt herself flush as she said, “How long have you been up?”

He moved back across the room to her, his long, strong limbs, his innate power and beauty, taking her breath away all over again as he answered with a soft kiss, followed by, “Good morning.”

One kiss turned into another, and then another, until all she could think about was how much she needed him.

“You have no idea how much I want to stay here with you,” he whispered into the curve of her neck right before his tongue came out to taste the skin below her earlobe.

She shivered, wanting him to stay with her—wanting him to be inside her again—so much she thought she might burst apart with her need. If circumstances had been different, maybe she would have pulled him down onto the bed with her and convinced him to let his professional responsibilities slide for an hour. But she couldn’t stand the thought of being any more trouble than she’d already been.

So instead of pulling him closer, she laid her hands flat on his chest. “They’ll all be waiting for you.”

His eyes were dark, full of desire, as he looked down at her. With a badly muffled curse, he straightened up. As soon as he stepped back, she threw off the covers.

“I’ll just be a second.”

“I’m heading over early to set up. You don’t need to rush.” He moved closer again, pulled her naked body against him. “God, you’re lovely. You make me want to call off the shoot today and just stay locked in this room with you.”

She wanted the same thing, but that want was too big, like an ocean trying to swell and crash inside of her, so she joked, “We’d starve.”

“What’s one day without food if I’ve got you?”

She knew he couldn’t be serious, and yet, he sure looked like he was.

Stepping out of his arms, she headed for the bathroom. “I just need five minutes and then I’ll come help you with the shoot today.”

His eyes were dark with the desire that was always there . . . and something she needed a moment to put her finger on.

“I really appreciate your help, Chloe.”

That was it, she realized as warmth spread through her. He appreciated her. And not just because of what had gone on between them in bed.

They smiled at each other. She was just leaning in to turn on the shower when she heard him say her name again.

Feeling surprisingly comfortable being naked around him, she said, “Mmm?”

“Remember that first night I found you in the tub?”

Another flush accompanied her smile. “I honestly don’t think I’ll ever be able to forget.”

"Me, either," he agreed with a wicked grin that said he had no intention of ever forgetting, and then, "I can't help but wonder what would have happened next if we'd known each other better that night."

"You're not the only one," she murmured as she turned on the hot water and stepped beneath the spray. She could feel Chase's eyes on her through the glass door, even after it had fogged up.

Chloe smiled, feeling pretty and so wonderfully feminine as she soaped up and washed her hair. She had already been looking forward to tonight, after the shoot was done, when she and Chase could do all those wonderful things they'd done the night before.

But now that he'd put that image in her head of the bathtub, of what the two of them could do together in it . . . now her anticipation was all but running away with her.

By the time she got out of the shower, Chase had left the room. She wrapped one towel around her hair and another around her body. As she blow-dried her hair, she tried not to look too closely at the bruise on her cheek. It was fading a little bit. She'd actually forgotten about it last night when she and Chase were making love. Because he didn't look at her like she had anything wrong with her.

Because he looked at her like she really was lovely.

Moving back into the bedroom, she saw that Chase had folded her jeans and T-shirt and placed them on a soft chair in the corner. God, she'd like to burn those clothes. But they'd been what she was wearing to paint her little apartment a more cheerful color when her ex had surprised her.

Yesterday, she'd forced herself to put the horrible clothes back on because she'd been planning to leave after saying goodbye to Chase. But now that she wasn't leaving until the end of the shoot, she couldn't help but think of the rack of beautiful clothes in the living room.

Clothes she didn't have the money to pay for.

Her stomach sank as she looked again at her ratty jeans. Would it really hurt if she wore another new outfit or two? She would pay Chase back as soon as she could.

Knowing she was rationalizing things, she made herself face the real reason for wanting to wear the new clothes: it would be as good as a promise to Chase that she really wasn't going to leave. She owed him that, at the very least.

She poked her head into the living room to make sure no one else was inside the guesthouse before walking over to the rack of clothes. "Just coming to find something to wear," she explained to Chase.

His answering smile told her he understood the message she was sending him. Chloe had never been able to say so much to a man without saying a thing. Probably because she'd never been able to find a man who really understood her.

Not until now.

The thought made her legs a little shaky as she headed for the rack of clothes.

"The clothes are going to look great," he said just before tugging at the towel around her body as she walked past, pulling it down below one breast, "but this might be even better."

And then his lips were on her, tugging, sucking, and she was dissolving into one big puddle of need. "You're going to be late," she reminded him breathlessly.

"Don't care." His words were muffled against her other breast, which he'd uncovered with another tug at the towel. A moment later, it was on the floor and he was lifting her up onto his lap, her legs going around his waist.

Someone could come in, Marcus could stop by any second, one of the models or Jeremy might need a word with Chase before the shoot began. But instead of voicing all—or any—of those concerns, Chloe worked to unbutton and unzip his jeans.

He pulled a condom from a pocket and then—*oh, yes!*—a moment later he was lifting her hips up and then down over him and he was driving into her. Their mouths devoured each other and his hands were busy, one cupping and squeezing the curve of her ass as she rode him in the seat, the other on her breast, teasing her sensitive flesh between his thumb and forefinger, a beautifully sensual pressure that shot straight through her to her core.

She was coming that fast, her inner muscles squeezing and clenching around his shaft until he pulled her even closer and groaned her name into their kiss.

Her heart raced as she tucked her head against the crook of his neck. He tasted clean and sexy, like a man who'd just given a woman incredible pleasure at the kitchen breakfast bar.

"Just like I said," he murmured against her hair, "I'll take you over breakfast any day."

She couldn't believe she was sitting there, naked on his lap, her legs still wrapped around him, with a smile on her face.

But she was.

"Last night . . . now . . . it's been amazing. Just amazing."

She felt his arms tighten on her for a moment, wondered if it had been the wrong thing to say, to tell him what she was feeling when she was in his arms.

But then, he was giving her bottom a light smack and saying, "Go find some clothes before I take you back to the bedroom and make us really late," and the easiest thing was just to tell herself that everything was okay.

Their fling was going great. And it was still just a fling.

Definitely just a fling.

Ten minutes later, they were headed out to the vineyards. Wisps of early-morning fog lingered beneath a rising sun that promised warmth. And yet, despite the beauty all around them, despite the fact that the shoot was going well, despite the fact that Chloe had willingly trusted her body with him again and again, something grated inside of Chase.

No question about it. Chloe was right. Their night together had been beyond amazing.

But the whole honor thing was still bothering him, a feeling that he should have had more control, that he should have waited until she was even more ready for everything he wanted to give her—and that he should have waited until more than just her body wanted to be with him.

Because he wanted more from her than just a few nights. He wanted a hell of a lot more than just a fling.

They were standing near Marcus's huge infinity pool, which looked out over the rolling hills, when his brother walked over to say, "Good morning."

Chloe turned to his brother with a wide smile. "Hi, Marcus." She gestured over the pool. "You really have a lovely home."

Chase watched Chloe flush as the adjective she'd used registered.

Lovely. It was his special word for her.

"It's just stunning," she amended a moment later, as if she had recognized the same thing, that the word was now off-limits for anything but what he saw when he looked at her.

They all took a moment to appreciate the killer view. Marcus turned to Chase. "Sorry I wasn't able to check in with you yesterday. Something came up in the city that I needed to go deal with."

Chase didn't have to hear Jill's name to guess that it had to do with her. "Everything okay?"

His brother's eyes held shadows that Chase hated to see. Damn it, if anyone deserved to be happy it was Marcus. Especially after he'd given up so much of his own life for Chase and his six brothers and sisters . . . and still did.

"Anything you need my help with, just let me know." Chase made sure to keep his offer light, easy. But he wanted to make sure Marcus knew he was there to be a sounding board for whatever was going on with Jill. Just because Chase didn't really like her, didn't mean he couldn't help, right?

Jeremy rounded the corner, saying, "Who's got coffee?" in a voice that sounded like death. When he saw Marcus standing there, he stumbled and would have fallen into the pool if Chloe hadn't caught his arm in the nick of time.

"M-Marcus, hi."

"Good morning, Jeremy," Marcus said with a small smile for Chase's assistant. "Feel free to have at my coffeemaker."

Their parents had raised them to accept everyone—gay, straight, whatever—and Marcus had always dealt well with Jeremy's adoration, careful not to feed into it, or give any false hope, without being mean about it.

Still, when Jeremy opened and closed his mouth without actually saying anything, Chase was glad when Chloe wrapped her hand more firmly around his arm, and said, "I'll go with you to make coffee and you can tell me what we're working with today. I can't wait to get my hands on more beautiful clothes."

When they'd disappeared inside the house, Marcus said, "Is Chloe working for you now?"

Chase quickly explained about Alice getting sick and Chloe filling in.

"Sounds like she's saving the day left and right for you," Marcus noted. He looked back into the house where they could see Chloe and Jeremy laughing together as she made Jeremy that much-needed cup of coffee. "Have you thought about adding her to your permanent team?"

"I want her to be more than a part of my team."

Marcus didn't say anything for a long moment as he turned his gaze back to Chase. "Have you told her this?"

"No." He already knew what she'd say if he did. That it was too fast. That she wasn't ready for more. That it was just a *fling*. "I need to find out what happened to her the night I picked her up first."

Marcus's eyebrows went up in surprise. "She hasn't told you yet?"

"No, she hasn't. Not yet."

"But you're obviously sleep—"

Chase cut his brother's sentence off with a killing look, and Marcus held his hands up. "Look, you know I like her. She's great. Really great. But if you've asked her what happened and she won't tell you, then maybe you should do a background check, or ask people we know in San Francisco to see what they know."

Even as Chase shook his head at his brother's suggestions, he appreciated what Marcus was doing, that he was trying to help. But they'd always been different personalities. Marcus took over for people and did whatever he could to solve their problems. Whereas Chase believed in being patient. Over the years he'd honed his patience as he'd waited for the perfect light, for the perfect shadows, for the perfect colors and the perfect subjects for his photos.

He knew deep in his gut that Chloe didn't need someone to solve her problems. Instead, she needed someone to love her, to support her, while *she* solved them.

Soon, very soon, he hoped she'd trust him with what had happened.

The only problem was that even then, even if she eventually trusted him with her past, with her troubles, he wasn't yet convinced she'd choose to stay with him . . . or that she'd choose to love him.

Chloe did even better her second full day of working on the shoot, as if she'd been born to the job. Even when he did a host of water shots, needing each of the models to get into the water, she wasn't afraid to get right in there with them. After falling in, she emerged with a giggle, then repeatedly held her breath and went under the water to make adjustments with needle and thread and clips and pins.

He was switching to a different camera when he was stopped by the sweet sound of her laughter. Unable to keep from staring, he saw her there in the pool, surrounded by sun and blue sky and a group of people who had all come to quickly adore—and respect—her.

Dinner with the models and crew that night was full of laughter, especially when Jeremy urged Chase to share his stories of life on the road.

As flan was brought out for everyone, Chloe was wiping away moisture from her eyes from laughing at one of his better tales. "Please, be serious. No matter what anyone says, I refuse to believe you actually walked into the cage at the zoo with the lions."

"I most certainly did," he said in a mock-offended voice. "They were eating out of my hands."

"More like preparing to eat your hands," she shot back.

He shrugged, spooning up some dessert to feed to her. He couldn't have been more pleased when she ate it off his spoon without even the slightest hesitation.

"See," he said for her ears only, "eating right out of my hands."

She rolled her eyes, but the flush that began to creep across her cheeks told him she was only just realizing how close the two of them had been tonight. He'd repeatedly touched her hands, brushed stray locks of hair away from her expressive face and just plain stared at her like a lovesick teenager all night long.

"Did your mother know you did this?"

He grimaced. "Not exactly."

Everyone else was talking about other things by now, but Chloe clearly didn't want to drop the story about the lion photos. "Please tell me you were younger. And way stupider."

He put on his most solemn face. "I was." He waited a beat. "It's been at least a year since that assignment." He could see her trying not to smile. And failing. "Would you have been worried about me, lovely Chloe?"

Her mouth parted slightly at the word *lovely* and he realized his mistake when he went from half-mast to rock-hard in a millisecond. He'd needed to join his crew and models tonight for dinner. But every second he was here with the group was one less he was alone with Chloe.

"Would it have mattered if I was?"

He held her gaze, suddenly serious. "Yes, it would have mattered. If I had known you back then, I never would have risked everything for the perfect photo."

"No?"

He slid his hand over hers beneath the table. "No."

But he'd risk everything for her.

Thirteen

Later that night, as soon as they stepped inside the guesthouse, Chase kissed Chloe the way he'd been dying to kiss her all day. He kissed his way from her sweet mouth to the pulse point in her neck and felt her heart race beneath his lips, his tongue.

"You have such lovely, soft skin." He slid the straps of her silky top from her shoulders. "Such lovely, responsive breasts." He pressed kisses over the swells that rose up out the top of her bra. "And you make such lovely little sounds when I'm kissing you."

When he looked back into her eyes, they were dark with desire. Along with the growing emotion she simply wasn't able to hide from him.

He'd wanted to take his time with her tonight, wanted to love her slow and easy, take all night if he had to. Instead, he was saying, "I can't wait another second," just as she said, "Hurry." She slipped her panties off as he yanked off his pants and boxers.

"Please tell me you have a condom," she said and, thank God, he did have one that he'd stashed in his pocket that morning just in case an opportunity arose to sneak away from the shoot and make love to her.

A moment later he was sheathed and lifting her up so that her dress was bunched up around her waist. She had her arms wrapped around his neck, her legs around his hips as he drove into her.

She gasped out his name and he found her mouth and kissed her. But it was more than a kiss. And what they were doing together was so much more than a quickie against the front door.

Chloe's tongue laved the spot on his shoulder where she'd bitten down into a tendon as she'd come apart in his arms. "I didn't mean to hurt you." She looked stunned by what she'd done to his skin. "I've never done anything like that before."

Beyond glad that she was starting to really let herself go with him, he said, "You're the one who's going to have bruises from the door if I don't get you into the bath right away."

Her legs still wrapped around his hips, he carried her through the house to the bedroom. Continuing to the bathroom, he kept her right there on his lap as he turned on the taps and tested the water. "Perfect."

After pulling her dress off and removing her bra, he lowered her into the tub. She seemed reluctant to let go of him.

"Aren't you coming in, too?"

He didn't say anything at first, just let himself drink her in. He loved the way she'd held on to him. Being with her like this was so natural, so right. Chase knew he could never be with a woman who spent her life worrying about what she ate, about whether or not she had cellulite or a little extra flesh on her stomach. He spent all day with women—and men—who were obsessed with what was on the outside.

Chloe's natural self-confidence, which he was watching return by leaps and bounds with every hour that passed, along with her very real beauty, was the perfect antidote to all of that self-conscious preening. He loved the fact that her nails weren't painted, that she wasn't waxed bald between her thighs, that she hadn't dyed her hair or whitened her teeth. She looked like a woman should.

"You're staring at me."

"Yes, I am. And you're so beautiful that I'm going to be staring a whole lot more."

She blushed. "Come join me in the tub."

But even though he was desperate to get in the water with her, all day he'd been thinking about the conversation they'd had that morning.

"Remember that first night I found you in the tub?"

"I honestly don't think I'll ever be able to forget."

"You're in the bathtub again." He paused. "And we know each other better now."

"We certainly do," she said softly.

The question hung silently between them: What would have happened that night if she'd trusted him? And was there any chance that she trusted him enough now for what he was asking her to do?

There was only one way to find out.

"I've wondered a hundred times how that night could have played out differently," he told her in a low voice.

And then he saw it—renewed excitement and arousal moving across her beautiful face. Looking down at the water, she licked her lips and took a deep breath. When she looked back up at him, she was transformed: a sensuous creature from head to toe.

"Why don't we find out?" She didn't give him any time to catch his breath before she said, "I think I'm going to soap up now." Her voice was husky, and almost enough to have him forgetting about the whole thing and just diving in there to pull her down over him again.

Instead, he made himself take one step back, and then another, until he was backed up against the sink. He yanked off his T-shirt and stood there naked, his erection throbbing hard against his stomach as he watched her reach for the soap.

That first night when he'd walked in on her in the tub, he should have left the room immediately. But wild horses couldn't have dragged him away. Hell, the entire house could have been falling down around them and he still would have stood there, unable to do anything but stare at Chloe in awe.

Tonight, he was again standing in the bathroom, watching her slowly, sensuously, begin to run a bar of soap down her outstretched legs. She had such smooth skin, such pretty thigh and calf muscles, such lovely toes.

Slowly, she lowered her leg back into the water, then lifted the other.

His erection was a living thing against his lower stomach, a heartbeat away from dragging the rest of him across the room and into the tub to get at her. Knowing he had to hold on to something to keep from reaching for her, he grabbed a towel off the rack beside him and gripped it tight enough to tear it in two.

Chloe didn't need to look at Chase to feel the heady strength of his desire from across the room. She loved how powerful she felt, teasing him this way. And she loved the fact that he wanted it just as much as she did.

God, she thought with a barely repressed moan, it was going to be so good when he finally joined her in the tub.

It was so tempting just to give in to that need, to throw the soap down and reach out for the gorgeous man standing on the other side of the bathroom watching her with utter lust.

But the anticipation of that moment would only make it sweeter when it finally came.

Still, she had to work really, really hard to keep her voice steady as she continued to play their sexy game. "Just give me a sec, okay? And then you can hand me that towel." She couldn't repress a small smile as she looked at him and said, "You don't mind waiting, do you?"

"No."

Not bothering to hide her grin at how strangled the one short word had sounded, she dipped the lavender-scented bar of soap back into the water.

Once wet, she began the slow process of running it over her collarbones, and then lower, and lower still.

The tips of her breasts had already beaded tightly beneath the heat of his gaze, but as she came closer and closer to them with the suds, she couldn't believe how much more sensitive her skin felt. Almost as if one touch from her soapy fingers—combined with the devastating desire in Chase's eyes—would be enough to have her crying out his name again.

The soap slipped from her fingers and water splashed up onto her face.

Chase's voice came from across the bathroom, low and borderline desperate. "I think the bar of soap slipped between your legs."

She had no idea what came over her then, how on earth a wanton seductress could have taken her over so quickly. If ever there was a time and place for reticence—for fear—to lift their ugly heads, it was here. It was now. And the truth was, a large part of her was shocked by how her hidden desires were bubbling up one after the other with Chase . . . and that she was actually letting them out.

The smart, rational thing would be to end the game right away, before it went any further. She should be doing everything she could to keep the truth of who she really was from Chase, should be making sure that he could never come back one day in the future and hurt her with it.

But when she looked up at him, she simply couldn't find a way to reconcile all of those fears with the beautiful man clutching the towel for dear life. And, ultimately, her body didn't really care about her latent fears at present, or the fact that he was so far out of her league with his glamorous lifestyle, while she'd been barely scraping by as a waitress. Not when such beautiful satisfaction awaited her in his arms.

Which was why she found herself saying, "Maybe I would have better luck looking for it on my hands and knees."

Chase blew out a pained breath. "I'm not sure I'm going to survive this."

Moving slowly, carefully, in the slick and soapy tub, she sat up until she was kneeling. Water streamed off her breasts. Reaching into the water for the soap, she said, "Ah, there it is, slippery little sucker."

A moment later she was going fully onto her hands and knees, lifting enough out of the water that she could feel cool air rushing between her thighs, over her belly, before picking the soap up and moving back into a kneeling position.

She could hear Chase's heavy breathing as she pushed her wet hair off her chest and shoulders with her free hand, then ran the bar of soap over her collarbones, over her arms, across her stomach and then, finally, her breasts.

She ran the soap over one breast, and as her nipple stiffened into an ever tighter point, he groaned. The truth was, Chloe could barely stifle her own whimper of need as she asked, "Everything okay, Hotstuff?"

She had no idea how she managed to ask the question in such a steady voice.

He choked out a strangled laugh at his nickname. The nickname she'd given him that first night when he'd walked in on her in the bathtub. "Everything is perfect." His voice wasn't quite as steady as hers. He nodded at her naked body in the tub. "You're going to be really clean."

Yes, she would. Because she wasn't done yet. Not by a long shot.

Cupping her hands in the water, she lifted them and poured water down her chest. Suds washed down over her breasts and rib cage and stomach.

When she'd washed the soap off her chest, she picked up the bar of soap and looked straight at Chase. A muscle was jumping in his jaw, and his hands were tightly fisted on the sides of the towel. She couldn't see his hard-on behind the towel, but she didn't need to.

"Just one more place I need to get nice and clean." She didn't take her eyes from her hot voyeur as she lifted up to balance on her knees, allowing the cooler air to caress her skin. She moved her knees apart several inches in the bottom of the tub, then took the soap and placed it just below her belly button.

Chloe felt like she was all nerve endings. The soap slipped away from her again, but this time she wasn't about to retrieve it from the bottom of the tub. She desperately needed to touch herself and her breath left her lungs in a rush as her fingertips brushed over her sex.

"Don't stop." Chase's breath was coming out just as fast as hers. "Please don't stop."

She let her fingers continue stroking, sliding through her wetness until she could feel the tremors building from way down deep. Suddenly, he was there with her, his large body wrapped around her, his warmth taking away any chill that remained. In one hard stroke he pushed inside her to the hilt and she pushed back against him just as hard, wanting him even deeper, even closer.

The water splashed all around the room as he held her steady with one arm around her waist while driving into her again and then again as she begged him for *more, more, more* until the orgasm she'd been teasing him with joined with Chase's impending release, swelling big enough to break through her entire soul like a tidal wave.

Chloe smiled at him as he dried her off and Chase loved the way she leaned into his touch, rather than away from it as she once had. Picking her up, he moved to the chair in the corner of the bedroom and pulled her onto his lap. She curled into him like a contented kitten.

"Thank you for trusting me."

Her head shot up from where she'd had it against his chest. Wariness had crept back into her expression as she said, "I like you, Chase. A lot. But—"

He should just keep his damned mouth shut. He should enjoy what they were doing and give her more time. But, damn it, he was ready now. And he wanted Chloe to be ready, too.

"I know you won't trust me completely yet. Even if I don't like it, I understand. At least, I think I do." He waited for her to say something about what had happened to her, and when she didn't, he worked to push down the disappointment. But he knew he'd blown it when the words, "I don't want no-strings-attached," shot out of his mouth.

She immediately stiffened on his lap and tried to pull away. Just as he'd known she would.

"But that's our agreement."

"No. I never agreed."

"You did!"

"You wanted no-strings-attached and I was hoping I could convince you otherwise. Just like I'm hoping you'll allow yourself to trust me completely one day."

"I'm not looking for a relationship. You know that."

"Yes, but I don't know why. Tell me what happened."

"I didn't run from one guy to end up diving straight into a relationship with another one," she began, and he could hear the reticence in the tone of her voice, could see how much she wanted to end their conversation in the lines that appeared at the sides of her mouth.

Her hand lifted to cover her cheek again and it nearly killed him not to put his hand over hers and pull it back down.

Which was why he'd never admired her more than he did when she dropped her hand and said, "But you're right. It's not fair for me to be so vague. Not to tell you what happened." She sighed and her eyes filled with shadows. "In a nutshell, I was married and it wasn't great."

"Even from the beginning?"

She shook her head. "No. At first it seemed great. Well, okay, at least." She scrunched up her nose. "Honestly, I've asked myself that question a hundred times. Why did I fall in love with Dean in the first place?" She took a deep breath, one that shook through her all the way to his lap. "You know what I think I've figured out?" she asked in a very soft voice.

More glad than he could ever express that she was finally talking to him like this, he gently replied, "What's that?"

"When we were looking at your family picture

and every time you talk about them . . ." Her words fell away momentarily before she continued, "I wanted that. So badly. I wanted to be part of a family that was warm and fun and loved me."

"You were an only child?"

She nodded. "But it wasn't just that. My parents have never really been that open with their feelings. I know they love me, but I can't remember ever hearing it. I don't remember many hugs."

Chase's heart broke for the little girl inside of Chloe that longed for those hugs. He wanted to make up for each and every one of those hugs she hadn't gotten, starting now, he thought as he pulled her closer against his chest.

"When I met Dean I was young and stupid and desperately looking for that warmth." Her eyes lifted to meet his. "Turns out I had awful instincts—at least, I did when I wanted something so badly to be true that wasn't." She shrugged as if she was trying to make it all less of a big deal. "He was nice at first. And I was so happy to finally feel like I had somebody. That I was part of a team. But we weren't really a team. After a few years, Dean started to control me, what I did, who I saw. He liked keeping me as a pretty possession. Like his fancy house and his shiny car. I was just one more pretty thing to bring out from the locked cabinet to show off to people."

Chase wanted to say a thousand different

things to Chloe about how stupid her ex had been. He wanted to tell her it wasn't her fault for believing he'd been a better, kinder man than he actually was. He wanted to rage at the unfairness that her ex had turned on her.

But Chase didn't want to do or say anything that would make her stop talking to him. So he forced himself to swallow it all and simply ask, "When did you decide to leave?"

"One day I was sitting at the country club with a bunch of his friends' wives that I really didn't have anything in common with, and I realized I'd been entirely swallowed up by him. I tried to talk to him about it, but he wasn't interested in listening." She swallowed hard. "That was the first time he scared me."

Chase worked to keep his muscles from tensing with rage beneath her. "What did he do?"

"Nothing physical. But he'd started drinking more and more and it was like he wasn't listening to anything I'd said. When I woke up the next morning, all of my quilting stuff was gone. My fabric. My machines. Everything."

This time Chase couldn't stop himself from saying, "What an asshole."

Her mouth was tight as she said, "A few weeks later, after I finally accepted what the rest of my empty life was going to look like with a man who didn't actually love me, I filed for divorce and I moved to Lake County."

"Somehow you must have known it wasn't safe for you to stay in the city."

She shook her head, saying, "No," then paused, frowning. "Maybe. Maybe that's why I felt like I had to leave." Her frown deepened. "I love San Francisco," she told him, "but I felt like I needed to start fresh. I didn't want his money, I just wanted my freedom back. Freedom to work on my quilts. Freedom to choose my own friends. Even the freedom to wear ratty jeans or shoes that don't have a designer name on them. My apartment never really felt like home, even though I wanted it to. Even though I needed it to." She blew out a breath. "But that was okay. I told myself I could eventually make it home, because I thought filing for divorce, leaving him and moving away had worked. I didn't hear from him for months, so I thought he'd accepted the divorce." She moved her hand up to her cheek and touched the fading bruise. "Evidently, he hadn't."

"What happened the night I found you?" Chase could hardly get the words out between clenched teeth.

Her eyes darkened. "I was getting ready to paint my living room when I heard someone at the door." He could feel the shock of that memory radiating from her tight muscles. "Dean was standing there and I was so surprised to see him I let him in without thinking, without even once second-guessing that I wasn't safe with him. But then I realized he was drunk. I don't know how I could have forgotten how much he was drinking toward the end, but I had. I don't know, maybe I made myself forget things I didn't like remembering."

"That's natural, Chloe."

But it was like she couldn't hear him, couldn't do anything but relive what had happened with her ex-husband.

"He said, 'You're not getting away from me. You're mine.' I couldn't believe he had the nerve to come to my new town, to stand in the middle of my apartment and tell me that. I didn't think not to be angry, not to say that I wasn't his. I told him to go away, that we'd talk later when he wasn't drunk."

Chase knew what came next. "There's nothing worse for a drunk than hearing that he's a drunk."

She nodded. "He told me to shut up and said that he'd made the mistake of letting me get away with too much when we were married and that this time he wouldn't."

Chase echoed the words, "This time?"

She closed her eyes. "His exact words were, 'You're coming home with me right now. And this time you'll do what I tell you to do.' "

Chase barely bit back a string of curses as she continued, saying, "He'd never been like that before, had never just outright scared me. But I didn't want to back down, didn't want him to think he could control me anymore. So I told him I was already home. I told him I wasn't going anywhere with him and that I wanted him to leave. Now." Her words hollowed out even more than they already had. "He lost it and grabbed my hair and when I pulled away he punched me."

She lifted her hand to her cheek, but he was already there with his, cradling her soft skin, wishing like hell that she'd never had to be hurt. Knowing he never wanted her to be hurt again.

"I was stunned for a minute. I honestly couldn't believe what he'd just done. I kept waiting for him to start apologizing, to admit that he was completely out of control. But the look on his face, it wasn't sorry. It was like he was finally victorious, looking at me there with his mark on my face. I was so freaked out that he was going to do it again, or something worse, that I didn't think. I just grabbed the nearest paint can and swung it at him. And then while he was down, I grabbed my bag and ran."

She was shaking from recounting the story to him and he hated that he'd asked her to go there, that he'd made her relive it all.

"Chloe, sweetheart, you're all right now."

She closed her eyes tight. "Do you know what I was doing the whole time I was driving away in the rain? I kept wondering, why was I so stupid? That's probably why I crashed into the ditch.

Because I couldn't pay attention to anything but that voice in my head that said I should have seen it coming."

"Looking for the good in people is never stupid."

She opened her eyes. "But being blind and naive is." She gave him a small smile that never reached her eyes, before moving her hand from her face to his. "I know you must have guessed some of this as soon as you saw the bruise on my cheek. But thank you for not pressuring me to call the police. I will. I know I have to. For once in my life, I've got to fight for myself. For my own life. And know deep inside myself that I can win that fight."

From the moment Chase had met Chloe, every last one of his protective urges had come to the fore. Again and again, he'd wanted to jump in and take care of everything for her.

Never more than right this second. He wanted to get in his car and track down the bastard and make sure he never came near her again, make absolutely sure he never had another chance to lay a hand on her.

Only, damn it, he knew that if he did that, if he wrapped Chloe up tight and made sure everything was soft and easy for her from here on out, wasn't that nearly as bad as the way her ex-husband had stolen her freedom from her?

How was he going to find a way to love her without smothering her need to be free?

"You'll win." He knew it with every fiber of his being.

Her fingertips moved across his lips. "So much faith in me," she said softly. "I'm so glad you were the one who found me in the storm."

But they both knew that didn't really change anything. Because he couldn't just tell her, "Hey, you know what? I think you're ready for a new relationship." Not when she'd just made it abundantly clear to him that she wasn't.

As if she were reading his mind, she said, "So if I can't be your girlfriend, is that it?" Her words were soft, but clear. And steady, even as she added, "Does that mean this is over?"

Chase had never been so torn between what he wanted . . . and what he knew he should do. But Chloe had just been completely honest with him, despite all the reasons she could have come up with not to trust him.

He owed her the same.

"I should say yes," he finally gritted out against her fingertips. "If I had one single ounce of decency, I would say, yes, it's over." He took her hand in his. "But obviously I'm just as much of a scumbag as any other guy, because the thought of not touching you again, of not kissing you again, of not making love with you again . . ." His gut clenched tight, as if an invisible fist had gripped it. "I can't even imagine it."

He held her gaze, knowing his was as dark, as

heated, as hers. Chase knew he shouldn't keep pressuring her to give him things she wasn't anywhere near ready to give, even as he said, "If the choice is to take what you're offering or to walk away, I choose this. I choose you. I choose whatever you're willing to share with me. Even though I'm never going to stop wanting more from you than just awesome sex. Even though I'm always going to want to change your mind."

"Chase, I—"

He put a finger over her lips. "I know you're not ready and I know I shouldn't push you. I know it sounds crazy that anyone could fall this fast. I know it might not seem like it makes any sense, but damn it, I don't care if it's crazy. And I don't care if it makes sense or not. I can't help the way I feel. And I can't stop myself from loving you."

Chloe's eyes got big at the word *love* and a moment later, when she scrambled off his lap with sudden, fierce strength, it took everything Chase had to let her go.

Chloe had been honest. Painfully so.

So had Chase.

She'd even offered to walk away from him. She'd tried to be honorable, just as he'd been with her.

But Chase was clearly a realist. Just as she was. And they both knew that their physical connection was undeniable. Unstoppable.

"I know you don't want to hear that I'm falling in love with you," he said softly. "But that doesn't make it any less true."

Oh, God, she shouldn't want to hear that he was falling for her, not when it scared her to death to know how deep his feelings ran. And yet, she couldn't deny the warmth that spread through her at knowing what she'd come to mean to him.

He was standing now, facing her. Waiting.

There were a million excuses she could have made, a dozen lies she could have tried to tell.

But she couldn't.

"I'm sick of lying to myself. I can't do it. Not with you." The admission came out before she could pull it back, and she willed herself to be brave.

Fortunately, it was easier to be brave with

Chase than with anyone else. Because she knew that he loved her.

"The truth is that I won't be able to control myself around you, either. The truth is that even though I can't give you what you want, even though I should be the one to let you go find someone who's capable of loving you the way you deserve to be loved, I don't want to walk away from you. From this. I can't give you what you want. All I'm capable of giving right now is sex. Just sex."

Oh, God, what was wrong with her? Why was she letting herself get in any deeper than she could handle?

"Then that's what we'll do." He held out a hand to her. "Have lots and lots of great sex." He paused, his expression serious. "But not until you feel better. Not until you're not shaking anymore from having to relive that night." He lifted her hand to his lips. "I'm sorry I made you go back there, Chloe. I'm so sorry."

"You needed to know," she told him. And, surprisingly, she felt a little lighter for having shared her story with someone who cared for her. Deeply, truly cared.

She walked all the way into his arms. "I feel much better," she told him.

"There's no rush," he said, even though both of them knew that there was, as their days together ticked down. And she didn't want to waste another second thinking about what Dean had done. Damn it, hadn't she vowed that he wouldn't steal this from her, too?

"I really do think I'm ninety-nine percent of the way there," she said. "Think you're up to helping me get that last percent back?"

Chase stared at her for a long moment before his mouth moved into a sinfully sexy smile. And then his lips were sliding across hers so softly she almost couldn't feel his kiss.

But her body reacted instantly.

A few seconds later, he kissed her again. Just as softly. She tried to kiss him back, but he pulled away before she could. Another kiss, too gentle and quick for her to do more than just wait for it.

No, damn it! If they were going to do this "just sex" thing, she couldn't let him give her these soft, senselessly enticing kisses. From here on out she needed to make sure things stayed physical, not emotional.

Having sex, not making love.

Hot kisses, rather than sweet.

Amazingly, she knew exactly where to start. "Let's—"

He pressed another one of those soft kisses against her lips.

"—go—"

Another kiss.

"—outside."

That finally stopped his mind-bending onslaught and it occurred to her that he'd been trying to kiss her into submission. A gentle capitulation.

And, oh, if he did that long enough, gave her enough of those sweet kisses that stole her breath and made her heart pound with wanting . . . well, she could see that he just might end up drawing a promise out of her that she wasn't ready to give.

A promise in return for pleasure.

Chase had told her he wasn't going to give up. But she was just as firm in her position. So if he was going to try to make tonight about emotion, she was going to make sure they erred on the side of the physical.

Her resolve firmed just as he came at her with another one of those sinfully sweet kisses aimed straight at her heart. Pulling away before it could land, she led him to the French doors and out to the balcony off the bedroom. She didn't need to hear his questions to know he was wondering what the heck she was up to.

Well, he'd just have to wait and see.

At the last second, she realized they were going to need one more thing before leaving the room. "Where are your condoms?"

Out of her peripheral vision, she could see his erection grow bigger, taller. "In my bag."

"Get one." She smiled at him, a smile that felt wicked and different. But not bad. Liberated. "At least one."

His eyes narrowed, a muscle jumping in his jaw, at her command.

She gave him another wicked smile, along with the brush of her hand across the stubble beginning to cover his jaw. "You don't like me telling you what to do?"

"On the contrary," he responded, his words raw and rough, "I like it a great deal."

Darn it, she was trying to keep a handle on things here. He shouldn't be able to turn everything on its ear with just a few words.

The night air still held some of the warmth of the day, but it was cold enough that she could feel it slide across her overheated skin. It felt good, like a splash of sense. Just enough sense to keep her purpose in place, but not enough to have her put a halt to being with Chase altogether.

When they were all the way outside, she turned back to him, plucking the condoms from his fingertips—he was clearly a hopeful, and extremely virile, man given the stack he'd brought out—and placing them on the balcony railing within easy reach.

She let herself look at him for a long moment, the way he stood before her in the moonlight, utterly confident in his nudity. Of course he was. Any man—any person—this beautiful should be confident.

He took her hand and his thumb rubbed

sensuous little circles against the inside of her palm. "I knew the instant I saw you."

"What—" She should stop this, move back to playtime. But her mouth was a traitor with another question. "What could you have possibly known?"

"Nothing," he replied with perfect honesty. Honesty that immediately cut through any protests she might have made. "And everything."

She didn't understand.

Or, rather, she didn't *want* to understand.

She needed to keep things simple. Sex and heat. That's what their connection was. That was all it could possibly be until she had her life figured out and back on track.

"We're good in bed together," she told him, and then, to make sure they stayed on the purely physical track, "That night at your brother's house, out on his porch, what did you want to do to me?"

His eyes burned into hers, a whole new level of intense. "You know exactly what I wanted to do to you."

"Show me, Chase."

A second later, he had her backed into the railing, one hand in her hair, the other on her hip. They'd been like this enough for her to recognize the way he liked to hold her.

She liked it, too. So much. There was sizzling pleasure in his arms. But comfort found her there, too. A sense of safety that he would always hold her just right. Not too tight. Not too loosely, either.

Fortunately, his mouth descended on hers just then, sending her thoughts into flight.

She hadn't thought he could kiss her better than he already had. Oh, how wrong she was.

This kiss was hotter, went so much deeper, was so much more dangerous, than any that had come before.

She couldn't breathe, didn't even care that she was quickly losing her hold on reality as her sole focus centered on his mouth, to the way his tongue found her most sensitive spots, to the way his teeth knew just where to bite, just how hard to tease her. And then, oh, God, he was doing just what he'd done before, running kisses across her cheek, then down to her neck, to the hollow of her collarbones.

The anticipation of what he was going to do had her trembling even before his tongue slid against her skin.

She held her breath, only to have it come gasping out as he made contact.

"Lovely, Chloe." His seductive praise was a whisper just below her earlobe and she shivered with unrepressed delight as his teeth found her there and lightly pressed into the sensitive flesh.

"You didn't bite me there."

"I wanted to."

A whimper escaped her as she realized that she

was a fool to think she could lead Chase anywhere. His gentleness did not preclude his power over her emotions.

He laved the small bite before moving his attention back to her shoulders. She never would have thought that she'd be sensitive, reactive, on that part of her body.

How incredibly wrong she was.

Chase lifted his head. "Too many clothes."

She was on the verge of opening her mouth to remind him that she was naked when it hit her: he was pretending. Pretending they were rewinding back two nights. Giving her the fantasy, per her request.

His fingertips moved to her shoulders where the silky straps of her dress had been. Slowly, deliberately, he slid those phantom straps aside. "Lift your arms for me."

There was no reason for her to raise her arms. She didn't have any clothes on, no dress to get off. Her breasts were already there, bared—and aroused—before Chase.

It would have been enough for her if he'd laid her down and taken her on the wooden slats of the deck, right then and there. But, oh, wasn't it so much sweeter to play this game?

To pretend.

And to lose herself in heady anticipation.

Moving her hands and arms as if she were trying to slip free from the straps of a dress, she lifted them up and shimmied, just as she had two nights ago.

She went to lower her hands when Chase said, "Just like that."

She waited for panic to take over, for the urge to lower her hands. He'd promised not to hold them in place again, and he was keeping to that promise. But wasn't asking her to do it almost the same? And shouldn't she be feeling something other than the heady warmth that was moving through her, head to toe?

"Lovely."

He ran the fingertips of his free hand over the swell of her breasts and she arched into his touch. One broad fingertip began slow circles over her skin. Slowly, way too slowly, he came closer to the tightly puckered skin that was so desperate for his touch.

"Chase," she moaned when instead of giving her what she needed, he turned his attention to her other breast.

"Mmm?"

He didn't look up from the torturous circles he was making on her flesh. Her arms trembled from the way she was holding them, but she didn't lower them.

"Please," she begged, "I need—" She bit her lip on another moan as he came almost to the tip, then backed away and ran his finger down in the hollow between her breasts.

He paused his hand there, right in the center of her chest, where her heart was beating so hard for him, then leaned forward before she could get her brain to kick into gear, and kissed her softly.

Thoroughly.

Possessively.

The hairs on his chest teased her breasts, driving her even crazier than she already was.

And then, before she could shift or blink or beg, he lowered his head and took one of her nipples into his mouth. She needed to lower her arms so that she could steady herself by holding on to him, so that she could grip the back of his head and hold him there—*oh, yes, right there!*—while he gave her the pleasure she'd been craving.

Everything narrowed down onto the lash of his tongue upon her, the coiling heat inside her belly, his warm breath against her chest. Chloe lost all track of time as he laved her breasts, as he loved every inch of her torso—the peaks, the curves, the hollows, the shadowy undersides, the spaces between her ribs. And then he was moving lower still, dropping to his knees, holding her waist with his large, strong hands, holding her there for him to devour.

His tongue and lips and teeth held no mercy as he destroyed her soul, knocking down her defenses one inch of skin at a time.

And then he was nudging her legs open wider, before covering her with his mouth, and she was holding on to him for dear life, knowing she'd never live through this pleasure, that it was too big, too all-encompassing, far too sweet to be real.

To be hers.

She thought she heard the words, "You taste like heaven," and then his tongue was going deeper, replacing his fingers inside of her, sending her rocketing off into another impossible orgasm.

Her legs began to crumple but he was already there, holding her steady.

Not letting her fall.

Later she would let herself marvel at the fact that she'd been standing stark naked at a public winery with a man's face between her legs, crying out so loud that anyone on the property could surely hear. And had to know exactly what was going on.

But now, tonight, how could she possibly care about any of that? Not when all that mattered was pleasure.

No. That wasn't what mattered. Not really.

It was Chase.

He was what mattered.

The thought nailed her straight in the center of her heart just as he shifted, standing up. His hands were still on her hips when he kissed her. She tasted herself on his lips; but more than that, she tasted him. Tasted his hunger. Tasted his need.

Tasted just how much he cared about her.

Loved her.

She wanted to pull away from that truth, from him, from her past, from her own fear, but even if he hadn't chosen that moment to say, "Turn around for me, lovely girl," even if his hands hadn't been helping her do just that, she wouldn't have had a chance in hell of leaving him just then.

He had her, body and soul.

And not just because of the orgasms.

Moments later, she was facing the moonlit vineyard and he was placing her hands on the rails. "Hold on," he said softly, seductively. "And don't let go."

She wanted to think he was talking about the rail, but she knew what he really meant.

He wanted her to trust him. He wanted her to believe that his love could be enough to change her life.

Tears rushed her even as her arousal spiked higher than ever before at nothing more than the sound of Chase ripping open the condom wrapper.

"You're even more beautiful like this than I knew you would be."

She turned her head, a light breeze taking her hair with it as she looked at him over her shoulder. "Chase."

He positioned himself at her entrance, so hot and hard she could hardly believe it. She held her breath, waiting for the moment when he drove into her, when he filled not just her body, but her heart, too.

But he remained still, his eyes on hers.

"I love you, Chloe."

She gasped as he finally took her. Her head fell forward, hung down as she gripped the rails and took what he was giving her, as she pushed back against him just as hard. His hands moved from her hips up over her waist as he took her, and soon, his palms were full of her aroused flesh.

Never. She'd never done anything this decadent. This depraved. This delicious.

This beautiful.

She'd made this plan to have sex outside to make sure things stayed purely physical. Entirely on the surface.

It should have been impossible for them to deepen their connection while having sex standing up, out on a balcony. It should have been inconceivable that she would feel even closer to him while he had her bent over the rail with her breasts in his hands while he was thrusting hard, deep, into her.

If ever there was an act that should be just sex, it was this, a man and woman who had been perfect strangers just days ago, desperate and panting as they came together.

And yet . . .

Somehow it was beautiful. So beautiful that her eyes were damp.

And her heart was fuller than it had ever been.

In perfect unison, he pinched the tip of one breast at the same moment he slid the fingers of his other hand between her legs.

She shattered.

Chase lifted Chloe into his arms and carried her back inside the bedroom. Her eyes were closed, and as she blinked to try to open them, he pressed a kiss on one eyelid.

"Shhh."

A kiss for the other.

"Time for bed."

She snuggled in tighter to him, his exhausted sex kitten.

Again and again, she amazed him.

Humbled him.

Her playfulness, her willingness to take a risk despite her past . . . he wasn't sure she realized that she was showing him all those things out on the balcony.

He knew she'd wanted to prove to him that she could play in the "just sex" big leagues. Instead, she'd trusted him—trusted herself—with something different. Daring.

Sex in the bathtub had been mind-blowing.

Sex on the balcony, watching her grip the rails so hard her knuckles turned white, watching as she gave up control and bucked against his hips to drive him deeper inside . . . there wasn't a word for what that had done to him.

Well, maybe there was.

"Love." He whispered it against her cheek, felt her stir slightly, even though she was almost out.

He would have been perfectly happy if the only place they ever had sex was in bed. Well, not *perfectly* happy, but the fact was, regular sex with Chloe was a million times better than crazy sex with anyone else.

Only, the truth was that Chloe was a woman who liked—who needed, who craved—adventure. He wasn't sure she realized it yet. But he did. And he wanted to live those adventures with her. Beside her. Within her.

He laid her down on the bed, her head upon the pillow, and when she didn't loosen her hold on him—even half-asleep, she couldn't fight what they had together—he slid beneath the soft sheets with her. She immediately shifted to curl against him in the way they'd slept the past two nights: her back to his front, her hips cradled against his perpetual erection. She pulled his arms around her like a blanket and settled deeper into his arms with a contented sigh.

Lovely.

His.

Fifteen

One more day.

One more night.

Chloe had twenty-four hours left to be with Chase in this fairy tale. She wanted each of those hours, those precious minutes, to last forever, knew that she would be counting them down until the buzzer rang and she left.

She needed to leave. Because, as she'd told him last night, she needed to do this on her own.

Didn't she?

All day, as she'd worked with everyone, as she'd gone to check on Alice and found her much improved in her hotel room, Chloe had gone around and around with it in her head.

At first, it had been easy to tell herself she needed to keep her distance from Chase because *all men were evil.*

Which had turned out to be completely laughable. Because while her ex was certainly unhinged, Chase didn't have an evil bone in his body. In a million years, she'd never have thought she'd find a guy like him on the side of the road in the middle of a hailstorm, on what she'd thought was the worst night of her life.

She shouldn't believe he could have fallen in love with her. Not in only three days.

She shouldn't be replaying that moment over and over when he'd said, *"I love you."*

Lost in her troubled thoughts, her hands stilled on the lace of the corset she was tying for Amanda.

"Do you need me to suck in tighter?"

Chloe frowned. *Suck in tighter?* What could Amanda possibly have to suck in? "No. You're perfect just like that."

Amanda looked down at herself. "I'm getting fat."

"No!" In the back of her mind she knew she needed to back off, calm down. But she'd spent too many years listening to Dean say that to her. She couldn't stand to hear Amanda say it about herself.

"You're beautiful, Amanda."

But although she could see that the girl enjoyed the compliment, she didn't truly believe it.

As the model walked away, Chloe wanted so badly for her to believe in her own beauty. In her own worth. She wanted to save Amanda from years of self-hatred. From bad relationships. From men who weren't worthy of even a minute of her time . . . let alone years.

She felt her lover's eyes on her and Chase's pull was so strong that she couldn't stop herself from staring back and suddenly wondering, yet again, Was that what she was to him? Was she simply a woman he was desperate to save because he was a protector to his core?

No. She knew better than to think that. Especially when he'd never done one single thing to try and take her power away.

Instead, hadn't he given her the tools to empower herself? Hadn't he asked her to use her talents, her skills, to create beauty? To grow stronger?

And then, like a ton of bricks raining down from the perfectly blue sky, the real truth of the matter hit her: it wasn't Chase that thought he needed to save her, to coddle her so that she never had to face danger again.

She'd been doing that all by herself.

Hiding out here at the winery, not picking up the damn phone and calling the police, not forcing herself to face the fact that she was going to have to find a way to protect herself from Dean once she was out on her own again.

It was just what she'd done in her marriage. She'd hidden from the truth of how bad it was because it had seemed so much more painful to deal with the truth.

Standing in the middle of the vineyard with Chase's eyes still on her, she knew he didn't deserve to be dragged into her mess. And until she could be worthy of him by knowing how to stand on her own two feet, she couldn't be with him for real.

Just then, Beyoncé's "Single Ladies" started blaring from the portable stereo, and Amanda dragged her over to the group, who had all started dancing in their beautiful silk dresses.

Chloe had always loved to dance, loved to feel her limbs, her muscles, grow loose and warm. The sun was still in the sky, pouring down over them, and when the rubber band around her ponytail fell out she let it go, shaking her hair to let it move around her face.

As she danced and Sara grabbed her hips to shimmy into her, Chloe could almost pretend again that the past ten years had never happened. Yes, she'd been hiding out from reality, but getting to be with Chase and the models and his crew these past few days had done so much to strip away the layers she'd never wanted to be there in the first place.

Yes, she knew this feeling of freedom, of joy, was only temporary, knew that trouble was waiting for her outside of the fantasy of this vine-covered world, but she still had a few more hours of joy left, didn't she?

"She really is pretty."

Chase turned to see Ellen standing beside him. He'd been utterly enraptured watching Chloe dance with the models.

But it was more than beauty that made it impossible for him to take his eyes off her.

Day by day, minute by minute, she was transforming. She'd already been a butterfly, even standing on the side of the road, dripping wet with that horrible bruise marring her soft skin. So it wasn't that she was emerging from her cocoon.

Rather, the colors on her wings were growing brighter, more magnificent, as the burdens, the fears she'd been carrying, fell away piece by piece.

"Inside and out," he agreed.

Ellen remained by his side, both of them watching the dancing. Surprisingly, this was the first time he'd run into her during the shoot. Almost as if she'd made sure to stay out of his way.

Feeling bad about the way he'd stood her up that first night, he said, "I really am sorry about—"

She put her hand on his arm and her touch felt strange. Wrong. The song ended and when Chloe looked over and saw them standing together, her expression tightened, narrowed.

Ellen quickly dropped her hand and waved. "Hi, Chloe!"

Chase watched Chloe's mouth turn up into a smile that wasn't entirely real as she moved toward them.

"Hmm," Ellen said, "she looks mighty possessive of you."

Chase didn't have time to tell her it was mutual before Chloe was there with them.

"Hello, Ellen."

Ellen smiled at her. "Wow, you have really gorgeous hair."

Chloe blinked, clearly surprised by the compliment. "Thanks."

The late-afternoon breeze whipped up, blowing a strand across her face. Chase reached out, slid his fingers through the silken strand as he tucked it behind her ear.

He felt her breath catch more than heard it as their eyes locked. He'd waited all day to touch her again, for the chance to fill up his senses with her softness, her sweet scent, her innate sensual responses. Her hand came up to cover his, holding his palm against her cheek in an instinctive reaction to his touch.

Until Ellen broke the spell by asking, "How have the two of you enjoyed being here this week?"

Chloe dropped his hand like he had the plague and a faint blush stained her already flushed cheeks. Clearly, she'd only just realized she and Chase had been holding on to each other in front of Ellen.

"It's been like living inside a fairy tale," she said softly. She gestured out across the gently rolling mountains, covered in even green rows. "It must be marvelous coming here to work every day."

Ellen nodded. "It's pretty great. Except for when we get a bridezilla in, demanding to know why the grapes aren't in fuller bloom for her big day. But really, that's the only time it kind of sucks."

Chase was glad to hear Chloe chuckle, her discomfort at seeing Ellen again—and accidentally touching him in front of the other woman—receding.

He liked seeing that possessive glint in Chloe's eyes. Loved it, actually. He doubted she even realized it was there—and that she'd continually been moving closer and closer to him, unconsciously staking her claim in front of a possible rival.

She might have repeatedly told him she couldn't be with him, but that was her head talking. Her heart seemed to know better.

He knew better, too.

"Marcus wanted to be here to say goodbye to everyone, but he was called into the city suddenly," Ellen told them. "He sends his apologies."

Chase had a bad feeling about his brother's frequent trips to the city. He'd always tried to keep an open mind about Marcus's girlfriend, Jill. But Chase had never been all that crazy about her. None of the Sullivans were. Yes, she was beautiful, but her beauty wore thin beneath the layer of ice she walked around in. The stick up her ass didn't help much, either.

Chloe's face fell. "Oh, no. I really wanted to see him again before I left, to thank him properly for giving me a place to stay this week."

She pulled the plump, soft flesh of her lower lip in between her teeth. Chase couldn't keep his eyes from landing there, didn't have a prayer of keeping the rest of his body from responding in kind.

He'd never wanted a woman like this. Not just with his body. Not just with his brain. Not just with his heart.

But with his entire soul.

Ellen looked more than a little confused. "You'll see him again, won't you, Chloe?"

Just then, Sara yelled, "Chloe, I can't get out of this stupid thing! It's starting to freak me out. Can you help me?"

Relief sweeping across her lovely face, Chloe said, "I've got to go help the girls out of their clothes. It was very nice to see you again, Ellen." She held out her hand and the two women shook goodbye, at which point she turned and fled any more questions.

"Wait a minute," Ellen said, still confused. "Why won't she see Marcus again? Aren't you and Chloe together now?"

Chase ran a hand through his hair. The frustration he'd had a hell of a time keeping at bay during the day's shoot was eating straight through his gut.

"It's complicated."

Ellen looked back at Chloe, who was unbuckling one of the models' bondage-inspired evening dresses. "It doesn't really look all that complicated from where I'm standing. Heck, I practically got singed when you guys touched."

He knew Ellen was right. There shouldn't be anything complicated about a guy falling in love with a girl. Funny, in all the years of women falling for him, he'd never thought it would end up like this—with him losing his heart to a woman who was so afraid to lose hers.

And now, all he had was one final night to try and talk her around from *couldn't* to *forever.*

He felt Ellen's hand on his arm again. "A few nights ago, I was a little disappointed that things didn't happen between us, but honestly . . ." She flicked another glance at Chloe. "I hope this works out for you. She's very sweet. You make a beautiful couple." She smiled widely at him. "How about I block out a weekend for you next year, just in case?"

Chase immediately saw a breathtaking vision of Chloe in a long white dress waiting for him surrounded by vines.

"Good luck, Chase."

Ellen walked away and he turned back to watch Chloe carefully wrapping up one of the dresses they'd used that afternoon. He'd never relied much on luck before, never liked counting on something so elusive, so unpredictable. He'd always figured on talent and hard work to get him where he wanted to be.

But this time, Chase was afraid luck was exactly what he needed.

Sixteen

Several hours later, Chloe waved goodbye to everyone in the van as it drove toward the Sullivan winery gates. "I'm really sad your shoot is over." She looked wistful as she said, "It meant so much to me the way you all included me on the shoot."

"You were an important part of it," he told her.

This time she didn't argue with him or try to downplay her role, but simply said, "You made me feel valued. Secure. Everyone did. And I enjoyed myself so much." She smiled up at him. "Even better, I feel like I've made some friends."

"You did," he replied as they walked back inside the guesthouse. It was always hard to shut the door on a good project. Especially this one, which had turned out to be so incredibly special.

But, at the same time, he was glad that it was just down to him and Chloe now.

He slid his fingers through hers, lifted her hand to his mouth and let his lips linger on her knuckles. "Would you go out on a date with me, Chloe?"

Surprise flickered in her eyes. "We've already talked about this."

"I'm not talking about the future. Just tonight. That's all I'm asking for."

He could see her uncertainty, the way she was grappling with what she wanted . . . and what she felt she should be doing.

Finally, she said, "We both know I'm a sure thing tonight," one side of her mouth moving up into a little smirk. "You don't need to spring for dinner first."

He wasn't ready for the spark of anger that lit in him at the fact that she still seemed to think sex was enough for him, wasn't ready for the impulse that had him challenging her with the words, "Are you saying you want to have sex?"

Her eyes were tormented as she lifted her chin and came right back at him with one tortured word.

"Yes."

His mouth came down over hers, but even then he was careful with her, despite the fact that he was pushing down her shorts and panties.

"Chase," she moaned against his mouth, urging

him on by pressing her hips into his hands, helping him strip her lower half bare.

He gauged her desire, her need, and knew that it was as big as his before saying, "I promised to always give you what you want. Tell me what you want."

Her eyes were dilated almost to black and he could see everything she was trying to block out, everything she was trying so desperately to hide from.

"Please just take me."

He pulled open her shirt, his mouth finding her nipple through the pink lace bra. At the same time, her fingers were on his zipper, pulling, yanking, and then he was in her hand and she was wrapping her long, slender fingers around him, stroking him.

He'd just promised her anything she wanted, vowed one more time to give her everything. And even though his heart felt like a bomb had hit it at the way she kept trying to put distance between them, he lifted her hips with his hands and told her, "Wrap your legs around me."

He drove into her before either of them could take their next breath and her flesh tightened, grasped, clenched around him. He knew she wanted him to drive into her mindlessly. He knew she wanted to pretend that what they had was just attraction.

But, damn it, he couldn't do it.

Even for her, even when she'd just asked him point-blank to do her, he couldn't just take her like an animal against the front door.

"Chloe."

Her eyes, which had been closed tight, opened slowly, blurry with lust. And all that emotion she didn't want to feel. All that emotion that she was trying to push away because it hadn't come at the right time or place. Because she wasn't ready for it. Because she thought she needed to be strong and walk away from him tomorrow morning.

"I can't do it, sweetheart. I can't pretend this is just sex." Chase needed to look into her face, wanted her to have to acknowledge the truth of what was between them as he said, "I love you."

She sobbed out his name before kissing him like she'd die without his kisses.

His body took over then, pure instinct as he drove into her, as she lifted herself up over him, then down so that they were connected utterly. Perfectly.

He felt her inner muscles contract a split second before she gasped against his mouth. And then her head was falling back and she was driving her pelvis into his, entirely lost to the pleasure, to the way their bodies sparked and charged together.

Somehow he rode out her climax, every pull and tug of her clenching heat against him. He never wanted to have to leave her, never wanted to have to let her go.

But when she pressed her mouth against his shoulder and said the word *"Love"* so softly he almost couldn't hear it over the beating of his own heart in his ears, he fell all the way over the edge.

"Chase?" He'd carried her over to the couch and pulled a blanket over them. She'd only just caught her breath. "I know I'm always asking for this, but can we start tonight over again?"

She could feel his smile against her ear.

"Of course we can."

Chloe shifted so that she was partially sitting up on the couch, but still in his arms. "They've all just left and now it's time for me to say, 'I'm really going to miss everyone.' "

His eyes were steady on hers. "This is my part, right?"

She knew he was teasing her and was amazed by how forgiving he was, rather than lashing out at her for trying to reduce what was between them to just sex.

"Yes, this is your part."

"I'll miss them, too, but I'm glad we're alone now."

She wanted to say she was sorry for hurting him. For the way she kept hurting him. For the fact that she wasn't saying "I love you" back.

But all she could say was, "I'd like to go out on a date with you, Chase." When he didn't immediately respond, she took a shaky breath. "Please say yes."

His eyes were still dark, still intense, as he said, "Yes."

Her chest, her stomach, everything hurt. Ached for this beautiful man. She made herself smile. "I should probably put on a new shirt."

He looked down then, seemed to notice the torn fabric for the first time. "I was too rough with you. I didn't mean to do that."

She silenced him with a kiss. "No. You would never be rough with me." She climbed from his lap and pulled a dress from the rack of clothes before leaving the living room. "It will just take me a few minutes to shower and change."

Chase sat with his head in his hands. What the hell had he just done? He'd all but attacked her up against the door. Chloe didn't deserve to be treated like that. She was precious. He should have been gentle, no matter what.

And he should stop blurting out how much he loved her over and over. It only made things worse. It only made her feel more cornered. More like things were out of her control.

Knowing he'd only end up taking her against the bathroom tiles if he joined her in the shower, he went into one of the bathrooms neither of them had used and quickly soaped down. He was already thick and throbbing again at the thought of Chloe naked, with water streaming over her body, just down the hall.

He turned the water to cold and forced himself to stand beneath the icy spray.

He really wanted this to be a date. A real date. Not just a prelude to more sex.

Seventeen

"Wow, this is stunning," Chloe said. "I don't think I would ever get used to this view."

They were sitting at the corner table at Auberge de Soleil, high in the hills of Napa Valley, and Chase knew exactly what she meant. But it wasn't the view he'd never get used to admiring.

He couldn't manage to drag his eyes from his date.

The waiter came by and handed them each a glass of champagne. "Your brother Marcus wanted to let you both know that he hopes you enjoy your evening with us."

"I should have known he had eyes all over this mountain," Chase said with a crooked grin as he lifted his glass to Chloe. "He probably won't even let me buy my girl dinner. Always trying to assert his older-brother status." He grinned at her. "We'll just have to make sure we order the most expensive things on the menu."

Chloe shook her head, obviously still surprised by his brother's gesture. "It must be so amazing to be from a big family. To know that they're always there for you."

He wanted to tell her that being with him meant the entire Sullivan clan would take her in—and protect her—as one of their own. He wanted to give it to her as another reason why she never needed to be frightened again.

Instead, not wanting to break the spell, he said as cheerfully as he could, "Sometimes it's great. Sometimes it's a pain in the ass. Now, if we could forget about Marcus and the rest of my siblings for a moment?"

She looked up at him, their eyes linking, sparking, as she nodded. "Forgotten."

"Good. Because I want you to myself tonight."

"Tonight," she echoed, "I'm yours."

Warmth infused his chest—hell, his entire soul—just to hear her say those two words.

I'm yours.

Chase lifted his glass. "To rainy nights."

She tipped her flute against his, murmuring, "To rainy nights," in a husky voice.

He continued to hold his glass against hers. "And to one very lovely woman that a storm brought into my life."

Her eyes were glassy as she put her flute to her lovely lips and took a sip.

• • •

"You know," she said a while later, after eating some of the best food she'd ever tasted, "this just might be the most romantic dinner date I've ever been on."

"I figured you and I were long due for a little romance."

Chloe cocked her head as she looked at Chase. Really let herself look.

At first, she'd been too blown away by his outward beauty to really see much. And then, she'd been afraid to stare because of what she might see in his eyes when he looked at her . . . and what he might see mirrored right back at him.

How could he not see that he'd been romancing her every single second since he'd met her on that rainy road and told her to get into his car?

She smiled at the memory of that first night. How she'd wanted him despite herself—and liked him a great, great deal more than caution warranted.

She let herself pretend, for just a few moments, that this really was her life. That Chase was the man she'd been with for years. That they went on romantic outings to Napa Valley starred restaurants all the time.

And that she was happy, not just for one night. But always.

Because she was loved.

Really and truly loved for who she was.

"It's another reason why your photos are all so beautiful. You aren't just creating the fantasy for all of us. You want to believe in that fantasy, too, don't you? I swear, your whole life you must have had to fend off women with big, long sticks."

He gave her his best version of lecherous. "Just one really big stick."

She couldn't help but laugh. "I set you up perfectly for that, didn't I?"

The waiter came to refill their water glasses just as she asked, "Are the rest of your brothers like you? Big and tough on the outside, but gentle romantics on the inside?"

As the waiter left, Chase pretended she'd just wounded him, his hand over his chest. "I once picked up a novel on my sister's bed that used the words *velvet-covered steel* to talk about the guy's junk. I'm pretty sure what you just said reduced me to a velvet-covered marshmallow. Our waiter may never look at me the same way again. He's probably calling the club now so they can kick me out of it."

Chloe laughed again, loud enough that a few heads turned to admire the beautiful couple in the corner. "Being a nice person doesn't in any way change the fact that you're all man."

"That statement would have had a heck of a lot more impact if you weren't half giggling as you said it," he informed her, half joking, half serious.

Still giggling, she said, "Sorry. Although I'm not sure I'll ever be able to get the words *velvet-covered marshmallow*—or the image of it—out of my head."

"I plan on making damn sure they're gone later tonight," he promised, heat flickering in his eyes along with the laughter.

"Are any of your other big, strapping brothers closet romantics? It will just be our little secret."

She couldn't help it—she loved hearing about his brothers and sisters, imagining how nice it would be to always know that they were there for you. To laugh with. To joke with. Even to argue with.

Chase shook his head. "I'm pretty sure doing anything that moves doesn't qualify as romantic. Apart from Marcus. He's the only one who doesn't play that way anymore, although he definitely used to before he met his girlfriend."

"Doing anything that moves." Chloe worked to tamp down the sudden twisting in her gut and tried to keep her voice light. "As long as everyone knows the score, I guess that's okay."

But Chase instantly saw through her. "I'm not going to lie to you. I used to be one of those guys."

She swallowed, hating the thought of Chase so much as looking at another woman. Kissing another woman. Touching another woman. Making love to another woman.

Her stomach lurched and she abruptly put down her fork. “Okay. Thanks for being honest.”

He reached across the table, taking her hand in his. “I don’t want to do it anymore. I don’t want to be that guy anymore.”

She wanted so desperately to believe him. But she knew firsthand that it wasn’t that easy. “But isn’t it exactly what you’ve been doing with me?”

“No.”

“Yes,” she countered. “We met, I moved, we had sex.”

“You’re different, Chloe. You’re special.”

Angry at herself for how badly she wanted the fairy tale to come true, she asked, “How can you possibly know that? In the four days since we met, you and I have had sex nearly every moment that we’ve been alone. That fits the criteria pretty perfectly, doesn’t it? Odds seem pretty darn high that you’ll move on to your next shoot and find another woman who can’t get enough of you.”

She could see that flicker of frustration on his face. The same one that had him taking her up against the front door a couple of hours ago.

Why did she keep pushing him like this? Why couldn’t she just accept that he meant what he said about her?

But she knew why, knew that deep down she was afraid she was the same twenty-two-year-old girl who had fallen for her ex’s lines, his pretty words, for a warmth she'd so desperately wanted to believe was there . . . and ended up marrying a man who didn't know—or like—her at all. Because when she thought back to her marriage, hadn't she believed her ex was rescuing her from her life? She couldn't bear it if she was foolish enough, was needy enough, to make the same mistake twice.

That first night when Chase had found her on the side of the road, she'd worried that he was too good to be true. And now, she could have sworn that he wasn't, that he really and truly *was* that good.

Could there be any chance that she was wrong?

Chloe didn't know what she expected Chase to say, if she'd thought he would drag her into the back of the restaurant to teach her another lesson about just how good they were together, but she definitely didn't expect him to reach into his jacket pocket, pull out an envelope and put it on the table.

She looked at it, then up at him just as he said, "I didn't fall in love with you because you're so lovely it hurts to look at you. I didn't fall in love with you because you make love like a dream. Although I love that you do."

She swallowed hard. Those three sentences had just made the list of top ten sweetest things any man had ever said to her.

Her hands trembled as she picked up the envelope.

She could tell there were pictures inside it. And she was afraid to look at them.

Not because she was worried about not looking pretty . . . but because she'd learned over the past few days that Chase saw everything.

Especially the things people were trying their hardest to hide.

Finally, she slipped a finger beneath the flap and pulled out the small stack of photos.

She was laughing in the photo on top of the stack. Her mouth was wide-open, her head was thrown back, as she looked at something on Amanda's phone.

"She was showing me one of those funny auto-correct lists."

Tentatively, Chloe turned to the next photo. She was laughing again, this time in the middle of the pool, after falling in while trying to help fix Amanda's hat at just the right angle.

A smile moved onto her lips before she realized it was coming. "I had such a great time with everyone," she said softly before turning to the next photo.

Chase had captured her talking with Marcus that night at the party at his house. She'd been loose because of the wine and had let down her guard with Marcus after a surprisingly fun day with everyone. It was obvious just how desperate she'd been to let happiness take root within her heart again.

Thrown off by what Chase was showing her about herself, she moved on to the next picture, one where she was packing up dresses and a half dozen beautiful fabrics were spread out across her lap.

She'd never seen herself look like that, had never see herself dreaming before.

Emotion threatened to swamp her, so she quickly moved to the next picture in the stack.

Oh.

If only she'd stopped with the fabrics, with the dreaming, with the desperate longing for happiness.

The final picture was from that first afternoon out in the vineyards, when she'd looked up at the end of the day and Chase had his lens pointed at her. She remembered the terror of knowing she hadn't hid her feelings for him. Feelings she hadn't even been able to understand because they were so raw, so new.

So pure.

"Ask me again how I know you're special, Chloe."

The pictures dropped from her fingers onto the table.

She didn't need to ask.

Chase had shifted his seat so that he was sitting close enough to hold her hand beneath the table.

"Thank you," she said softly, her throat clogged with emotion. "It's been a wonderful night." She licked her lips, squeezed his hand with hers. "A perfect night."

Oh, God, she was going to cry, could feel the tears building up, threatening to spill. All it would take was one sweet word, one heartfelt look, and she'd be a goner.

She was working so hard on holding those tears back that she didn't notice Chase standing up until she felt him gently tugging at her hand. Blinking up at him in confusion, she rose to her feet and let him lead her across the room, his hand on the small of her back, simultaneously comforting and arousing. He pulled her into his arms and they were dancing to the song the three-piece jazz band in the corner had just begun playing.

"The Look of Love."

Chloe lifted her face to his in surprise. "This song." She flicked a gaze at the band, then back at him, shaking her head. "It's almost like they know about—"

Her voice broke before she could finish the sentence. But she had to. Had to admit it to herself. To Chase.

Her voice so soft she didn't know if Chase would even be able to hear her, she whispered, "It's like they know about the way you look at me. About the way you've always looked at me."

And she now knew from seeing that picture

he'd taken of her in the vineyard that first night, it was the way she'd always looked at him, too.

With love.

And with his large, strong body cradling hers, with his heart pounding against hers, Chloe pressed her face into his shoulder . . . and finally let her tears come.

Chase had never felt like this before, like his heart was breaking one beat at a time as Chloe softly cried while they danced.

He wanted to give her everything. He wanted to slay all her dragons. He wanted to hold her close and never let her go. He'd told her he loved her, but he knew she still believed she needed to leave him to prove that she was a strong person.

She'd told him the night was perfect, but she was crying.

His whole life, he'd always known exactly what to do. Women hadn't been much of a challenge, but now he knew that was because he'd never really cared before.

Until he'd fallen in love with Chloe.

Chase wished there was a simple answer, wished he could convince himself it was as easy as taking her ex-husband apart for ever hurting her in the first place, and that once he dissolved the threat to Chloe's well-being, everything would be fine.

But how many times had he and his brothers

gone out to avenge a wrong against one of his sisters, only to end up the bad guy, only to have them cry, "I'm not a baby! When are you going to let me stand up for myself?"

How the hell was Chase going to let her go and do what she believed she needed to do?

And how much would she hate him if he couldn't do it?

Eighteen

By the time the song ended, Chloe had managed to recover her grip on her emotions, thank God. Glad she hadn't put on much makeup, she quickly wiped away her tears while Chase led them outside to a beautiful lavender-and-rosemary-scented terrace complete with a bocce ball court.

"Bocce ball used to be my favorite game to watch as a kid," she said to try and bring some normalcy back to things after crying all over him. "I would sneak out to the park where they had a couple of courts and watch families play together."

"Did you play, too?"

She shook her head. "Not officially. It seemed like only the wealthy families had their own balls and even courts in their backyards. But when there was no one around I would play with the tennis balls I'd collected."

She let go of Chase's hand and moved onto the empty sand court and picked up one of the heavy balls. "These are the fancy balls I'd see other people playing with." She laughed softly. "If anyone ever saw me, they probably thought I was making a mockery of the game with my tennis balls."

She was surprised when Chase took off his jacket and rolled up his sleeves. "Show me how it's done."

Chloe almost told him she hadn't intended to end their überromantic evening by rolling balls in sand for points. But wasn't that exactly one of the things she loved most about Chase—that there were no hard-and-fast rules in his life? No *shoulds*. No *have tos*.

And, best of all, no *shouldn'ts*.

Slipping off her heels so she wouldn't leave big divots in the sand with the sharp points, she picked up the tiny white ball. "This is the jack. We toss it out, then try to see who can get closest to it with our own balls." She picked up a blue ball and handed it to him with a grin. "Since you're all man, why don't you be blue?"

He put his hand over the ball, somehow managing to pull her closer rather than just taking it from her. His mouth settled down over hers in a way that was at once familiar, yet shockingly surprising, and Chloe couldn't stop herself from twining her free hand around his neck and going up on her tippy-toes to kiss him right back.

When the sound of a passing car reminded her that they were on a public court in the middle of the resort, she forced herself to pull away from his sinfully delicious mouth.

His thumb brushed across her lower lip. "I like this game already."

She blushed at the heat in his words, even though there really wasn't a single reason left to be blushing in front of Chase anymore. Not after all the ways they'd made love, the number of times she'd come apart with his mouth and hands on her.

But something told her she'd always blush with him, that those butterflies would always be there, flying around inside her belly whenever he gave her one of those hot, intense looks.

She wanted so desperately to look toward that future, to envision what it could look like, to let herself dream of little girls and boys with his eyes, his tanned skin.

But she couldn't let herself do that tonight. She could only be with him right here, right now.

"Tell me how we score the game," Chase said, pulling her from her dark thoughts.

She explained that the team with the balls closest to the jack scored the points for each round.

"I have an idea," he said when she'd laid out the

rules, and she couldn't miss the wicked undercurrent in his voice.

"I can't wait to hear this."

And the truth was, being with Chase was so wonderfully exciting, so exhilarating, that even playing a simple game was more fun than she'd ever had before.

What would a life with him be like? Would each day be better than the one before?

Lost in her thoughts, she was surprised to feel his fingertips lightly skimming the skin beneath her chin. She looked up at him and her knees nearly buckled from the desire—and love—shining in his eyes.

"Do you want to guess my new spin on the rules?" he asked in a husky voice.

"Every time a person loses a point, they have to give the other one a kiss?"

He moved his mouth so it was barely a breath from hers. "So innocent," he whispered against her lips.

It took all the breath she had left to tease back, "But you want to change all that, don't you?"

"Don't you?" he asked, his question a caressing challenge to her fantasies.

Oh, God, she almost came right there, in the middle of a bocce ball court in Napa.

"Yes." The word was released from her lips before she knew it was coming and his mouth captured hers again, far too briefly.

"If I win this game, I also win you for the night. If you win, you win me for the night."

Oh, God, they weren't going to play tonight for a pointless score . . . they were going to play for each other instead. The wicked suggestion had her body immediately responding with a flood of warmth low down in her belly and at the tips of her breasts.

"If I win," he said in a low voice that thrummed through her veins faster, hotter, than a shot of tequila, "you'll be mine tonight for anything, everything, I desire."

She felt her lips open, felt air rush from them in the reverse of a gasp. "Anything?"

"Anything."

No. God, no, she shouldn't want what *anything* entailed.

"Everything?"

He ran his fingers over a lock of her hair. "Everything, Chloe."

She'd already done more wild things with Chase this week than she had before in her whole life. Bathtub sex. Outdoor sex. Up against the wall sex.

She tried to tell herself there couldn't be more, but it was no use.

She knew there was. Simply because she'd already been fantasizing about it. About doing all of those forbidden things she'd once wanted, things she'd been told were wrong to want.

"And if you win, lovely Chloe, I'm yours to do with as you wish."

Oh, God. She honestly didn't know if she wanted to win . . . or lose.

Chase had never played bocce ball before, but he and his siblings had often played similar games where they hurled rocks at a target. At the outset of the game, Chase had been fairly certain he'd win. It didn't take him long to realize he should have known better.

By the time they were down to the final point, 14-13, Chloe's lead, he told her, "You're really good at this."

She smiled up at him. "I know."

He loved the playful way she kissed him, none of those dark shadows in her eyes for the time being. "Are you trying to distract me?" he asked.

"I would if I needed to . . ."

He had her in his arms before she could finish her sentence. "You just gave me a good idea." He dropped his eyes to her lush mouth, so lovely, so soft. "Prepare to be distracted."

"You can give it your best shot," she challenged him.

"Now you're in for it," he said, and then he was kissing her and the game was momentarily forgotten.

It nearly killed him to follow through on his plan and abruptly let her go. "Your turn."

Her eyes were fuzzy and unfocused. "My turn to what?"

He smiled at her, a devious smile that told her he had her right where he wanted her.

Her eyes cleared. "Right. The game." She gave him a mock-hard look. "Prepare to be destroyed, Hotstuff."

But as she bent over to pick up a red ball, he knew he was long past being destroyed by Chloe.

She was his, damn it. Just as he was hers.

It wasn't one of them having power over the other. It wasn't a matter of control, of wanting to be in charge.

She had to lift up the hem of her dress every time she got into position for a shot. Her legs were strong and gorgeous, her feet bare and pretty on the sand. There wasn't an inch of her body he didn't desire, from her toes to her eyebrows.

Just as there wasn't any part of her heart that he didn't love.

"Stop looking at me like that."

"Like what?" he asked in his most innocent voice.

"Like you're the big bad wolf and I'm Red Riding Hood."

"Hmm," he said, "now there's an idea for another game to play tonight." He paused a beat. "When I win."

He barely heard her muttered, "Like hell," before she let the red ball roll from her fingertips.

Her ball slammed into his with perfect precision, knocking his blue ball completely out of the game.

Straightening up, she gave him such a gleeful look—so pretty, so pure, so sweet to the core—it was all he could do not to fall on one knee in the sand and propose to her right then and there.

"One more perfect shot and I win," she told him with great satisfaction. "And then you're mine."

He could sprint around a track, row across a lake, without losing his breath. But with Chloe, it happened all the time.

He saw the way her hand trembled as she picked up the final red ball. She looked at him, held his gaze for a long moment before turning back to the game and letting the ball go in one graceful roll, where it landed right next to the jack.

And she won.

But instead of turning to him with a victorious cheer, she simply stood and stared at the balls. Finally, she turned back to him. "I guess we should go now."

He wanted to tell her it was just a game. He wanted to pull her into his arms and tell her there was nothing to be worried about.

But something stopped him—the same thing that had stopped him from heading into the city over the past four days and taking her ex apart.

Chase knew Chloe's strength, could sense how deeply rooted it was in her from that first moment on the side of the road.

But it wasn't enough that he knew it.

Chloe needed to know her own strength, too. And that loving him wouldn't ever diminish it.

Walking over to where she stood, he held out his hand to her. And waited for her to make up her mind about tonight. About whether she was going to claim not just her spoils . . . but all of him, body and soul.

Finally, she reached back to him and, just as their fingers slid together, said, "It would have been so much easier if you had won."

"I know," he said, "but I never stood a chance of holding on to my heart with you." He held her gaze. "Not for one single second."

Nineteen

Anything.

Everything.

Chloe's mouth grew drier and drier during their drive back to Marcus's winery, her heart pounding harder and harder.

She tried to talk herself around all the reasons she shouldn't be freaking out.

1. She wasn't a scared virgin.
2. She and Chase had already had sex lots of times.
3. He loved her.
4. And she was pretty damn sure she was falling in love with him.

Oh, God, that was exactly the problem.

She loved him.

Chloe wasn't actually sure it would be easier to be the one in control of their lovemaking tonight if she didn't love him, but two bodies coming together, a tangle of mouths and hands and limbs that were a world apart from emotion, from love, seemed so much easier all of sudden.

Just sex. That had been what she'd wanted. Or, at least, it had been all she'd told herself she wanted from Chase.

But her heart knew better.

Her heart had always known exactly what it longed for.

And her heart would never deny that love—pure, honest love—was all she'd ever wanted. All she'd ever needed.

A part of her was surprised that Chase hadn't tried to ease her nerves during the drive. She could feel his concern, just as much as she could feel his desire. She knew he didn't like watching her sit beside him with her insides shredded and torn. But instead of jumping in to save her, instead of trying to smooth everything over for her, he was giving her space to work things out on her own.

God, she only loved him more for that, for the faith he had in her to know the right thing to do, even when she was convinced she didn't have the first clue.

As they drove through the Sullivan Winery gates, Chase reached for her hand and she could feel his confidence, his love, settle in through her skin, shimmying in past her flesh to her bones, all the way down to her soul.

A smile finally came to her lips, the first one since she'd won their game and realized what she'd done to herself.

"Let's go in."

They let go of each other's hands only long enough to get out of the car. It felt so right to walk beside Chase, to feel his strength, his steadiness, beside her. Instead of waiting for him to open the door, she put her hand on the unlocked doorknob and pushed it open, leading the way into the living room.

"That first night, when you brought me here, I was scared," she admitted. Strange how that was the easy part of her admission. Harder, so much harder, was saying, "Somehow, even then, even when I didn't think I'd ever be able to feel anything again, I wanted you." She put her hands on either side of his face. "I wanted to touch you." She brushed her fingertips over his jaw, then up against his cheekbones and into his hair. "I wanted to know if you'd make my skin burn the way it is now." She pressed up on her tippy-toes and said, against his mouth, "And I wanted so badly to taste you here."

Her lips barely brushed his, just enough for her to know that he tasted a little like the chocolate from their dessert and the wine they'd had during dinner. But mostly he tasted like Chase . . . the beautiful man who had brought her back to life.

She slid her hands through his soft, dark hair, then down the back of his neck to his shoulders. "I wanted to undress you and see if you were as perfect as you looked." She could feel his heart beating against her palm as her fingers went to the buttons at the top of his shirt. "I had a hunch you would be," she whispered as she uncovered his chest, one glorious inch at a time.

She pressed her lips against his bare skin and a low groan rumbled from his chest, but he didn't try to take charge of her night with him.

She couldn't keep her hands from shaking as she worked to open the rest of the row of buttons, pulling the hem of his shirt from his pants before slipping it off his shoulders and letting it fall to the floor behind them.

"I've never really had a chance to just look at you." Even as she said the words, his muscles across his chest and abdomen were flexing and tightening. “You look a little tense,” she murmured, enjoying being in control like this so much more than she ever would have guessed.

She moved close again and pressed her palms flat against his chest and began to stroke over his pecs, the indentations of his abs rippling as she caressed him.

“Does that help?” she asked him in a naughty voice.

“Yes.” His lie was raw.

Hungry.

Borderline desperate.

She leaned in, pressing her lips to the curve of his neck and shoulder. “Then I’ll have to do it more.”

She licked at his skin, wetting it before she nipped at him with her teeth. For a moment, she knew how a vampire must feel, how hard it must have been for Edward not to sink his teeth into Bella’s sweet flesh in those vampire movies she’d watched alone.

He groaned again, his skin and muscles vibrating against her outstretched hands.

Somehow, she dragged her mouth from him to continue what she’d started.

He was hers for the night.

Hers.

Chloe planned to wring every ounce of pleasure, of joy, from these precious hours, from every sweet minute with Chase.

Placing her fingers over his belt buckle, she

began to work the leather. His skin was warm everywhere she brushed against it and her little hum of happiness sounded in the silent room.

"Lovely." Chase's compliment resonated through every cell in her body, coming to a stop right behind her breastbone. "The way you look when you're undressing me . . ." He paused, waiting until she lifted her eyes to his. "You undo me, Chloe."

She swallowed at the look in his eyes, at the fact that she felt like he was caressing her, stroking her, without even touching her.

His mouth was a distraction from her plan to strip his clothes off the rest of the way, but such a wonderful one. With her hands still on his belt, she went back up on her toes and kissed him softly again.

They both knew this kiss was a promise of what was to come, a promise that he'd know exactly what he meant to her by the time the sun rose in the vineyard outside.

Her breath came in short little puffs as she drew back and turned her attention to his pants. His zipper came undone a moment after she drew his belt apart, and then she was pushing his clothes away, watching with pleasure as his trousers dropped to the ground. Chase stepped out of them, moving closer to her as he did so, close enough that she could feel the heat of his thick erection against her belly.

He was gorgeous, sinfully so, standing before her in only his boxers. But she wouldn't be satisfied until she had stripped him bare, just the way he always stripped away all the layers of protection she'd tried to wrap herself in.

Every time they'd made love, Chase hadn't just removed her clothes; he'd slowly begun to strip away her fears. Her hesitations. Her long-held belief that she couldn't ever have the love of a man as good as this one.

She wanted to tear the cotton from his hips . . . but at the same time, she wanted to go as slow as she could to savor every moment of discovering Chase.

In the end, her hands took over from her brain, moving to hook a thumb into each side of his boxers. She had to lift the cotton over his erection, and once she'd cleared it, she stopped, mesmerized.

"You make me want to do things I haven't wanted to do in a long time."

He didn't need to say the words, *Then do them,* for her to hear them. She didn't need his silent urging to help her move to her knees before him, either. And she certainly didn't need his encouragement to lean forward and press her tongue against his hard flesh.

"Chloe."

His hands, which he'd kept so carefully at his sides until now, came into her hair.

She felt hungry, wild, and so damn happy to be right where she was with Chase against her lips. If anyone had told her a week ago she'd love being like this with a man again—with any man on the planet—she would have known them to be certifiably insane.

But, oh, it was beyond lovely to taste Chase, to feel his hands tighten on her hair, to know that she was driving him insane with pleasure with her tongue, with the slightest scratch of her teeth over him. As she opened her mouth wide enough to suck him in between her lips, his thigh muscles tightened, hardened almost to stone, against her hands where she was holding on to him.

His pleasure was hers, too, as she drew him in deeper. She could feel how careful he was to let her lead, and though she loved him for it, she wanted to feel him lose control, wanted to know that she was the woman responsible for breaking his control to pieces.

Pure feminine instinct driving her every move, she moved one hand from his thigh to cup the tightening flesh below his erection, and then the other to wrap around the base of his thick shaft. Her tongue lashed circles on his sensitive skin.

"You've got to stop," she heard him say as if from a long distance away. "I can't hold back much longer."

She didn't want him to hold back. Despite the fact that her body was crying for his touch, regardless of how good it would feel to drag him down on the floor with her so that she could climb over him and take him into her, she wanted this more.

So instead of stopping, she simply gave over everything she was, gave everything she had, to pleasuring the man who'd shown her that there didn't have to be a limit to joy.

She could feel him growing bigger, thicker, in her hand, could taste his arousal on her tongue. But she needed more, needed all of him, and as she took him in deep again, she moaned over his hard flesh without thinking about what that vibration would do to him.

A second later his deeply pleasured groan was followed by his vow of love, a vow that reverberated throughout the room as his shaft began to pulse and grow between her lips. She had to open wider for his thrusts, for the increased girth that filled her mouth as he pressed in hard against the back of her throat and he gave her everything she wanted, all of his control.

And as Chloe kneeled there before him, with her hands on him, she gave up the last vestiges of her control, too.

Chase hadn't seen this coming, hadn't thought Chloe winning him for the night meant she was going to blow his brains with her mouth and tongue and hands.

Sweet Jesus, he didn't think his legs could hold him up after the most explosive orgasm of his entire life.

When he could finally open his eyes again, he looked down to see Chloe still kneeling below him, looking at him with a sweet smile that belied what she'd just been doing to him. She looked as hazy with arousal as he still felt.

"You're so yummy." Her voice was husky. Happy.

She was acting as if he'd given her everything she'd ever wanted by coming in her mouth.

Every time they came together, she blew his mind in some way. They could spend the next seventy years together and he knew he'd never cease to be amazed by the lovely woman in front of him.

As Chloe slowly stood back up, as she rubbed herself against him in her sweet yet sensual way, she said, "I'm so glad I won you," right before she licked over his chest.

After coming hard enough to blow the top of his head off, he should have been sated, at least for a few minutes, but all it took was one stroke of her tongue against his chest for the blood to start rushing to his groin again.

Chase cupped her hips, loving the feel of her soft flesh against his palms as he pulled her up against one of his thighs, slipping it between hers. Her gasp of pleasure as he pressed against her sent a hot whoosh of breath over his chest.

She was still in charge of their night and he knew he needed to let her lead, but he needed to touch her, needed to give her even a fraction of the pleasure she'd just given him.

She moved her mouth to the other side of his chest as she rocked against his thigh. He could feel how hot she was, could feel the damp proof of her arousal.

Chase had thought he was prepared for this night, that he was up for giving himself over to Chloe, that he could handle anything she dished out.

What an idiot he was.

Nearly two decades of as much sex as he wanted with models and actresses hadn't prepared him for making love to a woman he was actually in love with.

Moment by moment, he was learning that love made everything different.

Bigger.

Better.

So much sweeter.

"Chase?"

He looked down to find the woman who was tying him up in such incredibly pleasurable knots looking up at him with determination.

With hope.

"I know what I want next."

Thank God he'd just come or he would have

erupted simply from the heated anticipation in her voice. "Anything," he vowed to her. "Everything," he promised.

"I want—" She stopped speaking as if she'd suddenly run out of air and her eyes darkened with uncertainty.

"Tell me, Chloe. Tell me what you want. Let me give it to you. Give it to yourself." Her eyes widened at those last words and he knew he'd hit home with them.

"I want to give myself up to you." She took a shaky breath. "I want you to—" He could see that she was scared again, his brave, lovely girl who'd just taken him into her mouth without so much as a pause. "I want you to tie me up."

He forgot how to breathe, actually couldn't remember how to draw breath into his lungs for a split second.

Tonight was about so much more than sex. He knew that. Had known it from the start.

He hadn't really known how much more, though, hadn't thought she'd want to knock down every last barrier she'd had to erect around her body—and heart—tonight.

He wanted to tell her she didn't have to do it, that she was already the bravest person he'd ever known, but before he could, she lifted her chin as if she could hear the words he hadn't yet said.

"It's my night. You're mine. For anything. For

everything," she said. The determination was back. "This is what I want." She slipped her hands through his. "This is what I *need.*"

"I love you." He dipped his mouth down to kiss her once. Twice. A third time. "Should we go see how strong those bedposts are?"

Her eyes flashed dark with arousal . . . and with the fear she was so hell-bent on breaking past.

No matter what, Chase knew he was going to show her how good giving control to someone you loved—and who loved you right back—could be.

"Yes." She tightened her hold on his hands. "Please."

Twenty

Chloe stopped dead at the threshold of the bedroom they'd been sharing, and Chase turned to her, his eyes taking in her expression, the tight hold she had on his hands.

"Chloe?"

Knowing she needed to be strong—wanting to be strong not just for him, but for herself, too—she said, "I trust you," as her heart whispered, *I love you.*

She felt his large, warm hands cupping her face, stroking across her cheeks. His mouth dipped down to hers, sipping at her lips like she was the finest wine. “So sweet.” He licked across her lower lip, and she was shivering with the pleasure of it as he said, “So brave.”

She didn’t feel brave. She felt like an actress trying to assume a role she had no prayer of nailing.

But she wasn’t on the set of some movie. This wasn’t a TV show she could watch from a safe distance. This was her life.

A life she needed to reclaim, every single piece of it.

“Show me how good it can be, Chase. Show me how good it *should* be.”

He lifted her in his arms, so swiftly the breath whooshed from her lungs as her feet lifted off the floor. She loved being held by him, loved knowing that she was always safe with Chase.

He carried her into the large room and over to the bed. He didn’t let her down right away, not when he was obviously intent on kissing away all of her fears first.

When he finally pulled back to lay her down, she whimpered at the loss of his heat, the hard press of his muscles against her as he stared at her, his eyes moving slowly from her face to the swell of her breasts, almost painfully aroused beneath the thin silk of her dress. The skirt had lifted way up around her thighs and that was what he finally reached out to touch, stroking his palm up one leg, from her ankle to the sensitive skin of her thighs.

She moaned her pleasure, lifting her limbs to get closer to him, to offer him more of her body, to offer him every part of her.

"Do you have any idea what it's going to do to me to see you naked and bound for me? To know that you trust me enough to love you like that?"

A flood of arousal coursed between her thighs. She couldn't answer him, couldn't have possibly found any other word besides, "Please."

She'd sworn never to beg a man for anything ever again, but with Chase it wasn't begging; it was simply her body—her soul—needing, insisting on having, something she'd denied it for far too long.

And then Chase's hands were on the hem of her dress and he was lifting it higher and higher, up over her thighs and then her waist and breasts. She didn't need him to tell her to lift her arms, she was already there, helping him get the beautiful dress off. She was dying to be naked for him, dying to feel his skin against hers.

His eyes were everywhere at once—her face, her breasts, her thoroughly damp silk thong. "I've never wanted to take a picture of anyone more than I do right now."

She knew better than to ever let a man take pictures of her naked. She should have been surprised by the words, but the truth was, her trust in Chase went so deep, her faith in his goodness ran so pure and true, that she didn't have a moment's hesitation about his taking pictures of her in the nude.

"I trust you, Chase."

"No. Never." His hands moved to her hips to hold her with obvious possession. "If anyone ever found the pictures, if anyone else ever saw you looking this way but me, I'd have to kill him."

The love she felt for him was on the tip of her tongue, but before she could put voice to it, he was pulling her thong off and down her thighs, throwing it to the ground on top of the beautiful dress he'd found for her.

"I should wait until you're tied up to do what I'm dying to do to you."

Normally, she would have waited for him. But this was her night. And she was in control.

"I won you," she reminded him, and when he looked at her, his pupils were dilated nearly black with desire.

"Yes, you did," he said softly, his low, heated voice whispering over her skin, setting every inch on fire.

"You have to do anything I want." She licked her lips, biting the lower before adding, "Everything I want."

As she spoke, he was putting his hands on her legs, gently pressing her thighs apart.

"Look how lovely you are," he said, each word reverent, raw with passion.

She looked down her naked body to the flesh that ached for him. It was a heady feeling knowing this beautiful man was all hers. And not just because she'd won him in a game.

He'd given her his love.

And she wanted so desperately to take it.

"Taste me, Chase."

Her words were barely more than a whisper and she wasn't sure he heard her at first, but then, he was sliding one hand down from the inside of her knee to her thigh, closer and closer to her core, and she had to hold her breath until that glorious moment when he finally touched her.

There. Oh, God, right there.

She wanted to keep watching him touch her, was so incredibly turned on by seeing his large hand slide slowly over her, but it felt too good for any of her muscles to work. Her legs fell all the way open on the bed and her eyes closed as she lowered her head to the pillow and moaned her pleasure into the room.

Again and again, his fingers took her straight to the edge, but never taking her all the way there.

She arched her hips up into his touch, but as he continued to tease her, as the heat in her belly pooled and intensified, she was about to start begging for him to give her what she needed.

And then she remembered what she kept forgetting: this was her night.

Somehow, she found the strength to prop herself up with the pillows, to open her eyes and say, "I told you to taste me, not play with me."

She saw the wicked glint in his eyes, knew that he'd been waiting for her to guide him further. She shivered at the thought of all the delicious, decadent things she wanted him to do to her.

She was just opening her mouth to set him back on task, when he slowly lifted his fingers from between her legs and brought them to his mouth.

Oh, God, she couldn't believe she was watching him lick her arousal from his fingers.

"Is that what you wanted me to do? Is this how you wanted me to taste you?"

She would have answered more quickly if his hand hadn't moved back between her legs to stroke her to an even higher fever pitch.

She wanted to keep up with the sexy banter, but she couldn't, not until she'd had at least a little release so that she could think straight again.

"Watch what you do to me, Chase."

He answered with a low, borderline desperate groan, as she pushed against his hand, a silent plea for more. And when he said, "You're so lovely, Chloe," just the sound of his voice, the approval in his eyes, the adoration in his expression, had her right there, hovering on the edge of detonation.

A moment later, she lost hold of everything. Everything but complete ecstasy. She could barely catch her breath, certainly couldn't form words, but she didn't need to remind him of her original command, because before she'd even come down from her mind-blowing orgasm, his mouth was hot and wet between her thighs.

She arched against him, her hands going to his hair as she cried out again. She couldn't be this close again, couldn't possibly be right on the edge of coming entirely apart.

But, even though she should have known better by now, she hadn't counted on Chase. Hadn't counted on the way his tongue slipped and slid over her aroused flesh so perfectly, so sweetly.

So sinfully.

She had to look, had to open her eyes again and look down to watch him love her like this.

Obviously in tune to her every movement—every thought—as he swiped his tongue over her, he lifted his eyes to hers. She read lust, need and desire in them.

And so much love that all it took was one more swipe of his tongue for her to come apart all over again. Her skin was slick with sweat, her heart had never beat so fast, as he took her to that incredible place she hadn't ever realized was there waiting for her. Not until the first time Chase touched her. Kissed her.

Until he loved her.

When she finally caught her breath, she said, "I should be sated now," as he shifted up her body so that he could press soft kisses to her stomach and the underside of her breasts as he fondled them in his big hands. "I shouldn't need more."

"But . . ." he prompted, his tongue laving her belly button before his teeth gently nipped at the skin around it.

"But I do," she confessed. "I need so much more, Chase."

Chloe knew what would happen next. He'd rise up above her, she'd wrap her arms and legs around him and he'd take her the way she so desperately needed to be taken.

Instead, she watched as he moved from the bed and opened a dresser drawer. He pulled out four of the most beautiful pieces of fabric she'd ever seen.

"I've been saving these for you," he told her as he moved back toward her. "I was hoping you would be able to use them for your quilts."

She reached out to stroke the fabric. "Chase." Her eyes filled with tears. Gathering these fabrics for her was the nicest thing anyone had ever done. "I don't know what to say." But she did. "Thank y—"

He smiled down at her and pressed a kiss to her lips before she could finish. "You can thank me later, after I've made you scream with even more pleasure," he teased. He dragged the edge of one of the soft fabrics across her breasts. “Who knew this fabric would be so handy tonight?”

She felt her breath go in a rush. They’d come into the bedroom for him to tie her up, but she’d needed him too much to remember her goal.

“You’re going to tie me up with them?”

Giving her one of his beautifully sinful grins, he nodded. “And you’re going to have to be a good girl and not pull too hard on them when you’re coming for me so that you don’t ruin them.”

Seeing her obvious look of distress, he bent down to kiss her again. “I’m just teasing you, sweetheart. Yank as hard as you want. Come as hard as you need to. I’ll find you more beautiful fabric.”

She was so focused on what he was saying in his low, sexy voice, she was hardly aware when he lifted one arm and began to wrap the fabric around her wrist. But then she did notice, and she instinctively tensed.

He slowed his movements, more stroking the skin at the inside of her wrist than continuing to tie her up, and she relaxed into his touch. Trying to take her mind off her fears, she said, “Tell me more about what you’re going to do to make me come again.”

She liked the way he sounded surprised by his laughter. “Are you sure you can handle knowing?”

Her right wrist was attached by the fabric to the bedpost by the time he finished asking the question.

Oh, God, she wasn't sure about anything right now. Only that she needed to press forward with this, no matter what. She wouldn't let her true sexuality be stolen from her for one more night. Not one more goddamned night. This was who she was, who she'd been made to be, and Chase would never hurt her.

Only love her.

It would have been easier just to close her eyes as Chase worked from her wrists to her ankles, but she didn't want to let herself hide from any part of this. That's why, instead of waiting for him to lift her other arm up, she made herself put it into place for him.

She was rewarded with his smile, followed by his swift intake of breath as she purposefully shifted her hips against his erection when he moved to tie up her other hand.

"Thank God I'm tying you up, or I might just embarrass myself," he said in a low voice.

She couldn't believe he had her laughing when every single one of her panic buttons should have been pressed instead by the position he had her in.

"Give a tug on the fabric for me."

Even without her legs being bound, he'd tied her wrists securely enough to the bedposts that she couldn't get away or protect herself if she needed to.

She waited for the panic to take over, knew it had to be coming. Any second now it would swamp her and she would be begging him to untie her, to let her go back to safety, back to a place where she wasn't forcing herself to face down every goddamned fear.

But as the seconds ticked down, all she felt was the warmth of Chase's gentle caresses to her hip, to her waist, to her face. And all she knew was that he was looking at her as if she was the only person in the world who mattered.

And that was when she realized something she should have realized long before now: Chase was just as afraid as she was.

He was afraid that she wouldn't ever let herself love him back.

She would have reached for him if she could have, if her arms weren't bound above her head. "I'm scared, Chase."

He didn't hesitate even a single second before beginning to untie her.

"No," she said through a throat that felt dry and raw. "Not because of the knots in the fabric."

His hands stilled on her wrist. "Chloe, sweetheart, you don't have to do this."

She felt a sob rise up from her chest. "Believe me," she said, "I've tried not to."

She closed her eyes, but even with that sense

gone, Chase was everywhere, his scent, the sound of his breathing, his warmth against her bare skin.

Love.

She'd whispered the word against his neck once before. She hadn't been able to keep it inside, not when so much pleasure had been turning her inside out. It had been there on her lips, a silent vow to the man from whom she'd been unable to stay away.

She waited for him to ask her to actually say it, braced herself for it.

But Chase had never played by the rules and instead of making her admit her feelings for him, especially when she was bound before him and he had the clear upper hand, she was startled by a shifting of weight on the mattress and the warm caress of hands on her legs, down her thighs to her knee, massaging her calf muscle before finally reaching her ankle.

Her eyes flew open in shock. Here she'd been on the verge of confessing her love to him, and he was simply continuing to tie her up.

But, oh, wasn't it just the most lovely sensation, feeling him spread her thighs apart wider, watching him bend over to press a hot kiss to the needy flesh between her thighs right before he moved his concentration back to the fabric around her ankle.

"I love the way you taste," he said almost as if

in passing, and when his tongue licked over her again in a sinful assault on her every sense, she would have come off the bed if she hadn't been tied to it.

"So lovely," he murmured against her slick heat. "Always so responsive for me."

She moved her free leg to open herself to him even more.

"Only one more left," he said softly, and she was just on the verge of processing what he was saying, the fact that she was almost entirely bound, when his tongue speared inside of her.

Everything in her body coiled into that one spot that was about to explode, and she stopped breathing, stopped thinking, couldn't have remembered to be scared for the life of her, even as he shifted again and tied up her other ankle.

But he didn't give her synapses any time to start firing again, because as soon as she was fully bound, his mouth was back there, between her thighs, giving her more pleasure than any woman had surely ever known before.

And then she wasn't fighting her ties to try and get away from the wicked stroke of his tongue, the diabolical thrust of his fingers inside her clenching heat, she wasn't even struggling because she was not at all scared . . . no, she was tugging and pulling against her bonds for the simple reason that it felt good, so good to know that she was giving herself over, one hundred percent—every ounce of all her faith and trust—to the man she loved. He'd already made her come twice, but it didn't matter, because she already knew she'd never, ever have enough of him.

She could hear moaning, begging, in the room, but she was so far gone that by the time she realized she was the person making those desperate noises, her world was being split apart by a pleasure so intense only one thing had any chance of remaining.

"Love."

The word fell from her lips again and again until Chase was there with her, until his mouth was saying the same word against hers and then they were kissing and he was inside of her, thick and hot and so wonderfully big she felt like she might burst from how full her body, her chest, her heart, felt as he loved her. She couldn't wrap her arms or legs around him, but somehow, she felt closer to him than she ever had before as he lifted up onto his knees and slid up so that she could look down her naked body, slick with her sweat and his, too.

"Look at how lovely you are, Chloe. Look at how brave you are."

He hadn't pushed her earlier when the word *love* had slipped out of its own volition; he'd simply let her fear dissolve all on its own.

Her thighs were spread far enough apart by his

bindings that she could easily see him slide slowly in, then out of her.

The act was impossibly beautiful.

Shockingly sensual.

“How can you be the one who’s bound,” he said in a voice that shook, “and yet I’m the one who’s utterly helpless?”

She’d never known a man to be so honest with his feelings, with his emotions. She hadn’t thought it was even possible.

Chase was so much more than her knight in shining armor.

He was her own personal miracle.

“I love you.” Happiness flooded her alongside the incredible pleasure. “I love you so much.”

So quickly she wasn’t sure how he did it, he pulled her bindings loose. And then they were wrapped around each other and Chase was rolling them over so that she was straddling him, looking down at the man who had managed to find a heart so deeply buried she hadn’t even known it was there anymore.

In the end, it was the look in his eyes of love—a love that promised forever, a love that would never, ever let her down—that pushed her all the way over the edge.

Straight into Chase’s loving arms.

Twenty-One

Chloe woke up with her legs entwined with Chase's and his eyes on her as he propped himself up on his elbow. "Good morning."

She felt sleepy and warm and impossibly content. "Hi."

Chase gently stroked the hair back from her forehead with his free hand, but even though his touch was gentle, even though she was still pushing sleep away, she could feel how tense he was.

Their night had been so incredible, start to finish, she'd barely been able to keep up with it, with the incredible pleasure of simply being with Chase.

The perfect, romantic dinner.

The fun game of bocce ball.

And then lovemaking so sinful yet sweet, so totally beyond any ecstasy she'd ever thought to experience.

She had to tell him again, "I love you."

The tiniest bit of tension went out of his expression, out of his muscles, as he smiled down at her, then pressed his mouth to hers in a gentle kiss that somehow managed to steal her breath away without even trying.

She shifted on the bed so that she was sitting up against the headboard. The sheet didn't cover her breasts, but the last thing she was thinking about was modesty. She could feel herself stalling, hated that she was making things even more tense . . . but everything she was feeling had come on so suddenly that she was only just barely managing to process her emotions as they flooded through her.

"I don't want you to go." Chase's passionate words resonated all the way down to the very depths of her soul. "I love you." He slid his hands over hers. "You love me."

"Chase, I—"

He pressed one finger over her lips. "Please, just let me say one more thing."

She paused, then nodded.

"I know you want to prove some things to yourself. But you don't have one single thing to prove. You're an incredible woman, the sweetest, strongest person I've ever been fortunate enough to know. I don't have one single doubt that you can take care of the things you want to take care of by yourself." He caressed her cheek and she had to turn her face into his warmth. His love. "Let me help you. Let me be there for you. Let me be there beside you. Let me be your strength in numbers."

All night long as she'd slept in his arms, her subconscious had been spinning, working to figure out how she was going to deal with everything. She'd been basking in wonder at the sweetness in every one of Chase's smiles, at the heat of his kisses, at how good she felt with him, at how wonderful and unexpected his words of love were. She'd tried to convince herself that leaving was still the right plan, that it was something she *had* to do to know her own strength.

But love—the love she could no longer deny feeling for Chase—had changed everything.

Especially her stubborn belief that she needed to go it alone to prove that she was strong, to prove that she wasn't a victim. Who was she kidding? Only a fool would walk away from this man.

She'd been a fool once before. But she'd learned from her mistakes: she wasn't going to turn away from a love this pure, this real.

"That first night you found me," she said softly, "I knew I would never trust a man again. I knew it wasn't even possible. But then you walked into my life and turned it completely upside down. And suddenly, everything I knew, everything I believed, came into question." She shook her head. "I didn't want to ask myself those questions. I didn't want to make the mistake of hoping again. I didn't want to end up believing in the wrong thing again. It was easier, so much easier, just to cling to those old feelings. It was easier to tell myself—to tell you—that our connection was just physical. Somehow I had to find a way I could justify not denying myself your touch, your kisses."

Chloe realized it was just as well that she was naked with Chase on the bed as she confessed her innermost thoughts, her final secrets. She was done hiding anything from him. From here until forever, she'd willingly give him her body. Her heart.

And her soul.

"All along I think I knew our connection went way beyond physical. All along I think I knew nothing would be able to stop me from falling in love with you. No matter how many times I tried to tell myself that I was going to leave, that I needed to leave, that striking out on my own was the only option, another piece of my heart broke just trying to imagine leaving you. I thought being strong meant going solo, meant standing on my own two feet without needing anything or anyone to lean on, but then I heard you talk about your family. I watched you with Marcus and I saw the way you work as a team with your crew. You showed me that the real strength comes from learning how to trust again. You make me want to be brave enough to love again."

Chloe moved closer to Chase, the sheet falling completely off her lap as she went to her knees in front of him on the bed, his hands held tightly up against her heart.

"I still want to be stronger, I still want to be a better person . . . but when I'm with you, I'm already the strongest, the best, I've ever been. Your love makes me feel like I just might find the woman I've been searching for inside myself all these years." Her tears were falling now, one after the other, as she professed the truth of her feelings. "I know we need to leave this fantasy world soon, but I don't want to leave you. Not now. Not ever."

Her heart pounded hard, so ridiculously hard, as she waited for him to respond to her heart laid out bare before him, practically raw and beating on the soft white sheets.

But he didn't say anything at all, this incredible man she loved so much. He simply lifted her onto his lap and held her.

As all of her dreams finally came true, Chloe wanted to laugh with the joy of it all. She wanted to cry tears of appreciation for the little girl inside who had never been able to give up the dream of warmth.

And she wanted to love the man who held her heart with his.

Making her choice, she nipped at his lips with her teeth, once, then twice, then a third time. With each love bite she could feel him growing bigger, thicker, against her groin.

She didn't think, didn't have to worry about hiding any of her desires anymore, as she lifted herself up just enough to come over his erection, then lowered herself down over his thick shaft. He was big, but she was already more than ready for him, had been from the moment "Good morning" had left his lips.

And still, even as she could feel how hard it was for Chase to hold on to his control, he let her lead their lovemaking. But, oh, how she'd loved making him lose control. And how desperately she wanted him to lose hold of that control again and again until there was no more thinking, no more chances for either of them to stop and think and worry.

"Last night," she said as she lifted nearly all the way off him, "do you remember when I had you in my mouth?"

She slid back down onto him and he pulsed hard within her, nearly setting off her own answering explosion.

"You were so gorgeous like that, Chloe."

Each word sounded pained, she thought, as she slowly lifted up again. "Which part did you like best?" she asked in her most innocent voice. "Having me on my knees in front of you?" She blinked at him, eyes wide. "Or was it watching yourself slide in and out of my mouth?"

She felt it then, the vibration of a growl that started in the bottom of his lungs before erupting against her mouth as he covered her lips with his and kissed her hard.

Another second found her on her back, her arms pulled over her head and held in place by one of his hands at her wrists. Again and again he drove into her, and she wrapped her legs around his waist to take him deeper, then deeper still.

She wasn't even the slightest bit afraid of the way he was holding her, but before she could tell him just how good it was, how close she was to coming apart, he stilled inside of her.

"I don't ever want to take anything you don't want to give. But I want you too bad, need you too much, not to lose control one day."

She loved that he was so careful with her heart even when their bodies were on the verge of going completely out of control. And yet, she knew better now than to need these pauses. She didn't need him to reassure her anymore that she was safe with him.

"I love it when you lose control. I love knowing I can do that to you. I love knowing that I can share all of my fantasies with you, that sometimes you'll tie me up and other times you'll be the one bound and waiting for me to lick every inch of your body."

"I'll never forgive myself if I step over the line, Chloe."

"No lines, Chase. No boundaries. We don't need them, I know that now, when love is what's behind every kiss—" she pressed her lips to his "—when love is what prompts every bite—" she nipped at his shoulder, then laved the small hurt with her tongue "—when love is what has me begging you to take me harder. Faster." She clenched her inner muscles on him to reinforce her point.

She looked into his beautiful green eyes that had always looked at her with wonder, with laughter . . . and with love.

"I'm putty in your hands. And I love it. Take me, Chase. Turn me inside out." She licked across his lips before adding, "Cross a line. I dare you."

As soon as her challenge sounded in the room, everything became a blur as he spun her on the bed so that her hands and knees were under her.

Oh, God, she thought as he came into her from behind. She tightened her fist into the sheets and held on for dear life as he took her, his hands moving from her hips to her breasts and then back down between her legs in a perfect path of pleasure. How she loved it when he sprinted right over the lines and reduced her boundaries to smithereens.

Chloe no longer had any fears of being controlled and Chase no longer held back to make sure he didn't push her too far. All that remained was the sweet ecstasy of trust.

And pure love.

After a shower so long and wonderful that the water had turned cold by the time Chase finally washed the shampoo out of Chloe's hair, she told him, "I'm going to call the police and file a report. I'm also going to get a restraining order. I know I should have called right away. It wasn't that I was ashamed to tell the police what happened to me. I know that I have nothing to be ashamed of." Her eyes darkened as she said, "I just kept thinking I should have been smart enough to see it coming, that if I'd only realized how unhinged, how angry, he was about me leaving him, then surely I could have made sure he couldn't hurt me."

If he ever came face-to-face with her ex-husband, Chase didn't have the first clue how he'd stop himself from killing the bastard.

"You're so good, so sweet, so strong, that you can do absolutely anything you want, Chloe. Anything but blame yourself for other people's weaknesses."

"I know that now."

Last night at dinner, he hadn't shown her all the pictures he'd taken of her. Now, he went to his camera bags and pulled out another set of photos. "I took these. For evidence."

She took them from him and quickly looked through the different shots he'd surreptitiously taken of her bruise during that first day. "I should have thought to ask you to take these for me. But I—" She stopped, took a deep breath. "I wasn't ready to think about what I needed to do." Her smile was small, but it was there, at least for a brief moment. “Thank you for being smart enough to take these, to plan ahead when I couldn’t.” She reached out her hand to him. “Will you come sit with me while I make the phone call?”

Chase was a breath away from telling her that he would do more than sit with her for a phone call. He and his brothers would make sure, in no uncertain terms, that her ex would never come near her again.

Instead, he walked with her into the kitchen, handed her the phone and held her hand the entire time. When the call finally came to an end, Chloe looked shaken.

“Have I told you yet how brave you are this morning?”

“I love you, too,” was her response.

He pulled her onto his lap and wanted to hold her like that forever. But the quiet left her far too susceptible to replaying over and over in her head what she’d just told the police.

“I finally get to have breakfast with you.”

She lifted her head from his chest in surprise. “Breakfast?”

“You’re about to be blessed by another of my talents.”

He raised his eyebrows in a faux-lecherous way to remind her exactly what talent she’d just been party to experiencing. He missed her warmth, her softness, when she slid off his lap, but he was beyond glad to see her smile back as he slipped on a flowery apron.

"I swear I won't say a single thing about marshmallows," she said with a giggle as he turned so that she could tie it in the back for him.

When he turned back to her, her eyes were dancing, thank God.

"Definitely still Hotstuff." She reached for a pair of scissors from the butcher block on the kitchen island. "How about I go pick some pretty flowers to match your very pretty apron?"

She jumped out of his reach before he could give her beautifully curvaceous rear a smack. Loving the sound of her laughter, he said, "Little Red better go before the wolf shows her he's hungry for more than pancakes."

Her lingering laughter, along with the words, "Promises, promises," followed her out the front door.

Chase stared after her for several beats, so incredibly thankful for all the blessings in his life, the biggest one of all being the woman he loved.

She'd told him this morning that she wasn't worried about his stepping over the lines—no, she hadn't just told him with words, she'd showed him with her body what she wanted to give, what she wanted him to take—but he knew there were bound to be times when he made her mad, when he acted on her behalf without thinking. Lord knew he and his brothers had done that enough times with his sisters, all in the name of protection. Not just because they were older and felt they knew best.

But even though Chase knew he and Chloe were bound to butt heads in the future, he also knew their love was strong enough to survive a little conflict.

And boy, oh, boy, was the making-up part of their future "discussions" about boundaries going to be fun. He was grinning as he grabbed flour from the pantry, then reached into the fridge for eggs and milk.

First, he was going to blow her mind with the pancakes . . . and then he was going to blow her mind in an entirely different way that would have her forgetting about breakfast altogether.

Twenty-Two

Chloe had been dreading making that phone call to the police for so long that she'd assumed her stomach would be in knots for hours, if not days, afterward. But she didn't feel weak or shaky. Just the opposite. She felt so much lighter now, like she could sprint up the mountain and not even be winded when she got to the top.

The lavender planted in front of the guesthouse was in full bloom and she could smell it as the sun warmed her and the flowers and the grapes growing on the vines all around the stunning Napa Valley property. Smiling, she moved to the plant with her scissors and had just started cutting a thick bunch when she heard a sudden sound behind her.

The instant it took her brain to realize that Chase wouldn't be sneaking up on her was a moment too long to jump out of the way of the hand that came down over her mouth.

The scissors fell out of her hand as a man yanked her hard against his body. "You little bitch, I saw you in there playing house with that guy."

Dean.

How had he found her here?

And how had he gotten onto the property? There was a gate, with a remote control needed to open it. But she knew, even as the questions ran through her brain one after the other, the answers didn't matter.

The only thing that mattered was that Dean had found a way in.

And he obviously wanted to hurt her. Again.

Chloe worked to still the panic inside. If she let fear rule her, she wouldn't be able to think straight enough to fight back. To fight for the life she deserved.

In place of fear, she let fury fly free.

Because she wasn't going to run this time.

No, she was never running again.

Her ex-husband's hand was smooth and sweaty across her face as he hissed in her ear, "Are you begging him to do all those dirty things to you, you filthy slut?"

He was even angrier today than he'd been at her apartment. His pride had to be pretty badly battered at the way she'd knocked him out with the paint can. And after living with him for so many years, Chloe knew how his brain worked: he figured since she hadn't gone to the cops yet that she must be too scared to tell anyone what he'd done to her.

She knew what he expected her to do. He expected her to take what he gave her. He expected her to cower. Just like she must have all those years that they were together. He hadn't even needed to use force during their marriage to get her to surrender her power to him. All he'd needed to do was look at her like she wasn't worth a damn thing—and she'd believed him.

Well, she knew a hell of a lot better now what she was worth. And who she was.

Using his underestimation of her to her benefit, Chloe bit down on his palm as hard as she could. She tasted his blood in her mouth as he screamed in pain.

Taking her chance, she kicked behind her,

hoping she was nailing his family jewels, and dove for the scissors.

Chloe almost had them when her hair was yanked back, hard enough for tears to spring to her eyes. Somehow she bit back her whimper of pain, knowing now that Dean would get off on that.

"I tracked down your car and bribed the tow truck driver to tell me where he picked it up," he bragged. "He said the call came from this winery, but I didn't think you'd already be in the sack with some guy when I got here." He yanked her hair again, hard enough that her vision almost went black with pain. "Tell me what he's doing to you. Now!"

She knew what would happen if she told him the truth. He'd hit her again. She could see how much he wanted to do it.

Oh, God, it had hurt so much the first time, but Chloe knew all she needed was to get a few inches closer to the scissors. And then she'd make damn sure the tables were turned.

Permanently.

Moving her mouth up into an insolent smirk, she said, "You couldn't handle knowing how good he is. How much better he is than you."

Just as she'd expected, his fist came at her. Only this time, she wasn't afraid, wasn't simply trying to get away like she had that horrible night when he'd come at her in her apartment. She wasn't able to move far enough to completely avoid his punch, but the shock of being hit paled against the victory of grasping the scissors in her fingers a few seconds later.

His fist was halfway to her face again when she ducked, turned and aimed the sharp tip of the blades at the man she'd once made vows to in front of her family, all because she hadn't been brave enough to trust her own heart.

She finally trusted it, damn it. Finally loved. And she wasn't going to let anyone take the love she deserved away from her.

As she nailed him with the tip of the sharp scissors right beside the dark bruise and cut she'd left him with when he'd attacked her in her apartment, Dean's screech of pain had him stumbling back . . . straight into Chase's path.

Chase's fist landed square in the middle of her ex-husband's jaw, the crack of bone against bone sounding loud and horrible in the once tranquil vineyard.

Dean's eyes actually crossed as he stumbled back, but Chase didn't stop there, just kept slamming his fist into her ex-husband's face again and again until he looked like a bobble-head doll with his head wobbling around on top of his skinny neck.

A voice in Chloe's head—a fairly small, quiet voice—told her she should stop Chase before he did permanent damage. But before she could, Dean's legs fell out from beneath him.

He hit the ground hard and she expected him to be unconscious, given the loud sound his skull made when it landed in the dirt, but he still blinked up at her, groaning as a line of blood trailed from his mouth.

Chase was down on the ground beside him a moment later, his hand around Dean's throat. "Apologize to Chloe."

She'd never seen Chase like this, completely letting loose his fury, his rage. Yes, she'd known all along just how strong, how powerful, her lover was, but it was still amazing to watch him protect her like this.

When her ex didn't say sorry fast enough, Chase tightened his hand around Dean's throat to the point where he started coughing.

"I'm going to give you one last chance to apologize to her."

Dean's eyes started to roll back in his head, but Chase wouldn't let him pass out, shaking him until he groaned again.

"Apologize right now. Or else."

The menace in Chase's low-pitched voice had Dean's eyes opening and his gaze locking with hers.

"I'm sorry, Chloe."

She couldn't speak, could only nod.

Dean started to pass out again, but Chase shook him. "You're not done yet, asshole."

She'd never seen her ex-husband look so

miserable. His face was bloody and bruised, he was crying and he had dirt smeared in with the snot running from his nose.

"Are you ever going to come near her again?"

Chase emphasized his question by banging Dean's skull into the dirt a few times.

"No." Dean was sniveling now. "Never. I'll never bother her again."

His eyes finally rolled all the way back in his head and he went out. Cold.

Chloe was staring down at her ex-husband, lying on the ground, looking smaller to her than he ever had before, when Chase's fingers brushed warm and gentle across her smarting cheek.

She turned her gaze to him as he pulled her into his arms. "Chloe, sweetheart. He hit you. Again."

But she didn't care about her own face, not when she could still hear the shockingly loud crunching of bones smashing together each time Chase had nailed Dean with his fist.

"Please tell me you didn't hurt your hand."

"I'm made of steel, not marshmallows, remember?" he said with a small smile. "It's going to take more than a few punches to hurt my knuckles." She could feel the anger, the fear for her safety, radiating off him. "Bloody hands are well worth the satisfaction of making sure he never comes near you again."

She knew Chase wanted to do even more damage to Dean to make up for what her ex-husband had done to her—not just the bruise on her cheek, but for years of controlling her . . . and not loving her right.

Chloe pulled both of Chase's hands into hers and held them over her heart. "You said you would do anything for me."

"Anything," he confirmed.

"He isn't worth it. He isn't worth any more of your anger. He isn't worth hurting your hands on his hard head when you need those fingers and knuckles working perfectly so that you can take your beautiful pictures. I want you to let the police take it from here."

A loud frustrated breath whooshed out of Chase's beautiful mouth. "It's going to kill me to let him walk away, Chloe. To know that he's hurt you and hasn't paid for it."

"But you will do it, won't you? You'll walk away. For me."

She watched him battle within himself, loving him even more for the way he wanted to take care of her.

Finally, he said what she'd known he would. "Anything, sweetheart. I'd do anything for you."

She went on her toes so that her mouth was a breath from his. "I know. And I'll do anything for you." She pressed her lips to his, then whispered, *"Everything."*

A few seconds later, she took the cell phone he handed her and called the police, telling them to come right away. And although she wouldn't let Chase tear Dean apart the way he clearly wanted to, she had no issues whatsoever with letting him tie her ex up with some heavy-duty rope. Tight enough that Dean came to.

Ignoring his groans, Chloe and Chase moved to the porch, where they kept an eye on her ex while they waited for the cops to arrive. She knew Chase didn't want to leave her for more than a few seconds and he zipped into the kitchen for ice faster than should have been humanly possible.

Pulling her onto his lap, he held the ice to her cheek just as he had that first night she'd met him, and softly said, "I'm so sorry, Chloe. I should have been out there with you."

"It's not your fault that he came after me here. Just like you said earlier, neither of us could have known what he was going to do next. But I'm pretty sure he won't hurt me again."

"No," Chase said in a low voice, "he won't. Do you know why?"

"Because he'd like to keep the teeth you left him with. And once he finds out there are five more sets of fists like yours . . ."

"You're right. He's scared senseless. But not because of what I did, not because of what I said."

"What do you mean?"

He smiled at her, a smile so filled with love—

and respect—that it took her breath away. "The reason he won't hurt you again, sweetheart, is because you had him. You didn't need me to hit him to make sure he didn't come at you again. You had already won the battle. The scissors were genius. And perfectly aimed." He looked a little sheepish. "You didn't need me to get in the middle of it all—I just couldn't help myself. Not when I've been wanting to take him down all week."

Chloe didn't care that grinning hurt her newly bruised jaw. She couldn't have held her smile back for anything. Chase believed in her. And he wasn't the only one.

She finally believed in herself, too.

"You know what I've realized this week?"

"That I'm a sex god."

The laughter that rippled through her felt like it was washing all the hurt, all the pain, away.

"Yes, Hotstuff, you are definitely a sex god. But also, I've realized that I like being a team. With you."

She wasn't sure she'd ever seen Chase look happier, not even when she'd told him she'd fallen in love with him.

And she was just as happy. Because she hadn't just been looking for warmth her whole life . . . she'd been looking to be part of something bigger than just herself, too.

A family. She wanted to know she was part of a family that loved her, no matter what.

Always.

Forever.

Just then the sirens blared through the Sullivan Winery gates and in moments the cop cars were pulling in front of the guesthouse. Chase held her hand the entire time she gave her report to the police officers. They would need an official report at the station soon, and Chase would be there with her for that, too.

After they'd watched them put her ex-husband into the backseat of one of their vehicles, Chase asked, "How are you feeling?"

Chase hadn't let go of her hand for one single second, and as the police cars drove away, she turned into his arms and rested her head against his broad chest.

"I'm a little sad," she admitted. "All those years . . . but I keep trying to tell myself none of them were wasted." She lifted her face to look into his beautiful eyes. "Because they led me to you, Chase."

Before she realized what he was doing, Chase was down on one knee in the middle of the garden. Reaching out for the lavender bush, he pulled off a flowering stem.

"Chloe Peterson, I love you."

She loved hearing those three words that filled her soul with such warmth—and endless happiness. But even if he never said them again, she would know what he felt for her simply by looking into his eyes.

"Will you marry me?"

Chloe no longer doubted that she was a strong woman. She also knew she didn't need to be strong with Chase.

Which was a very good thing, because her legs suddenly felt weak, her eyes were wet, and it was all she could do just to nod and whisper, "Yes," as Chase gently wound the lavender around her ring finger.

And as he stood up and kissed her, Chloe was amazed to realize that her fairy tale wasn't coming to an end, after all.

It was only just beginning.

Epilogue

Marcus Sullivan watched the waitstaff circulate through Chase and Chloe's San Francisco loft with trays loaded with some of his best vintages. They'd announced their engagement a month ago, and tonight they were sharing their joy with the entire Sullivan clan.

Everyone had cleared or changed their schedules to be here tonight. Even Smith had flown in for the weekend from Italy, where he was shooting a big-budget thriller. Chloe's parents were clearly overwhelmed, not just from meeting a big movie star, but by the entire Sullivan clan, minus Lori, who had gotten caught late at a video shoot for some hot new pop star. His mother, Mary, had been by the side of Chloe's folks nearly the entire evening, working overtime to make sure they were comfortable.

Standing off to the side of the group, Marcus was happy for his brother. Chase had picked a good woman. A perfect woman, really.

Marcus downed his full glass without tasting it and took another from the young waiter before he could walk away. He never drank to excess. Drunk had never been his style, and given that he was in the wine business, a predilection to overimbibing would have been more than a health issue; it could prove to be bad for business, too.

Tonight, however, Marcus didn't give a crap about business. Or remaining sober.

How could Jill have let him walk in and find her with—

His second glass went down just as fast as the first and he was reaching for his third when he realized his mother was coming toward him.

Just a handful of minutes ago, she'd told the entire crowd how very thrilled she was to—finally—see one of her brood take the plunge. What she hadn't said was that she'd always thought her oldest would have been first to the altar.

Marcus had thought that, too. Now he knew better.

Now he knew that the past two years of waiting for Jill to be "ready" for the next step had been nothing but a lie.

Working to head his mother off at the pass, Marcus said, "They're great together, aren't they?"

His mother looked at the happy couple with a smile. "She's perfect for him. Strong, creative, lovely."

Too soon, her eyes were back on him, just in time to watch him down his third glass. His tolerance was higher than most, but he didn't usually drink that kind of volume that quickly.

"What's wrong, honey?"

"Nothing."

But they both knew he was lying.

Marcus needed to get out of there before he ruined the party. "I'll be back in the city next weekend. I'll come by to see you then."

His mother put her hand on his arm. "Will Jill be with—"

Lori flew in through the front door just then, still wearing her dance clothes, before his mother could finish her sentence.

"Oh, my freaking God, I never thought I'd get out of that dance studio!" In an instant, Lori zeroed in on the happy couple, exclaiming, "My new sister-to-be!" as she threw her arms around Chloe. "We need to do a big group shot!"

Chase usually took pictures at family parties, but since he was the guest of honor tonight, Mary Sullivan had hired a photographer for the day. As the photographer took pictures of the Sullivans and Petersons, Marcus stood stiffly on the edge of the group. As soon as the picture-taking was done, he left before anyone could stop him.

He hadn't had a one-night stand in two years, hadn't taken a beautiful, willing stranger to bed for twenty-four wasted months. Like an idiot, he'd given up hot sex for the false promise of love.

Well, Marcus was a hell of a lot smarter now.

And, tonight, he was going to make up for lost time.

Center Point Large Print
600 Brooks Road / PO Box 1
Thorndike ME 04986-0001 USA

(207) 568-3717

US & Canada:
1 800 929-9108
www.centerpointlargeprint.com